VIPER FATALIS

FOREWORD

TOP SECRET//DR-ULTRA//DIA INTELLIGENCE

CPT. NATALIE NICKS

Since 1958, the American government has controlled the creation of future technology through an organization called the Defense Advanced Research Projects Agency, or DARPA. Aided by their secret division, DR-Ultra, they fight a shadow war to make sure cutting-edge weapons stay in the hands of the American military.

My name is Natalie Nicks. Like you, I had no idea about this hidden war until my first assignment as a newly minted Defense Intelligence Agency officer put me right in the middle of it. During a covert mission, I was targeted for assassination and almost killed by a suicide bomber. To honor my sacrifice, DR-Ultra used its secret TALON technology to revive me.

Now, equipped with several cybernetic enhancements, I work with an elite team of investigators called Reaper Force. We stand as the only line of defense protecting the present from the weapons of tomorrow. We aren't just fighting a shadow war; we are fighting to save the future of mankind.

My codename is Viper, and this is my story.

ALSO BY MARK CALDWELL JONES

VIPER FATALIS

AN ACTION-PACKED SCI-FI SPY THRILLER

MARK CALDWELL JONES

SAMURAI
SEVEN
BOOKS

For Maverick

"I exist in two places, here and where you are."
— Margaret Atwood

We know that no one ever seizes power with the intention of relinquishing it. Power is not a means; it is an end. One does not establish a dictatorship in order to safeguard a revolution; one makes the revolution in order to establish the dictatorship. The object of persecution is persecution. The object of torture is torture. The object of power is power.

— GEORGE ORWELL, 1984

PART I

NOBODY'S HERO

1

SIERRA VISTA, AZ

Natalie Nicks was completely surrounded by men who wanted to kill her. A wise man, or woman in this case, would realize the futility of the situation, raise their hands, and surrender. But she'd purposely put herself here, right in the middle of the action, dead center on target, at the greatest risk of being taken down any minute.

The choice had been a death wish of sorts. But not the suicidal kind. No, this was a direct challenge to the ole grim reaper. Come and get me, if you can!

Not that she wanted to die, but over the last many months, she'd flipped a switch, maybe a literal one, and something within her wasn't scared of the possibility.

She wasn't sure whether she was going crazy or living her best life. She hadn't felt this power-drunk since she was a teenager. Back when the grief from losing her parents and the effects of puberty hit like a hurricane, thrashing her life into an unmanageable mess. She'd been more rageful than a volcano back then, but couldn't do much about it. Things were different now. She had more power than she could handle, and she was definitely about to do something with it.

So here she was with about fifteen angry men who wanted her dead. Almost all of them had weapons: baseball bats, switchblades, shotguns, and rifles. They were mostly blue-collar types who moonlighted as a vigilante border patrol. And fancied themselves a barroom full of special operators. What they really were was a bunch of drunk middle-aged men with a hard-on for gun powder and violence.

She didn't care about any of them save one: Private First Class Joe Riley. That was the man she wanted to talk to about the stolen ground sensors. But before she could have that conversation, there was the matter of the mob.

She spun in a quick circle. Scanning the room as she went. In her mind, she imagined a compass on gimbals, like you find on ships out at sea. She marked the corners of the room with the points of the compass. Few people would understand the imagery. It was a trick her Uncle Wilco had drilled into her. Something he'd developed for himself as a Navy Seal.

Be aware, he'd lecture her of everything around you. Mark it in your mind, sweep all points of the compass, pick your target, then fight like hell and don't let up.

She'd never really put it to full use, all four directions that is, until this very moment and something about it was thrilling.

North: the pool table. And a group of four men, confused and hesitant, holding pool cues. Two of them were reaching for long guns in a rack mounted on the wall.

South: the bar and entrance to the kitchen. Two big men cussing her out and getting up from a table.

West: was the door she busted through. A couple of gray-hairs were drinking beer near the jukebox. Startled, but moving slowly, they'd be the last to engage.

East: the Ford F-150 truck. It had crashed through the main entrance. Three men were looking in it for the driver. She only had a few seconds before they realized no one was there and turned back on her.

North, South, East, and West.

She heard her uncle in her head. *Choose your first direction and clean it up fast!*

She looked around again and chose East. It was obvious by the way the men near the truck moved; they had very little training. But it wouldn't take much for them to get lucky. They may be out of shape and sloppy, but they could still kill her.

This brawl was going to hurt.

She hoped they were up for it. Because god knows, she surely was.

LESS THAN AN HOUR AGO, Captain Natalie Nicks had been in a more peaceful state of mind as she stood in the shadow of a limestone cliff, watching the encroaching darkness consume the last bits of a thistle-colored sky. A rush of frosty air flowed from the higher elevations of the Huachuca Mountains, through a forest of ponderosa pine, down into the canyon she'd picked for their rally point.

She checked her watch and was pleased they'd made it on time. The link up was on schedule and the objective's location was four klicks from her current position.

According to her intel, there was a small compound on the land there. It consisted of two metal storage barns and a ramshackle wooden structure. It had once been a hunting club, and now it was a biker's bar of sorts. This is where she believed they'd find Joe Riley and the stolen ground sensors.

She scanned the terrain. Once they left the foothills, and the cover of the scrub, they'd be on an open plain of the chihuahua desert. Nothing except a thin blanket of night would hide them as they approached their target.

To keep the element of surprise, they would need to travel quickly. Fast was not a problem for Nicks. These days she was equipped with cybernetic legs that allowed her to run at extraordinary speeds. But this wasn't a solo mission. Per her orders from DR-Ultra, she'd brought most of the Reaper Team—DIA Intelligence Officer Fatima Nasrallah and former SAS Sergeant Margaret Quinn. So she keyed her Satcom to signal they were in position.

Fatima moved closer to Nicks and nudged her in the ribs. "We're not going to infill by foot, are we? I have a new TV show I wanted to binge tonight."

Fatima was a thin, boney woman with skin tan as desert clay. She had a prominent nose and large rosebud lips perfect for blowing you a kiss after putting a bullet through your brain. Which she could easily do, because she was a deadly sniper recruited by the DIA after making a name for herself in Syria. She was a legend to those that had fought ISIS.

She skittered across the rocks with the ease of a tarantula. Her thick dark hair swung below her shoulder blades as she peered through the scope on her sniper rifle and scanned the horizon. The woman both annoyed and fascinated Nicks. But mostly she reassured her. She was a valuable ally who'd proven her worth time and again. Nicks was grateful she'd joined their team.

"You really don't read the mission briefs, do you?" Nicks grinned while throwing some serious side-eye.

Fatima muttered something in her native Kurdish while Nicks reassured her they weren't hiking any further and radioed their other teammate. "Send in the wheels," she said.

"Copy that, Viper. I'm on my final approach." Lee Park, affectionately called Mouse by the team, did little to hide the glee in his voice.

Park was a handsome Korean-American man in his late twenties. An accomplished engineer who already made a fortune from his inventions. He was a friend of Colonel Jack Byrne, their leader, and Byrne had recently convinced him to join the team. But he wasn't trained to be in the field, nor did he want to be. He enjoyed working from the safety of their headquarters.

Nicks could hear the jet-powered drone he was piloting. To her bionic ears, the UAV, still quite a distance away, sounded like one of the native hummingbirds Sierra Vista was famous for. It was anything but.

"I've got eyes on the drone," Quinn whispered to the two other women. Her excitement was apparent despite the black face paint.

Codenamed Gremlin, she was the team's quartermaster. The chief mechanic who managed their high-tech equipment. A stout English redhead with blue eyes and a British accent. She glassed the sky with her special optic monocle. The blip of an infrared strobe, pulsing on the nose of the drone, grew brighter as it approached. "Incoming in five, four, three, two..."

The drone zoomed over their position, releasing its payload and gunning its jet engines to climb back into the night sky. A pair of cylindrical airdrop canisters fell like bombs and whistled their way toward a flat spot a few yards from the mouth of the canyon. A quick jog from their current position.

This was a freefall drop. No parachutes and no explosions. Just the resonant baritone thunk as the strange missiles slammed into Arizona desert like two giant lawn darts.

Quinn trained her monocle on the canisters, then passed it to Nicks. Each was about five feet in diameter and they sat stiffly upright—two silver columns holding up an invisible roof.

"Looks good." Nicks said.

Quinn collapsed the looking glass and put it away. A Cheshire grin revealed her pearly white teeth. "I can't believe that worked."

"I never doubted it would." Nicks replied. She gave the signal, and the team left the cover of the overhang and made their way to the vehicles.

"Two DARPA Sandbugs upgraded and tricked out by the best mechanic in the biz, yours truly," Quinn said as she climbed into the first dune buggy. "Collapsible roll cages and infrared headlights so we can use night vision."

While they had many options, Quinn made sure the team used equipment in line with their fundamental mission—protecting their nation from the weapons of the future, while also testing those same weapons for the Department of Defense. These came fresh from DARPA's Ground X Vehicle program.

Nicks climbed into the other and took the wheel. Fatima climbed in with Quinn. All three strapped on helmets. Fatima and Quinn added their bone conduction headsets and checked their radios. Nicks had that hardware built into her cochlear implant, so they tuned their gear to her special frequency.

"You're both loud and clear," she said.

After a last check of the vehicle, the team added their panoramic night vision gear. Quinn fired up the infrared headlights and the invisible beams illuminated the desert in green sunlight. They could drive through the dark with ease and yet maintain total blackout. No one would see them coming.

As the team rolled out, Fatima asked. "Remind why we want Riley?"

"DR-Ultra's new ground sensors were being field tested at Fort Huachuca when they were stolen. The base is an electronics proving ground for the DoD and Riley was stationed there at the time." Quinn said.

"He's our prime suspect, but Riley is part of a volunteer militia that likes to hunt illegal migrants. The theory is they wanted the tech to catch more people crossing from Mexico." Nicks added.

"So you think we'll find the equipment and Riley at this place?"

"Intel shows the place has armed guards twenty-four seven. They're definitely hiding something there. I thought we'd wait until they were good and liquored up before we paid them a visit," Nicks said. "Just an ordinary repo mission. Should be no problem if these drunk skinheads are cooperative."

Quinn laughed. "No one we go after is ever cooperative. You don't think these bozos are different, do you?"

"I sure as hell hope not," Nicks said.

She stomped the accelerator and the team cut across the flat basin as if beckoned by an invisible scent leading them toward their unsuspecting prey.

2

Nicks pushed the speed as much as possible until they were within sight of the militia compound. There, she slowed to a crawl while Fatima scanned the perimeter with a spotter scope. The property backed up against Bureau of Land Management wilderness. The entrance faced Rock Ridge, a gravel road that broke off from Highway 92 and headed south into the Coronado National Forest. They were about three hundred meters out.

They parked the Sandbugs behind a stand of mesquite and draped them in camouflage netting and made the final approach on foot. About hundred yards out, they set up their first observation post.

Fatima's mic squelched, "All clear in my line of sight. There's a lot of activity in the bar but you're clear to move in closer."

"What the hell does that sign say?" Quinn asked.

"The Croaked Frog," Nicks said.

"Shouldn't it be the Dead Frog?" Fatima asked.

Quinn explained the cartoon frog was an old internet meme. Pepe the Frog. It was a favorite of white nationalists. In this neon version, they skewered Pepe with a giant frog gig. Two little x's over his eyes confirmed he had croaked.

Quinn reminded them, "As much as I detest this neo-Nazi bull-shit, we're using non-lethal force. Everyone's equipped with sedative bullets. DR-UItra's special blend of Ultiva. Hit anyone center mass, and it's instant lights out."

Fatima groaned. "That's disappointing."

"We're not going to kill them, but we're not going easy either. These guys stole state-of-the-art military tech like it was nothing," Nicks said. "Their social media profiles are full of gun photos, brags about AR-15s under their beds, and German shepherds in their back-yards. They think they're untouchable."

"They better not have dogs. I'm not killing a dog," Quinn said.

"Even if it's a Nazi?" Fatima asked.

"Got a point there," Quinn corrected herself.

"Don't worry, no dogs," Nicks said, crossing her fingers. She heard the drone still circling high overhead.

"Mouse, how does it look from your angle?" she asked.

"Thermal imaging shows you've got a packed house. The soft-ware is counting over fifteen men in front, a few stragglers in the back. Gait analysis shows your man Joe Riley is walking along the west side of the bar. Sending you video feed now."

"Damn," Quinn grimaced. "The intel package said to expect five or six men tops."

"There's three times that," Mouse confirmed.

"Protocol says we scrub the mission and come back another day." Quinn's tone suggested nobody would agree to that.

"What do you say, Fatima? Want to pack it in?" Nicks asked.

"You're asking me that?" Fatima shot her a glance full of daggers. "Hell no, let's get on with it."

That's what Nicks wanted to hear. She turned to Quinn, waiting for her answer.

Quinn said, "I'm good, you know that. Just need a change in tactics. This can't be a sneaky night vision raid with that many."

"You have a plan?" Fatima tipped her chin at Nicks.

"Absolutely I'm on it." Nicks shot from their hiding place like a bolt of lightning and ran toward the east side of the property where all the vehicles were parked.

"Did you check her for loose screws before we left?" Fatima asked Quinn through the coms.

"Apparently, not," Quinn said. "Look at what she's doing!"

WHAT NICKS WAS DOING WAS CROUCHING behind a beautifully waxed Ford F-150 that she wanted to hot-wire and drive off with except for—

"These stupid rednecks have ruined a perfectly good truck. Can you see *this*?"

"See what?" Fatima asked as she advanced to the northeast side of the perimeter and climbed onto the roof of one of the storage sheds. "Describe it. I'm busy counting the number of targets between us and Riley."

"This jerk-off has hung a pair of balls on his trailer hitch—"

Quinn laughed. "They're called *truck nuts*."

"Could it be any more obvious that he's compensating for something?" Nicks said.

"Wait—are you touching them?" Quinn asked, adjusting her monocle to zoom in on Nicks.

"Well, yeah, I wanted to see what they're made of." Nicks said. "They're so smooth, polished chrome—literally. Why can't they all feel this nice?"

Another burst of muffled laughter rattled over the mics until Fatima killed the banter.

"Heads up. Three men coming out the front entrance for a smoke. Careful, two are armed."

Quinn adjusted her position, and her rifle, and reported. "I've got the one on the right."

"I'll take the one on the left," Fatima said.

"What's the plan, Viper?" Quinn asked.

The team waited a beat. But there was no reply.

Nicks pushed against the truck with both hands flattened against the tailgate. For several seconds, the truck didn't budge. Then, slowly but surely, the vehicle crept forward.

"What the bloody hell are you doing?" Quinn asked through the coms.

"Just a minor distraction," Nicks said.

"And you call me crazy?" Fatima added.

Nicks didn't argue. Why should she? It was crazy. Her muscles flared with a fresh surge of energy, and her bionic limbs filled with power. Her grip tightened. Small dents formed around her fingertips. The truck overcame its inertia, picked up speed, and headed straight for the bar.

When the rolling Ford F150 truck caught the attention of the three men outside the main entrance, the first laughed as if it were a hilarious prank. Adjusting his beer, he nudged the other two and pointed.

The second man appeared to have more common sense. He dropped his cigarette and sidestepped out of the way, pulling out his handgun as he moved. He fired at the truck, but before he could hit Nicks running behind it, Fatima took him down. He was fast on the draw, but she was faster.

The third man turned and attempted to escape through the door, as if he'd be safer on the inside. The truck hit him mid-stride, picked him up, and plowed through the entrance with a satisfying crash. That's when the team went into action.

"Cover me. I'm going to enter from the west," Nicks said. "Gremlin, take the south entrance and clear the kitchen."

"I hope you know what you're doing," Fatima said, sighing into her coms.

"I'll let you know if a few minutes." Nicks ran around the north end and angled herself at the entrance on the west side of the building, picked up speed, and threw all her momentum and body weight against the door.

It burst off its hinges like someone had rigged it with explosives. It sailed into the middle of the bar and knocked over a collection of table and chairs.

"Fucking mothers!" Fatima shouted, making adjustments to cover Nicks from her vantage point. Quinn cursed as well and headed for the back entrance.

Then Nicks walked through the shattered doorway like she'd been there a hundred times before.

EAST. That was the direction she'd chosen to clear first. It was definitely the most chaotic section of the bar.

Three men buzzed like hornets around the thing that had just invaded their hive. The truck, now half in the building and half out, had taken out a divider wall and crashed into the bar before coming to a stop. It pinned two men in place like they were waiting on their next beer. The flimsy plywood and tin roof had collapsed, opening a hole over it.

Two men worked together to pry open the passenger door. A third grabbed a baseball bat, while another loaded a shotgun.

"If that driver ain't hurt yet, he will be, stupid motherfucker!" Mr. Baseball Bat seemed intent on beating the driver to death.

When they realized the truck was empty, they turned around and went after Nicks.

Nicks punched the man with the shotgun before he even knew she was there. A left hook to the kidneys with her cybernetic fist was all he needed to drop the gun. As he doubled over, Nicks kneed him in the face, putting him down for good.

She turned into the path of Mr. Baseball, who was coming for her, swinging his bat like a hillbilly light saber.

Nicks karate-chopped through the bat, striking the skinny man in the bridge of his nose. The redneck Jedi went down in a shower of splinters.

Behind her, two more militiamen hit the floor, thanks to well-placed shots by Fatima. Unconscious assholes were piling up. Nicks took a moment to breathe it in. *Now this was a real party.*

FATIMA NASRALLAH SCANNED THE BAR. The stunned militia were shaking off Nicks's surprise attack. Every man still standing wanted a piece of her.

One silver-bearded bruiser, hidden behind an upturned table, aimed his pistol at Nicks as she leapt across the room to confront another man.

Fatima lined up a chest shot.

Bang!

Silverbeard shouted as he went down. "Jesus-H-Christ, I've been shot! Help me!"

A militiaman in Willie Nelson braids looked at Silverbeard, who now appeared dead, and turned whiter than a Klan hood.

"Help your goddamned self," he said and headed for the nearest exit.

"One more tiki torch down," Fatima said. "Another on the run, headed out of the building. Probably gone for good. But Viper, you've got several on your six I can't scope."

"Just take care of what you can, I'll do the rest."

NICKS HAD CHOSEN North as her next direction. The men by the pool table seemed the biggest threat now that Fatima had taken care of Silverbeard. She lunged just as two of the men had taken rifles from a gun-rack mounted on the wall.

Nicks grabbed the pool table with both hands and flipped it, flattening them against the wall. They lay there like smashed insects, moaning under the wreckage. Their rifles useless now.

"Watch out!" Fatima yelled.

Nicks glanced over her shoulder as a red-faced man smashed his pool cue across her back. Turning around, she caught the second swing, ripped the cue out of his hands, and broke it over her knee. Now she had two effective clubs. She batted her attacker in the face, unhinging his jaw and sending him to the floor.

The next man slashed at her with a large hunting knife. Nicks dodged and charged him with one of the splintered cues. She hit him with such ferocious speed, he was impaled through the shoulder and pinned to the wall behind. Nicks allowed a quick smile as the human dartboard strained in agony to free himself. Fatima shot him and put him to sleep.

Cursing, the remaining militiamen circled her. The bravest of the bunch was a bald body builder wearing a mechanic's uniform who jumped Nicks from behind. She pivoted, but another man grabbed her by the hair and yanked her like he was tugging a dog on a chain.

Nicks's head snapped back. A large bicep clamped around her neck—the mechanic's attempt to subdue her with a headlock.

Panic flashed through her when she gasped and found she couldn't breathe. The man was surprisingly strong.

She fumbled for his wrist and squeezed, giving no mercy. He shrieked as bones snapped under her bionic hand. When his arm fell limp in front of her, she used it as leverage, flipping the man over her, straight into the bar back. Mirrored glass and liquor bottles exploded in a loud crash.

The remaining men ran for the exit. Nicks turned right and found one last holdout, An overweight man was hiding next to the jukebox still playing heavy metal. He shook as he leveled a tiny pistol.

"Freeze, you goddamned bitch, or I'll—"

Before he could finish, Nicks closed the gap between them with her bionic speed, palmed his head like a basketball, and dunked it into the jukebox.

The turntable needle scratched across the little forty-five, ending the music and opening up space for the moans of the wounded men littered around the bar. She'd cleared all four directions and turned the clubhouse into an emergency room. But then she realized she'd almost forgot her actual target.

Joe Riley was gone.

3

Maggie Quinn opened the creaky screen door and entered the back of the building. She cleared the first room, which was a storage area filled with trash and kitchen appliances. Then moved through a short hall toward the sound of chaos, which took her into the kitchen.

Here, she surprised the cook. The lanky man in a stained chef's apron leapt out swinging a greasy meat cleaver. Quinn dodged and swept the butt of her rifle across his face. He faltered, dropping to a knee; she pulled the rifle around, taking aim at his big, bald head. He swung the cleaver again. She leapt backward toward the stove, firing one shot into the chef's chest, putting him to sleep. For good measure, Quinn smacked him again with the butt of her rifle.

When she stepped over him, she hit a puddle of kitchen grease, lost traction, and tumbled. The slip was a bit of bad luck and worse timing because their target burst through the kitchen, rabbited right over her, and continued out the back door before Quinn even realized who it was.

She keyed her coms. "Dammit, I missed Riley. He's outside, headed south on foot!"

Joe Riley fled out into the dark desert, cussing as he ran. Quinn charged through the back door chasing after him, but the young man was considerably faster.

Nicks was above them both on the roof. Her feet pounded the tin shingles like blacksmith hammers as she ran across the top of the building.

Fatima radioed in. "He's out of my line of sight. It's up to you two."

"I've got him," Nicks said. Taking a giant bionic leap off the end of the building, she hurled herself through the air. Her legs pedaled an invisible bike until she closed the gap and landed on Riley in mid-stride.

The two tumbled end-over-end through the dirt. When they came to a stop, Nicks was the only one who could stand. She'd used Riley to pad her fall, and he was in some serious pain. He grabbed his leg and cursed Nicks.

"What the fuck! You broke my goddamn leg!"

"Ah ... it doesn't look too bad." She rolled him over and checked. Maybe a fracture she thought. Then she frisked him. "That's the downside of having old-fashioned human legs—they break."

"Old-fashioned legs? He screamed. "Bitch, I'm going to kill you. Let me up. Let me up!"

Nicks didn't let him up.

Riley was pale with close-cropped blond hair. He was Nicks's height, about five seven. All skin and bones, barely any meat on him. But he was wiry and seemed to be in army shape, so she restrained him with a pair of flex cuffs she'd carried in her tactical vest.

She grabbed him by his one good leg and dragged him through the dirt back toward the shack.

Near the back entrance, Quinn and Fatima were securing other prisoners. They worked as a pair and cuffed everyone, even if they were unconscious. Then they gave each man a low-tech duct tape blindfold, and laid them, one-by-one, in orderly lines behind the building.

Nicks pulled Riley to his feet. Despite his injury, she directed him to hobble to a stack of dirty milk crates near the back door.

"Got some bad news for you, Riley," she said, forcing him to sit down.

"Yeah? What's that *bitch*?"

Nicks back-handed him across the face, knocking him off the crate. He squirmed in the dirt, moaning. Then hissed at her through his bloody teeth. Another string of obscenities rolled out, which Nicks interrupted with a swift kick in the ribs. His eyes rolled backward as if he might pass out.

Nicks grabbed him by one hand, a purposeful display of her unusual strength, and dropped him back on the milk crate.

"You want the good news. Here it is: I won't break your other leg, if you cooperate."

He looked up at her with a hint of fear in his eyes. "Who are you?" he asked, his tone was less venomous.

"The question of the moment is not who I am, but who are you? Joe Riley, the all-American solider? Or Joe Riley, the dumb-ass Nazi?"

"That's nothing but free speech. I get to believe whatever I wanna believe."

"No, that's a court martial. Because you can't be a member of this skinhead club and wear a flag on your shoulder at the same time. The army has a force-wide ban on membership in racist organizations. Didn't you know that?"

"I haven't done a damn thing except have a few beers with some friends."

She leaned in closer. "What about stealing a shipment of ground sensors?"

He flashed a shocked look at her. Everyone realized she'd struck a nerve. "I don't know anything about that. Anyway, if you're some kind of cop, I've got rights. What are you, FBI? Homeland Security? I know you're not military police."

Fatima and Quinn stepped up next to Nicks.

"No, she's none of those things," Quinn said. "She's a lot worse. Someone who doesn't mind sterilizing a wanker like you to get a little information."

Fatima threw the pair of truck nuts to his feet. It dropped with a dull thud. The dim starlight over them glinted off the polished chrome.

"Fuck, you're with the cartel, aren't you?" Riley said, looking at Nicks with genuine concern.

Nicks shook her head in disbelief. "Did I hit you too hard, Riley? What cartel?"

"You really don't know?" He seemed genuinely confused or worse, just plain stupid. "What is this then?"

"Enough bullshit. The ground sensors you stole. Where are they?" She shoved him off the crate again. Put her foot on his wounded leg and leaned into it. Riley screamed. "And what cartel?"

"Stop! Goddamn it, please!" he begged. "I'll tell you everything."

Nicks stopped and Riley spilled.

"They call him the Dragon. Some wetback weed farmer who thinks he's the next narco kingpin. One night, he ambushed my brother's militia with a truck full of men armed to the teeth. They had AKs and all this high-end tactical gear. He's on the warpath. Lopping his competition's heads off. He has the sensors!"

"You sold the equipment to a group of drug runners?"

"I didn't sell shit, lady. They kidnapped my brother, Frank. The dumb fuck got snatched up by those beaners. That's what I'm trying to tell you." His eyes pleaded his case as he spoke. "I thought he was dead. We couldn't find him for days; then, I got some texts. Sick photos of him. Hell, they ended up sending me one of his damn fingers in a padded envelope with a ransom note. Somehow they knew I was stationed at the base."

"The ransom was the sensors?" Nicks asked.

"They sure as hell don't need money, not from me. They wanted the tech."

"How would they even know about that equipment? It's classified." Quinn asked.

"You got me. I didn't know a thing about ground sensors. Not until they told me what to look for and how to find them." His eyes darted back and forth between Quinn and Nicks, as if he was trying to gauge whether they bought his story.

"So you're saying you traded those sensors for your brother? Where is he? We'll need to verify your story."

"You beat the shit out of him with a bat! Don't you remember, lady?"

"Riley, let's get something clear. If you're lying, I'll beat you with something a lot worse than a bat."

After a while, they confirmed Joe Riley was telling the truth. There was no trace of the sensors in the building, and Quinn found the brother's rotting finger in the freezer.

A search of Riley's phone revealed he'd taken snapshots of the stolen tech, and screen-grabbed images of the texts with the instructions on how to deliver it to the cartel.

When Nicks was satisfied the sensors were gone, the team bagged all the evidence they thought important, bandaged up the wounded prisoners, and sedated them.

In the morning, most of the militia would wake up broken and bruised but alive. Reaper Force would seem like a bad dream—one they wouldn't want to experience again.

Now, there was a new problem, and it wasn't Joe Riley and the Sierra Vista militia. Brand new, state-of-the-art DARPA equipment was on the other side of the border in the hands of a dangerous drug cartel, and Nicks and her team were back at square one.

PART II

DISTANT EARLY WARNING

4

SIX DAYS AGO, SOUTH OF THE US-MEXICO BORDER

R afael García never thought he'd die this close to achieving his dream, but it was obvious this was the end of the road. Death was *literally* staring him in the face. By sunrise, his backpack with the stolen ground sensors would be scattered among his bloody remains. But if he stood his ground here and now, his wife and son would be in the United States fulfilling his hopes by staying alive.

He aimed his gun and prayed the last bullet would find its mark.

Only an hour ago, his family had almost made it across the border. But the entrance to the tunnel had been too much for his young son.

Crudely built into a berm of the dusty chaparral, it resembled the mouth of hell. The passage sloped down into darkness, and roots hung like witch's hair from the ceiling. Tecate cypress and saltbush grew like fingers along the sides, camouflaging it well, especially as the sun set and the shadows lengthened across the Otay Wilderness.

"No, Papi. I'm not going in there!" Alejandro pulled away from him. "Not at night!"

The child threw himself into Araceli's tattered, dusty skirt.

"He's trembling with fear," she said. Tears welled in her eyes.

To be honest, Rafael didn't want to go in there either, but their only chance for prosperity was on the other side. His family had come too far, and his decision to steal from his former employer meant there was no turning back.

Rafael took off his stained cowboy hat, wiped his brow, and stared out over the darkening hills beyond the river. The purple light of dusk was fading fast.

"Let's make a fire," Araceli said.

"Yes, please!" their son agreed.

The boy, dressed all in black for nighttime travel, was exhausted and hungry. He was too afraid to leave their side even when he needed to relieve himself. He rubbed his tiny fingers against the secret pockets sewn into his clothes, likely fingering the Saint Christopher medal Araceli had hidden inside.

It was gut-wrenching to watch his son, only seven years old, trying to face something many grown men couldn't handle.

He dared not say anything, but Alejandro was right to be afraid. They were being hunted. He'd been aware of it for days. At first, a few strange sounds came at night. The smuggler he'd hired to lead them across the border dismissed them. Mule deer foraging for food, he'd said.

One night, things changed. The sounds got louder and more ominous. The smuggler was frightened enough to keep an all-night vigil. When he thought he spotted an animal, he alerted Rafael and headed off into the darkness to scare it away, but he never came back.

In the morning, all that was left of the man was a large bloodstain and a small revolver. Araceli had watched with disdain as he picked up the smuggler's gun. An act that betrayed his own fear but provided some comfort to his family as they continued onward north.

The Garcia's money the smuggler had carried was scattered to the four winds. Rafael and Alejandro spent hours scavenging for the loose bills, even though Araceli had demanded they leave it.

"It's cursed," she said. "Let it go if you want to live."

"It's our money. I worked for months to pay that swindler. Now, it's ours again. We need this!"

In the smuggler's backpack, they found a hand-drawn map and extra food and water the man had denied having. Rafael stuffed the items in his own pack along with his secret treasure, a foam-padded case with a dozen black metal devices the diameter of coffee cans. Each one sporting its own small antennae.

"Radios!" Rafael had told his wife and son. "I'll sell them in America."

But that was another lie in a long string of them. He'd driven a cartel crew down to the border to retrieve a truck full of similar cases. They brought the crates through the tunnel. Dozens and dozens packed with the strange devices. At gunpoint, he loaded them for the lazy crew boss they called Denada. Angry he was being mistreated, he'd impulsively hidden one case under his seat. A tax for the disrespect he'd suffered.

The next day, he'd packed up his wife and child, hired a guide, and made out for the border on foot. He would be his own man and build a new life away from the servitude he felt working for the narcos. Losing their guide was a setback, but with the map, they eventually made it to their final obstacle. The hidden passage to the other side.

Rafael pointed at the tunnel one last time. "This is it. All we have to do is go through and we're in America."

Alejandro turned away and hugged his mother again.

"We will camp here tonight," Araceli said, grabbing her son's face and mimicking Rafael's smile. "We'll go through the tunnel at first light; everything will be okay then."

"Okay," Alejandro agreed.

Rafael sighed, "Give the boy some of the mezcal so he can sleep."

She nodded solemnly and walked off to help her son gather firewood.

As they made their camp, the final bit of dusky light faded. The night air grew colder, and the moon rose. Clouds moved across the starry sky while Alejandro fell asleep in his mother's arms.

Just as Rafael relaxed, he heard the animal return. Closer. It seemed to bide its time, crouched behind a thick stand of cedar. Then it bolted like a horse, galloping away, cutting through the brush and out of sight. An alien whine akin to a howl echoed through the chaparral.

"The chupacabra!" His son startled, then burrowed into his mother's chest. "Don't let it get us, Papi."

"Now don't worry. A chupacabra only eats goats."

"But, he took the man. He'll take us too."

"No, son. We're safe tonight," he lied. "Monsters fear America."

Doubt passed through him like the long train of clouds gusting overhead. What kind of man was he to endanger his family this way? A desperate man. A naïve man, he thought, right as the moon broke through the overcast and shone down like a spotlight. Rafael had his first clear look at the thing stalking them. He'd seen nothing so terrifying—not in his worst nightmares.

"Araceli, *quietly*—make a torch like I showed you."

Rafael fumbled for the smuggler's revolver as Araceli ripped a piece of her skirt and wrapped it around a branch about the thickness of a mop handle. She lit it in the fire.

"Now, the tunnel. Take Alejandro, fast as you can. I will guard the rear."

She stood up with the torch, grabbed her crying son, and moved through the scrub toward the passage.

Rafael got up and carefully slung the backpack with the radios, money, and meager supplies over his shoulder. His hand shook as he pointed the dead man's revolver at the creature and walked backward —trying to keep himself between it and his family. But, as soon as he created some distance, the monster crept forward, ever so slightly following him.

He'd do all he could to stop it, even if it meant making the ultimate sacrifice. His wife and the boy had to be spared from this horror.

Surely, they'd find help on the other side of the tunnel. It no longer mattered if the border patrol caught them. In fact, he prayed for it. Let someone find them. Forest rangers. Racist gringos. Even the cartel's ruthless men please, God, anyone before it was too late.

He kept one eye on the creature and one on his wife and son as they descended into the tunnel. Sensing they needed more time, he stopped at the entrance. Despite his trembling arm, he aimed the weapon as best he could and fired.

The monster was undeterred. It kept coming. Using both hands this time, he aimed more deliberately. He squeezed the trigger, but his shot missed again.

"Run, Araceli. Run, Alejandro!" he yelled.

I'll meet you on the other side, he thought, firing the gun for the last time.

The gunshot echoed through the valley wilderness while all that Rafael had ever been, and hoped to be, was ripped from him, disappearing like a fool's dream into the darkness of his unknowing.

5

THE ANGELOS GROVE ESTATE, LOS ANGELES, CA

The grounds of Angelos Grove looked regal as the sun rose over the sprawling ten-acre estate and glinted off the Welsh slate roof. The palatial manor of gray stone, steel, and expertly carved marble rested in a multi-level bed of manicured greenery. Gothic gardens and neoclassical fountains spoke to the opulence demanded by the estate's first owner. Inside, luxury and state-of-the-art military equipment coexisted providing an unusual headquarters for Reaper Force.

Natalie Nicks and Maggie Quinn sat together on the veranda overlooking the reconstructed garden and pool area. Not too long ago, an audacious attack by Riza Azmara, the leader of the Dharmapala—a high-tech criminal syndicate—had damaged it. This morning, there was no sign of that terrible memory. All the reconstruction was complete. The gardens back in order. The pool, clean and inviting.

"So, are we going to talk about last night's op?" Quinn asked.

"Sure. What was your favorite moment?" Nicks asked with obvious sarcasm. "The part where we discovered our intel was wrong, or the part where we couldn't find the missing equipment?"

"The part where you tried to take down twenty men, single-handedly. What the bloody hell were you thinking?"

"Thinking? I wasn't thinking, I was *engaging the protocols*. Remember that little part of my programming? The part you've demanded I use, incessantly, since we started working together?"

Quinn rolled her eyes. "Oh please, don't lay that on me. As a friend, I'm just concerned. Project Starfire was hard on everyone. You've had an edge to you lately—not saying it's bad—just that I've noticed."

"No need to worry, unless I start punching team members."

Quinn laughed. "If that happens, I'll break out my new EMP rifle. One blast of that beauty will shut you down."

"Would that EMP rifle take care of the sigillum?" She rubbed the back of her neck and ran her fingers over the hard bump hidden below a skin colored patch.

"We've been working on that. Well, I have, but Mouse has been working on other things. A lot of things. He's kinda gone down a rabbit hole, one I'm not sure he'll ever come out of. But if he does, you'll be the prime beneficiary."

"Upgrades?"

"Yes! Upgrades!"

Adapting to changing technology was a daily occurrence for Nicks. In fact, technology was her job. Protect the present from weapons of the future. That meant making sure the United States maintained its technological superiority and making sure that advanced technology wasn't in the wrong hands.

Prior to the war with the Dharmapala, Nicks thought the job bordered on the mundane. They operated like glorified equipment managers, making sure bored soldiers didn't borrow the latest laser weapon for their trip to Burning Man. Sometimes they went after thieves selling restricted tech on the black market. Or they'd run surveillance on foreign scientists and report back on the technological advances of other countries.

Riza Azmara's attempt to take down DR-Ultra had changed

everything. The entire team had been threatened and almost killed. And the ensuing battle exposed dark secrets that Nicks had been blind to. In the end, she decided that even if it had shaken her faith in the leaders of her organization, she still believed in the mission.

She'd seen firsthand how dangerous it was to have advanced weapons in the hands of a terrorist organization. The thing in her neck was a perfect example. The sigillum was a device created by Azmara to enhance her unique power—the ability to control machines with her mind. While holding Nicks prisoner, Azmara had implanted the device in the base of her neck. Unfortunately, it was still there as a reminder of why her job did matter.

Quinn pulled Nicks's hair aside and ran her finger down the nape of her neck. "The patch is holding up. Masks it completely."

Quinn had tried everything to get the damn thing out of Nicks's neck. Finally, they settled on the patch to cover it. But Quinn had baked in some nanotech that blocked all signals coming in and out of the device as long as she kept the patch in place.

"Let's go check it out."

The two women retreated to the Cage, and Nicks took her familiar position on Quinn's examination table. Quinn pulled the high-tech scanner over. The NatScan, as she called it, filled a nearby computer monitor with information about Nicks's cybernetic body parts. Her two arms, two legs, and two ears were all TALON bionics.

Quinn hooked her fingernail under a skin-colored adhesive patch and pried it away until it revealed a bizarre silver skull about the size of a dime. It looked like a surface piercing you'd get at a tattoo or body modification shop. It was sinister and contrary to Nicks's style.

"Nothing new with this damn thing. You've still got eight booby-trapped fish-hooks in your spine, and if you attempt to remove any of them—"

"They electrocute my little lizard brain?"

"Yes, but don't worry. I've come up with some ideas on how to short it out safely. I just need to run more tests. Until then, just keep wearing the patch."

Nicks wasn't pleased but managed a half-smile. Azmara had controlled Nicks with the device. The experience was horrifying, and she never wanted to risk it again.

"Here's some good news to make up for my lack of progress in that department—" Before Quinn could finish, a blood-curdling shriek blared through the intercom.

"Who the hell is that?" Nicks said, jumping to her feet.

"I don't know, but it's coming from the new bunker!" Quinn got up and headed for the stairs.

"HELLLLLLP!" the person screamed again. They were in serious trouble.

6

The testing bunker was a colossal room. Engineers had created it during the repairs by consolidating two of the former lower levels into one space. Made of reinforced steel and concrete, it was now a refuge from future attacks. Its vaulted ceilings had been painted sky blue to make the long hours working deep underground a bit more tolerable. It was on that blue ceiling Nicks and Quinn found the source of the screams.

"Bloody hell! Mouse, you idiot!" Quinn yelled.

Their teammate, Lee Park, who was dressed head to foot in a black skin-tight suit, hung above them like a dark cloud spoiling the blue sky. Seeing him there, helplessly dangling, stuck to the wall by his feet and hands, reminded Nicks of a superhero. Except this super-hero had abandoned all heroic pretense. He was hyperventilating and seemed to be on the verge of a full-blown panic attack.

"How'd you get up there?" Nicks asked.

"Just get me down! Please!"

"Let go. I'll catch you." Nicks positioned herself under her frantic teammate.

"I can't. I'm *stuck!*"

"Then we'll do it another way." she said.

Nicks jogged to one end of the room, crouched like a runner at a track meet, then exploded out in a sprint that seemed impossibly fast. She leapt and bounded off a large equipment crate. Sailed through the air, grabbed Mouse around the waist and—*dammit*—came to a dead stop!

She hung from him in a tangle of arms and legs, swaying back and forth like a pendulum on a chain.

Mouse screamed again. Nicks clamped her hand over his mouth.

"Easy! I have sensitive ears, remember."

"How about we try a really tall ladder?" Quinn asked.

"Yes, please."

"No, I've got this." Nicks swung her legs up, straddling Mouse, and braced her feet flat against the ceiling. After tightening her grip on his waist, she gave Mouse and his suit a mighty heave, ripping them free. As they plummeted, Nicks twisted and landed catlike, cradling a very grateful teammate.

Mouse spilled onto the floor like Jello. His eyes were as wide as saucers. "Oh my god, you just saved my life. Thank you, thank you!"

"These saved you." She patted her bionic legs. "Maybe don't crawl around on a twenty-foot ceiling until you get your own pair."

Mouse stretched out on the floor like he'd fainted. He lay there with his eyes closed, muttering to himself. Quinn let him cycle through a few minutes of drama, then nudged him in the ribs with her boot.

"Get up dumb ass, I'll help you get undressed."

One eye cracked open, and Mouse smiled. He liked that offer.

EVENTUALLY, he took off the outfit which was designed like a wetsuit with a cowl, gloves, and booties. When he pulled off the last piece, it exposed a bright red rash around his waistline where Nicks had tackled him.

Quinn smacked him on his ass. "Next time, make sure this thing works before you scale the walls."

"It works," he said. "It just works too well."

"But how's it possible that thing held both of us up there?" Nicks wondered.

"I was hoping you'd ask. Follow me and I'll show you."

They returned to the Cage upstairs and walked over to Mouse's workspace, which was filled with tiny tool sets, anime action figures, about a hundred audio cassettes of old heavy metal bands, and a vintage Toshiba RT-2000 boom box with auto-reverse.

The most noticeable addition to his cluttered workbench was a multi-level terrarium. Mouse had several plexiglass tubes filled with bird of paradise flowers. A small iridescent-green lizard was licking nectar from the largest one.

"What's with the gecko?" Nicks asked.

"He lost his job selling insurance." Mouse roared with laughter and slapped his knee.

Nicks snorted, not at the joke, but at Mouse's ability to amuse himself with the lamest of jokes.

"That kills," he said.

"Jokes like that may get you killed—that's for sure," Quinn said.

Nicks glanced at Quinn, who was rolling her eyes. Sometimes she didn't know how the two of them worked together. She leaned in to admire the lizard. "Have to admit your pet's kinda cool," she said. "Hey, little guy." She tapped the glass. "He's cute."

"And aggressive. He attacked his brother." Mouse said.

"Oh no, where is he?"

"Dead."

"Damn, hope he had life insurance." Nicks kept a straight face.

Mouse laughed and slapped his knee again. "Good one, I'm stealing that."

Quinn sighed dramatically. "How about showing Nat what you've been working on before I decide to use you, and your stupid gecko, for target practice?"

"Yeah, of course." Mouse eye-checked Quinn to see how serious she was, while he hung the suit on its special mannequin. He pushed it closer to Nicks. "So as you saw, I'm still fine-tuning this. But for now, I'm calling it the spider-suit."

"Well, that makes sense." Nicks touched the strange fabric. It consisted of interlocking hexagonal tiles—a substance that felt like rubber to the touch. "Because you can climb walls like Spider-Man, right?"

"No." He pointed at his pet gecko. "Because it's based on Spider's biology."

"You named your gecko *Spider*?" Nicks shook her head.

Quinn gave herself a dope slap. "And they call him a genius—go figure."

"Anyway... explain." Nicks jabbed the suit with her finger again.

"It's a biomimetic textile called geckskin from the DARPA Z-Man program. Geckos have Velcro-like hairs on their footpads that attach electrostatically to sheer surfaces. This material mimics that."

"That's amazing, but I'd have to be pretty drunk to wear that body suit anywhere."

"He's just showing off. No one's going to make you test that bloody suit," Quinn said.

"Famous last words," Nicks murmured.

"We have something better for you. This deep dive into biomimicry gave me an idea for upgrading your bionics." Mouse said.

Quinn spoke next. "We've been studying how Azmara restrained you when you were captured at her base in Japan."

"Oh, I remember that all too well."

"Toroid mirror cuffs that disrupted your bionics." Mouse said.

Nicks nodded. "Whatever you call them. They sucked. The harder I pulled against them, the more pain I felt."

"We've come up with something to counter that in the future," Quinn said.

She placed a steel case on her workbench and opened the lid. A brand new TALON cybernetic arm was inside. "This is the Mark VII, and it kicks ass."

Nicks leaned over the table to admire it.

"This is a new right arm. A Mark VII. It has a similar tactical design as your current ones: graphene and boron carbide composite bone, but this is fifty percent stronger," Quinn said, pointing at the arm. "And the augstim muscles are twenty percent more powerful, because we've also improved the myoneural interface."

"Plus, it has two new features baked in," Mouse said. "Courtesy of yours truly."

He cued a video animation that showed a wire-frame image of the arm. All the bionic components could be seen interacting with each other inside the arm. As the camera zoomed in on the hand, tiny threads sprouted from the pores of the fingertips. Those threads wove together and continued to thicken.

"We equipped the fingers with a nanofiber interface that can augment Flux's networking abilities. You can hack almost any computerized device just by touching it."

The nanofiber grew like a vine, snaked into a computer port, and began downloading information.

"If you'd had this in Japan. Flux would've been able to hack those bloody cuffs and disable them on the spot."

Nicks eyed Quinn and nodded her approval. They'd both suffered because of Riza. So she liked the sound of anything that gave her an advantage over a monster like that.

"The other upgrade may be the most valuable," Mouse said. "You don't have the advantage of an optical prosthetic. So we figured out a way to use your cochlear implant to give you a similar edge."

Quinn tapped the wrist of the Mark VII and a speaker cone formed in the middle of the palm. Nicks heard a faint tone. Quinn picked the arm up and waved the hand in front of Mouse's pet gecko. In seconds, a three-dimensional image of Spider appeared on the screen.

"This upgrade is similar to LIDAR, it allows you to scan your environment with sound waves. Flux can take the sonograph and create a unique sound signature called an *earcon*. Using that you could track a target almost anywhere, even if your other senses were impaired."

"What do you think?" Mouse asked, obviously impressed with himself.

"Does it come with a Netflix subscription?" Nicks gave them a devilish grin. "If not, I'll keep the old arm." She was joking, of course, but part of her was hesitant. She was wary of her growing dependence on technology. Hadn't she already surrendered too much of her humanity to these upgrades? Even so, without it she'd be dead, and so would her team.

Quinn seemed to sense her struggle. "Don't worry. It'll take about thirty minutes in the surgical suite. It's not invasive since we designed it to be interchangeable with your current system."

"Yeah, the shoulder joint is the only delicate part. Your hand is interchangeable. We can take it off and replace it in seconds." Mouse tapped a hidden button at the wrist, flipped a switch, twisted a locking ring, and the hand popped off the arm. He held it up and playfully waved at Nicks.

Her eyes went wide. "Uh... that's new. You going to teach me how to do that?"

"Absolutely, I know you never read the instruction manuals anyway," Quinn joked.

"Okay, let's do it," Nicks said. "I'd hate to see all your hard work sit on the shelf and gather dust."

Quinn and Mouse looked at each and smiled. They seemed eager for her to test the upgrades. Quinn closed the Mark VII's case and said, "No time like the present. I'll prep surgery. Mouse, you run a final diagnostic on the arm."

Before they could even get started, Colonel Jack Byrne's voice came over the intercom. "All hands on deck," he said. "Penbrook just called an emergency team meeting. Starts in five minutes. Everyone meet me in the conference room."

"Good morning, everyone." Director David Penbrook materialized out of thin air. His form was an almost solid projection of his real self, which was thousands of miles away in his clandestine headquarters, Blackwood Lodge.

Penbrook was a pale, thin man, with dark graying hair that suggested he was in his late fifties or early sixties. He wore an expertly tailored charcoal gray suit, baby blue oxford shirt, and large designer eyeglasses with bold black rims. Notorious for his somewhat awkward social mannerisms, he quickly scanned the room, avoiding any direct eye contact, and offering no discernible smile.

Reaper Force stood at attention around a large conference table in the middle of the Cage, as his hologram sat down in a chair across from Nicks. Another ghostly form seemed to walk out of nothingness right into their midst. It was Penbrook's executive assistant, Marisol Flores.

Marisol was a thin, attractive, Hispanic woman with chestnut brown hair that fell just below her shoulders. Her most noteworthy feature was her mesmerizing green eyes. They were the same color as

Nicks's, but Marisol's sparkled as if cut from an emerald. Nicks wondered if she wore cosmetic lenses to enhance their color.

She had never paid much attention to the woman, but lately she seemed to have taken a more assertive role in managing Penbrook's schedule. Perhaps more like an excellent assistant should.

"Please be seated," Penbrook said. Marisol handed him a file, then leaned over and whispered in his ear.

The hint of a smile crossed Penbrook's face.

Once she delivered her message, she nodded respectfully to the team, eye-checked Nicks, and vanished into the ether.

Nicks dreaded what was coming next. Penbrook was notorious for his Spock-like mannerisms, direct speech, and frank attitude. He also loved analyzing their missions. Like a football coach, watching a game film, Penbrook would pick apart and second-guess the team's tactics when the missions didn't go well.

She'd always hated the terrible gut-punch of defeat. Whether it was during her time as an amateur MMA fighter or while going through Army Ranger school—failure was not something she handled well. Especially when other people pointed it out.

Penbrook opened the report in front of him, scanned the first two pages, and began the briefing.

"Your reports about the Sierra Vista operation are very troubling. Retrieval of these devices should've been quite easy."

Nicks nodded in agreement. "Disappointing, to say the least."

Coming back to the Cage empty-handed felt bad. All the clues and intel had guaranteed recovery of the missing equipment if they found Joe Riley. As acting team leader, Nicks had gambled on that lead and lost. Now they were empty-handed and she was to blame.

"Not to worry, Captain Nicks. I know your team will find a way to get back on track and complete the mission."

Nicks raised her eyebrows. She couldn't believe what she was hearing. Something about Penbrook had changed since the Project Starfire incident.

After that mission, Nicks had wondered if she would ever see

Penbrook again. She'd heard he'd faced disciplinary action for his role in the debacle. Whispers suggested his future role at DR-Ultra was uncertain. But here he was as if nothing had happened, continuing to be the one person with primary oversight of their team.

However, something was different. Nicks couldn't put her finger on it until now. It was as if someone had reprogrammed Penbrook. He'd developed an undeniable *personal* tone.

"To review, these particular ground sensors were created by DR-Ultra as part of the current Smart Wall Initiative championed by Senator Jason Snell. They've proven to be the best sensors DARPA has ever designed. Once a cluster of them is networked, they create an invisible tripwire. A web, really, that extends hundreds of feet above and below the earth's surface. We can't allow these to get into the hands of anyone, but particularly not those who want to defeat the technology.

"To that end, I've invited General Drummond here from the DIA to brief us on the Mexican drug cartel that might have the devices. He has a complete target support package on the matter."

Penbrook signaled Byrne, who patched Drummond into the feed. His image appeared next to Penbrook.

Drummond was a stern, hawk-nosed man. Close cropped silver hair stood out on his dark brown complexion. A grizzled war fighter with a dash of college professor, the kind that might kill you with his reading glasses if he didn't need them to deliver his report. He cleared his throat.

"Thank you, Director Penbrook. Good morning to all of you. As you must know, the DIA established the Joint Intelligence Task Force–Combating Terrorism to provide an enhanced analysis of terrorist threats to DoD interest. As part of that work, JITF-CT has developed a comprehensive database of drug trafficking organizations.

"As your operation uncovered, serviceman Joe Riley confessed to stealing the entire stock of Taproot sensors for a Mexican drug cartel that was holding his brother hostage. All the evidence suggests this group was the Draco cartel.

"The leader of this organization is believed to be Miguel Solis. His identity has been hard to confirm; he's known by the moniker El Draco. Currently, the Draco cartel is fighting several other cartels over territory in the Baja peninsula, and the lucrative Tijuana market. Unsubstantiated rumors say he has a secret manufacturing compound in the Valle de Guadalupe. But all satellite images of the suspected area are clean. We know his organization has a taste for advanced technology. Arrests of some of his lower level operators revealed they're one of the few cartels to use military-grade encrypted satellite phones.

"We are the DIA, not the DEA. We fight wars, not drug gangs, but we can't have El Draco's network exploiting brand new DARPA technology. I hope you can help us get it back. If you need more intel, please contact me directly."

Penbrook nodded. "Thank you, General. You've been most helpful. I've already sent copies of your information to the team."

Drummond said his goodbyes, and his image disappeared.

"Colonel Byrne, you have some additional information to share," Penbrook said.

"Yes, sir." Byrne pulled up a diagram of the sensors' components. "Consider what I'm about to tell you the worst-case scenario."

Byrne cued an animation of the Taproot sensor. It stripped away and lay each component out in sequence, as if being disassembled by an invisible hand. Its part number and description appeared under it.

"One of the most innovated parts of these sensors is its power source. The Taproot sensors are buried underground at a depth that would make them hard to find. They're left there for long durations. Current battery technology isn't practical for these, so we've outfitted them with a new generation of RTGs, used in satellites and remote radar installations. An RTG is a radioisotope thermoelectric generator. In other words, an atomic battery that generates electricity from the heat of radioactive material. Perhaps you can guess my concern."

"A dirty bomb?" Quinn's eyes widened in shock.

"Yes, that's right."

"You think this drug kingpin is building a nuclear weapon?" Nicks asked, the shock clear in her voice.

"We don't know what he's doing. I'm just covering all the plausible scenarios. We need to be on the lookout for anything."

Penbrook added, "The political situation on the border demands that we take contingencies serious. Maybe this cartel just wants to exploit the Smart Wall technology. Find holes in it before it's built. Or he may have something more nefarious in mind. Either way, your mission is the same. Get our sensors back and make sure we neutralize all leaks about the program."

Nicks chimed in. "Yes, sir. We'll develop a tactical response and get back to you with an update in the next few hours."

"Good. Every minute lost makes it harder to track down that equipment."

Drug cartels using state-of-the-art military technology was a dangerous scenario, no matter how you felt about the war on drugs or the border wall.

Like knights on a quest, Reaper Force had a dragon to slay, and a treasure to recover. But this was no fairy tale. The specter of a dirty bomb made their mission a sobering reality. They had to find this dragon fast.

The question was—where was El Draco hiding?

THE NEXT FEW hours involved a lot of pad thai and heaping portions of papaya salad from Night Market on Sunset, along with gallons of caffeinated drinks, as they dug into the minute details of the DIA target package.

They had all the intelligence ever gathered on El Draco's organization except for the specific information they needed most—the sensors's location. At least that was the case until General Drummond sent a new lead.

"The DIA just flagged a call from local law enforcement near the border." Byrne said.

The main monitor displayed the DIA report and an image of their new source. It was a picture of a handsome young man in a sheriff's uniform.

Byrne explained, "Background says this officer was active military. Served with your team, Nat. Deployed to Afghanistan. You remember the face?"

Nicks thought the man looked familiar, but the events in Afghanistan were her foggiest. That's where the explosion had happened. Where she'd almost died, and where the road to becoming Viper began. The trauma of the event made everyone and everything about that time especially hard to remember.

"He was a Ranger. Now he's a deputy with San Diego Sheriff's department."

Then she remembered and smiled.

"Yeah, I know him," she said. "His name is Brett Diaz."

PART III

WORKING MAN

8

DULZURA, CA

"**B**rett Diaz!" Sheriff Chet Turner had a fork in one hand and juggled his phone in the other. He hated cellphones; he was too old for the new technology. Didn't know what button to press, or swipe, or whatever. Somehow he hit the speakerphone, and the conversation boomed through the busy diner. Curious patrons turned his way, and he fumbled until he hit the right button and could hold the ridiculous thing to his ear.

"What's it this time? Kid sick? You're not hung over, are you?"

He wondered if he would have to give his protégé the monthly lecture on the perils of working for a rural sheriff's department. Away from the big cities, they made do with less. One sheriff. One deputy. Two vehicles. And three cubicles in a prefabricated metal barn they shared with the Rural Fire Protection District just east of the Otay Wilderness. Even though they oversaw a massive area, the Dulzura law enforcement community had zero luxuries, and they sure as hell didn't get sick days.

Diaz explained he wasn't calling in sick, he was calling in about something much worse.

"You sure he's dead?" Sheriff Turner asked. A few of the regulars turned his direction.

Edith Varnell, the server of the Colt 45 café, glided by the other side of the counter, offering to warm up the sheriff's mug.

Chet Turner held out his cup while he listened to Diaz explain himself. She poured in more coffee, and steam rose off the surface of the dark brown brew.

"Hold your horses," Sheriff Turner sputtered. "Give it to me in simple pieces. How much blood, you say?"

Turner listened intently. Nearby diners strained to eavesdrop.

"Sounds like a bad one. Yeah, of course. I'll be there in fifteen minutes."

The sheriff hung up the phone and rubbed his brow with his rough brown hands. Now in his late sixties, police work, ranching, and the sun had turned them to leather.

"Want me to cook up something for your lunch?" Edith asked.

"Not this morning, old gal. New deputy's rattled. Gotta go sort it out."

"Little green around the gills, is he?"

"I'll tell you the truth, no. Not really. He's an ex-Ranger, done quite a few tours, served in Afghanistan. But I think he's still adjusting to being out of the action, if you know what I mean."

"Does he got a taste for the dramatic?"

"Well, he's riled for a reason. He found a dead illegal on his own land this morning."

"That all?" Edith shrugged. "Once a damn week around here."

"That's the damn truth!" said a man at the end of the bar who appeared surprised at his own outburst. He shrugged and went back to slopping his eggs with a piece of rye toast.

"Well, this is not just someone dying of exposure. Might be a murder."

That bit of news brought out a chorus of murmurs from the breakfast crowd.

"Your boy has some spic in him, right?" Edith asked.

The sheriff shushed the older woman and scolded her in a sarcastic tone. "Now, Edith. That's not a politically correct term, you know that."

"Well, is he or ain't he? Brown enough, if you ask me."

"He's a good one and hates the bad ones. Something about gangs when he was a kid. This will stir him up even more. Seems whoever killed this poor fella got creative."

"That's why we need that wall. Forget the environmental impact nonsense those BLM boys spun up for the feds," Edith said. "That's if you ask me."

Sheriff Turner didn't have to ask her or anyone in the whole cafe their opinion on the matter. He could get an ear-full anytime he wanted. He knew what they thought because he thought it too. They differed on the particulars, but they all wanted to live in harmony with their neighbors to the south. It was the dangers illegal drugs brought to their community they hated.

"Damn cartels. Brutal sons of bitches." She handed him his check. "Maybe this Senator Snell fella will get his Smart Wall and we can all breathe easier."

"Maybe, so. Here you go." The sheriff passed her a few bills, then got up, dusted the crumbs off his uniform, and put on his black felt Stetson.

"Hope that's enough to make sure you keep this *quiet!*" He said emphasizing the last word so everyone in the diner heard it.

Amused patrons chuckled. He tilted the brim of his hat at the crowd and winked.

"Best be on my way. Thanks for the grub. Good as usual."

"See you tomorrow," Edith said as she cleared his dishes.

"Lord willing." Turner stepped out into the bright light of the early morning sun. The door closed behind him, causing the copper cow bell on the jam to clatter its warning to all those that had the ears to hear it.

9

About thirty minutes later, Deputy Brett Diaz was leading Sheriff Chet Turner down a worn deer trail that cut through a hedge of cypress and continued south toward the edge of his ranch.

Diaz walked in silence, questioning the decision he'd made to call the old man. The sheriff, high on caffeine, was full of patronizing quips about how many dead border crossers he'd found over the years. He dismissed Diaz's concerns and joked the deputy looked frazzled and tired.

"And you just started your shift, son."

Diaz didn't argue. His ebony hair was wet and stringy, plastered to his sweaty brow. His uniform was dirty and soaked through with dark stains of perspiration, outlining his wiry, muscular frame. Despite being a youthful twenty-nine, and having just shaved an hour ago, his ever-present five o'clock shadow suggested it was time to punch out and head to the bar. But there was a lot of work to do —unfortunately.

Diaz stopped and pointed to his discovery a few yards to the south of where they stood.

The sheriff grunted. "You said you found a body."

"This is it." Diaz pointed again as if the old man had missed it.

"Son, I wouldn't call this a goddamn *body*. The technical term for this is ... *remains*."

"Well, this is just the first of it. The poor bastard's been ripped to shreds," Diaz said. "You get any reports from the Border Patrol last night?"

"Not a one," the sheriff responded. "But I'll tell you what I did get this morning—a notice from the Department of Defense, of all places. Seems an army base in Arizona is searching for some stolen equipment."

The sheriff took out a crumpled piece of paper—a printout of an email—and handed it to Diaz, who gave it a quick glance and stuffed it in his back pocket. He was ex-Army, so it piqued his interest, but it didn't compete with the matter at hand. He hadn't shown Turner the worst of it.

"Come on, the blood trail is quite long."

Diaz led the sheriff farther on. The rest of the dead man was about fifty yards from the fence he'd built, and rebuilt, with his father years before. Diaz had tied police tape to four wooden stakes cordoning off a rectangular area about fifty by fifty feet. A string of human body parts littered the area, and a blood trail disappeared into a small cave-like entrance.

The two men walked along the edge of the trail, making sure they disturbed none of the evidence.

"I'll be damned, Diaz. What the hell?" The sheriff's growl was a mixture of bewilderment and outrage.

"That's what I was trying to tell you, Chief. It's ugly."

"Is that a tunnel?"

"I'm guessing so, but I haven't been down in it yet."

The sheriff took a small flashlight off his belt and shined it down into the hole.

"There's more in there for sure. Can't see much, but I sure as hell smell it."

That was the exact reason Diaz hadn't explored the hole yet. He was trying to ignore what his nose couldn't. The putrid air brought back memories of his service in Afghanistan. Most notably the carnage he witnessed after a terrorist attack in a small village called Jehanni. The pungent smell of blood. The lingering rot of death.

"Well, hell, I've never seen anything this heinous." The sheriff's complacency had vanished. Diaz could see the man was genuinely disturbed.

"You think this was an animal, maybe?" Diaz wondered.

"There are some strange tracks around here but no good prints." The sheriff walked in circles around the crime scene, staring at the ground as he went. Occasionally, he kicked at the brush and rocks in his path. "Anyway, what the hell kind of animal does this? This is absolute carnage. Plus, this man had this—"

With total disregard that would make a CSI tech blow a gasket, the sheriff reached down and picked up a small pistol. It had been half-buried in the dirt, partially hidden under a shrub, only a few feet from some mangled tissue that seemed to have once been a human hand.

"You think he wounded whoever did this?" Diaz asked. "Might explain all this damn blood."

The sheriff checked the gun. He showed the empty chambers to Diaz.

"He fired every damn round he had. Sure as hell hope, so."

Diaz took pictures with his smartphone.

"Gotta say, the blood trails suggest this poor soul did all the bleeding, or whoever's in that damn hole."

"We're seeing the same thing," Diaz said. "But I'm coming up short on theories."

"Has to be cartel business," the sheriff said confidently, like he was already dictating the report.

Diaz agreed it was as good an explanation as any, but he wasn't convinced. His white father had come from a long line of Texas policemen, while his Hispanic mother came from a more varied stock. Her family had a few Sinaloa drug runners in their ranks. He was familiar with their tactics.

"The cartels never put this much work into killing unless someone's going to see it. This poor bastard is out in the middle of nowhere. It doesn't make any sense." Diaz wiped his brow.

Sheriff Turner didn't seem to listen. The old man shook his head, took off his hat, and ran his finger around it impatiently. "When did killing anyone over drugs make a lick of fucking sense?"

They both looked at the tunnel entrance. Diaz sensed they were thinking the same thing. Someone needed to clear it, but neither of them wanted to do it.

The US Border Patrol had a special team called the Border Tunnel Entry Team. They called the men who worked on the team Tunnel Rats. Their Latin motto was *non grantum anus rodentum* which translated to "not worth a rat's ass." They borrowed the name and motto from the soldiers who cleared Vietcong tunnels in Vietnam.

Diaz wanted desperately to hand this off to a Tunnel Rat. But he knew Tunnel Rats only handled the big kind, ones with lights, rail cars, and electricity. The type of hole United States Homeland Security spent nine million dollars re-filling each year.

What Diaz had found was a "gopher hole" and not worth their time.

"I'll give you my flashlights and my shotgun, but I'm not about to step a damn foot in that hole," Turner grunted.

"You don't need to do that. I've got what I need," Diaz said, pointing at his gear he'd brought down earlier.

"Suit yourself." The old man shrugged. There was a tone of weariness in his voice. He said he wasn't worried about his age getting in the way of clearing the tunnel, he was just sick of pretending there was something useful about chasing desperate people through dank, muddy mazes. "If you're so hell-bent on coming to this country that you'd risk your ass in a shit-hole like that, then come on. Hell, we should have a clerk sit here with a crate of water bottles. When those illegals pop up, we should congratulate 'em and give 'em a goddamn passport!"

The old lawman had a point. But it was his job to investigate, and if he started now, he could clear the scene before his son got out of school. He didn't want the boy to see this.

He stepped down into the darkness.

"I'll be right here, scratching my balls, and saying the rosary on your behalf," the sheriff said. "Yell if you need help."

Diaz smirked. The only thing Turner might do was radio for backup. He wasn't about to come in after him.

"Sure will." He bent forward and duck-walked into the tunnel. He was a trim five-nine and a hundred and seventy pounds, but this was no easy fit.

The minute Diaz stuck his head in the hole, the sour smell got stronger. The tunnel was barely wide enough to turn around in, and he hoped he wouldn't have to make a break for it. For now, all he had to do was follow his nose and the flashlight beam. Within a few minutes, he'd found the source of the stench.

"Aw, goddamn it!" he said.

"You all right down there?" Sheriff Turner yelled.

"Yeah, but these poor people aren't!" Diaz said.

Diaz shined his light on a new horror. Two more mutilated bodies. The remains of a woman—and God help him—a small boy.

He called out what he'd found to the sheriff.

"I'm getting too old for this shit," the old man said.

Diaz was half the old man's age, but he felt the same way. Violent death had a way of aging the soul. He was tired of it. And taking the life of an innocent little child was the worst kind of violence.

This family, despite their obvious attempt to enter the country illegally, deserved justice. Brett Diaz was the only hope of that for over three hundred and fifty square miles.

He took a deep breath, muttered a blessing over the bodies, and got to work.

Ten minutes. Brett Diaz had been zoning out for a full ten minutes. Staring into the refrigerator and out through the kitchen window, he drank a cold longneck. His mind, still in the tunnel, tried to plan dinner and simultaneously comprehend what had happened to the murdered family he'd found earlier that day.

Death. Fish sticks. Tragedy. Mac and Cheese. And the mystery of how they had died.

Who had done that to them? It was disturbing.

His home wasn't far from the border but, in his estimation, far enough to remain sheltered from the more dangerous problems. He'd chosen the small ranch with its modest one-story house for that very reason. It backed up to government land in the shadow of Otay Mountain. The Tijuana River was nearby. It arched out of Mexico into the United States to touch the southern edge of Diaz's ranch before bending back across the border. This was the closest he would ever get to a piece of paradise, so he resented the murders had happened on the edge of his own land.

He looked out his window and caught sight of his son Will and

Will's buddy Evan. They were playing army and digging foxholes. He watched them for a few minutes and he relaxed.

Thank God the little guy had friends like Evan.

He worried so much about how the divorce would ultimately shape the boy's life. Let him be happy. Let him feel secure. And let him stay as far as he could from real foxholes.

He respected the army and didn't mind his son playing soldier. But he wanted something different for the boy. His time in special operations had almost been the death of him. Certainly, it had taken its toll, his marriage being the worst casualty. The divorce had been terrible and forced his wife, Erin, into rehab to kick a dependence on pain meds. While she worked on her recovery, on the other side of town, most of the parenting had fallen to him. It was a wonder the kid was functioning as well as he was. It certainly wasn't because of his stellar parenting skills. No, this was sheer luck, and he was grateful for every ounce of it.

Will turned around and caught him staring. They exchanged waves and a grin or two. The kid's smile melted him every time.

ABOUT AN HOUR LATER, Evan's dad showed up. Diaz greeted him in the driveway. Word had already spread through town. It forced him to chat about the bodies he'd found.

Eventually Gilbert called to his son. "Evan, come on. It's getting dark."

"Okay!" Evan said, and the two boys ran over.

"What have you knuckleheads been doing out here?" Diaz asked.

"Treasure hunting," Will said.

"Find anything?" Evan's father asked.

"Yeah, by the crime scene. We're going to be billionaires! We found the coolest things ever—"

Will slapped his tiny hand over Evan's big mouth and stepped in front of him.

"Sorry, Mr. Gilbert. That's official police business. Top secret." Will elbowed Evan in the ribs for good measure.

"Top secret, huh?" Diaz eyed his son suspiciously. "You know I'm the investigating officer, right? If you can't tell me, who can you tell?"

Evan laughed and Will grinned but stayed tight-lipped.

"We better go, thanks for having Evan over. Say goodbye, Evan."

"Goodbye, Evan," Evan said and ran to his father's truck.

Gilbert rolled his eyes and shook hands with Diaz. "Thanks, Brett. Have a good night."

Will gathered his top-secret treasure and squirreled it inside, while Evan and his father loaded up and headed out.

Diaz watched them drive away as the last glimpses of the western sun swept across his modest twenty acres. The serene vista infused him with a lingering peace of mind, reassuring him that the good always outweighed the bad. The borderland wasn't for everyone, but its allure charmed him, and he was sure it always would.

WILL SET up camp in front of the television. He fired up his console and played a building game that allowed its players to create worlds beyond his father's understanding.

Unlike most parents with kids this age, Diaz had never had to buy Will electronics. The kid had built his own game console one weekend during a manic phase of creativity.

"I'm hungry, Dad."

"I'm looking ... I guess I could make us some pork chops. Got a few in the freezer. That sound good?"

"We had that last night 'member?"

He didn't remember that at all.

He checked the pantry and found it bare. He had to get a better schedule. He was falling behind. He'd grown accustomed to Erin doing all these things.

"How about Chicken and Stars ... and some good ole Saltines?"

"Had that for lunch today." Will yelled over the chimes of his game—he'd just leveled up.

The nine-year-old was too smart for his own good. His new third-grade teacher had used words like gifted and prodigy. He'd advanced beyond his peers and taught himself computer languages with strange names like Python. Terms he needed to search on the internet if Will ever got off the computer. None of this praise made sense to Diaz, but it pleased him the kid was getting attention for all the right reasons. The exact opposite of his childhood experience. It was surprising and hard to accept something exceptional might spring from his gene pool.

"Just order a pizza, Dad. It's easier. I promise I won't tell anyone. Really, it's okay. You can get the kind with vegetables if you want."

He was smart, conscientious, and kind. The last trait neither of his parents had taught him by example. Life had knocked it out of them.

"Okay, pizza it is. Calling them now, you want wings?"

"No, but you get them, I know you like them."

"Want a beer?"

The kid paused his game and turned to his father. A grin wider than the big screen TV spread across his face.

"No, Dad. Are you crazy?"

"Maybe," he said, picking up the phone. He dialed the one and only pizza place that delivered to his location, Guido's Oven.

"Hey, yeah—Diaz. Yeah, that's the address. We need two mediums. One pepperoni and one of those, what do you call it? Supreme? No? The one with everything on it. Yeah, that. The Kitchen Sink. Do you have beer? I'm running low. No, okay. Two sodas, then. Yep, I'll pay in cash? How long? Okay, we'll be here. Goodbye."

Diaz camped out on the back porch, the local newspaper in hand, his head on swivel, eyeing Will through the open window, then back toward the dark Tijuana River.

"Homework done?"

"You already asked me that. I worked ahead. Did it all Sunday."

"All of it?"

"Yes, Dad..."

"You sure about—"

An enormous crash made them both jump. It had come from near the barn.

"What was that?" Will asked. He stopped his game again, put his controller down, and stood up.

"Clumsy pizza guy, I'm hoping." Diaz strained to listen more closely.

"No, dad. It's only been ten minutes. I've got a timer going."

"Well, maybe they're early."

"They're never early. We live in the middle of nowhere."

Another crash startled them. This time it was louder.

"If that's the pizza guy, he must be drunk!"

Diaz shot a disapproving glance Will's way. "How do you know what drunk is?"

Will shrugged. "Movies, I guess."

Diaz heard a strange trampling sound. A shadow moved across the backyard and into the cover of some trees at the southwestern corner of his property.

His son came up to the window. "Is that a deer?"

The land was home to many animals like raccoons, skunk, bobcat, and coyote. Mule deer who were less graceful than their whitetail cousins sometimes barreled through the brush. On the rare occasion, mountain lions came down from the higher elevations.

When they heard another burst of the strange galloping sounds, Will ran onto the porch, grabbed his father, and held tight. Diaz could feel a slight tremor in his son. The boy was scared.

One second later, Diaz thought he had good reason to be. An enormous shadow moved a few yards closer, its features now more defined in the faint moonlight. It was watching them.

He was hard-pressed to describe what he saw, but one word fit. Dangerous.

"Dad, what in the heck is that thing?" Will shrieked.

His father didn't know and didn't take time to discuss it. He went straight to his gun safe, at first reaching for his handgun. Then he remembered finding the dead man's pistol earlier that day. He tucked the handgun away and grabbed the shotgun, a box of shells, and a flashlight for good measure.

"Dad, you can't shoot it," Will said. "Maybe it's wounded or an endangered animal or something."

The boy's mind was working overtime to explain what he saw.

"I'm not going to shoot anything. Just being cautious, that's all."

The two of them stepped back out onto the porch. Diaz swung the flashlight across the yard, but whatever had been there was gone. They went back inside, closed the window, and engaged the double-bolt.

"I think you were right, buddy. Must've been a deer."

"But, Dad, it didn't look like a deer—"

Suddenly there was another crash, this time the strange trampling sound was in the front yard.

Diaz grabbed his son and pushed him into their hallway.

"Stay here!" he said.

"Dad, what's going on?" Tears welled in the boy's eyes.

"I'll check the front yard, then come right back to you. You stay here where it's safe, okay?"

Will's lip quivered as he agreed.

Diaz raced to the door. Opened it without hesitation. Shotgun leading the way.

11

D iaz threw open the front door and nearly gave the delivery boy a heart attack.

"Oh shit! What's going on, mister?" The kid yelled, backing away as he fumbled the pizza boxes.

"Jesus, kid!" Diaz quickly lowered his shotgun and pulled the boy through the door. "Get inside—*right now!*"

"So sorry, Mr. Diaz. I didn't think I was *that* late. By the way, there's something in your yard. Neighbor's dog, I guess, scared *the crap* out of me!"

Diaz scanned the front yard. Nothing was there. He shut the door and locked it.

"Apologies. For saying *shit*, I mean. Oh dammit, I did it again. To hell with it, you can take that out of my tip."

Spooked, confused, and possibly high, this kid was delivering curse words, not pizzas. He handed the two boxes to Will, who laughed at his colorful word choices.

Diaz grabbed his wallet. "How much?"

"Take as much out of my tip as you want, seriously. It's okay. I messed up. Just don't tell the boss. I really need this gig. It's my side hustle, you know. Trying to save up for a new turntable. DJ Nitro! You ever heard of me?"

Diaz smiled pleasantly as possible. "How much for the *pizza?*"

"$24.75, and I can take credit card."

Diaz handed DJ Nitro two twenties.

"Keep the change, kid."

"Wow, thanks Mr. Diaz." The kid pocketed the money, then glanced at the shotgun on his way to the door. "Is everything okay here?"

"Nothing big to worry about." Diaz said. "Listen, we'll keep everything that just happened between us, okay?"

"Sounds good, thanks so much. Enjoy your food and have a *super cheesy night*. Oh, we're supposed to say that."

Diaz gave the kid a half-grin. Will was already eating at the table.

"I'll watch you get to your car, okay? Lock the doors just to be safe."

The kid shrugged and mumbled something about paranoid cops, but made his way to his car.

Diaz took a deep breath as he locked the door, then made his way to the kitchen, rummaged through the refrigerator for a fresh beer, and joined his son at the table. It seemed they were both still on edge. Will was dealing with it by inhaling pieces of pepperoni pizza. After about ten minutes of manic eating, he stopped and eyed the window to the backyard.

"Dad, I'm not hungry anymore. Can we have this for breakfast?"

"Sure champ, no problem. You okay?"

He shrugged as he finished his drink.

"Dad?"

"Yeah?"

"Can I sleep with you tonight?"

"Of course. But you know you're safe here, right? I will always protect you. Don't forget that, okay?"

"I know, but ..." He played with the lace on his tennis shoe.

"You know, sometimes I like having a bunkmate," Diaz said. "Go brush your teeth and get ready for bed."

A smile returned to Will's face, and he rushed off to the bathroom.

If Diaz was honest, that exchange saved him the embarrassment of asking the same thing. He wanted Will close tonight. Something was out there, something that felt sinister, and Diaz sensed it wouldn't be the last time he came face-to-face with whatever it was.

Next time, he'd be ready for it. He'd make sure of that.

Diaz peered out the windows and scanned his property. The moon illuminated the wooded area in the southwest corner a bit more. Nothing was out there.

"Do you see that thing?" Will asked as he returned. He'd changed into his pajamas.

"Nope, I think *DJ Nitro* scared it away."

"What do you think it was?"

"Not sure yet. Cougar, maybe."

"Really? I can't wait to tell the guys!"

"Yeah? Well, like I said, maybe we keep this quiet until I know what we're dealing with."

"Can I tell Evan, at least?"

Diaz knew this was a perfect story for elementary school recess. Hard to deny the boy that.

"Okay, you can tell them. But, tell the truth. We *think* we saw a cougar, could've been a stray dog. We don't know what it was, okay?"

"Sure. I promise. It's totally top secret. Just between the two of us," Will said. "I swear on my cub scout heart."

Diaz laughed, snatched his son off the ground, and gave him a big hug.

"Okay, Mr. Top Secret."

"Dad, put me down. There's something else I need to show you."

Will rummaged through his things and returned with a black plastic case. "I think I should've told you about these."

"Is that the *treasure* you found?"

He opened it up. Inside the foam-padded case were a dozen black metal devices the size of hockey pucks. Each disc sported its own small antennae.

"I thought they were radios," Will said.

Diaz picked one up and inspected it while Will explained.

"I took one apart. Part of it is a radio. A transmitter, really. I want to keep that if it's okay, but this other part ... well, it's pretty dangerous for kids. Adults, too. See—"

Will showed Diaz the device's core battery covered with a red and white sticker. It depicted ionizing waves, a skull and crossbones, and a stickman running away from the danger. It was a radiation warning symbol.

Suddenly, the notice Sheriff Turner had given him earlier that morning came to mind. He knew what this was. The bulletin had been explicit.

Will was holding a treasure—*a very secret treasure*—one that the Pentagon was eager to get back.

Diaz didn't hesitate. He picked up the phone and made the call.

PART IV

FLY BY NIGHT

12

The sun hung over the Pacific Ocean, bathing the coast in its late afternoon warmth, when the ARES lifted off from the helipad at Angelos Grove. As programed, it flew south toward Dulzura, California. Nicks sat down and buckled in her safety harness.

She ran her hand over her upgraded arm. Quinn had wrapped it with a special regenaderm bandage, which would facilitate the self-healing artificial skin. An improvement over her old silicon sleeves. So far, she was pleased; the change was barely noticeable.

She leaned back, closed her eyes, and listened to the soothing sound of the rotors as they finished the vertical ascent and gave way to the jet thrusters. Soon they were at altitude and on the way.

The ARES was a welcome addition to their growing inventory of vehicles. They had cars, motorcycles, and the Sandbugs, but this was an upgrade—a low-maintenance sky taxi ready to go at any hour. Essentially an unmanned drone, it could fly and land on almost any terrain. A pilot wasn't required, and it was easy to modify for different missions.

Nicks's destination wasn't far. She'd been told it was a small ranch near the border in unincorporated San Diego County. And within the hour, the ARES descended from the turquoise sky, stirring up the ancient dust of the Otay Wilderness, and landed in a clearing between the Tijuana River and the ranch's fence line.

Quinn picked the secluded location because Nicks could drop in and do some quick reconnaissance unnoticed. And get the lay of the land before she investigated their new lead.

When the ARES cut its engines, the rear bay opened, and Nicks disembarked through the lowered ramp. It took a minute for her to realize she was in danger.

The man aiming his rifle at her was behind a nearby tree. A soldier, no doubt. His stance, uniform, and that fact that he seemed unfazed by the lingering rotor wash of the airship, suggested he was military.

The man had her dead to rights. Nicks imagined that arriving by the ARES was unsettling to anyone. This close to the border, it would be easy to consider her a threat. She raised her hands in surrender.

"I come in peace," she joked.

The man didn't respond. Instead, he maintained his position for a moment, watching her. When the ARES powered down, he stepped out of cover, still aiming the rifle at her head.

As he approached, she saw he was a San Diego County Sheriff.

"Nicks? Natalie Nicks? It can't be!"

The sheriff lowered the rifle, stopped, and stared—confusion evident in his eyes.

It had been a long time since she had seen him. He hadn't aged a day. In fact, he appeared more fit than she remembered him being in Afghanistan. She'd been living the life of a nun recently, and it was hard to ignore how handsome Brett Diaz looked in his uniform.

"But I saw you die ..."

His face was a mask of disbelief and awe.

Nicks lowered her hands, "Hi, Brett."

He rushed toward her, and they embraced.

13

Nicks examined the black case Will had discovered. She took out each remaining sensor and laid them out for a closer inspection.

"What your son found is a new security device called Taproot. It's an Unattended Ground Sensor or UGS. But these are light years ahead of what's available on the current market."

"So the outfit you work for made these?" Diaz picked one up. "What's it do when it goes off? Lights? Sounds? Badass Lasers?"

"Alerts someone on a computer somewhere. Honestly, I don't get that deep into the weeds on this stuff. They were being tested at Fort Huachuca to deploy them along the border."

"But how did they end up out here? On my land?" Diaz asked. "That's an entire state away?"

Nicks was wondering the same thing. These were some of the missing sensors, all right—but only a handful. There was a truck full of cases still unaccounted for.

"I'm not sure, but that's what I need to find out."

Nicks noticed Diaz was studying her. Really looking. She had studied him too. Something about the way he sat in that chair, at ease, confident, his dark eyes matching the dusky sky outside. It had been a long time since they'd spent time alone together. In the service, there'd been chemistry, but the mission, and other relationships, had been in the way.

Diaz broke the building tension by changing the subject. "We saw something strange last night. Couldn't make it out clearly, but it seemed to be a cougar."

"Are there many around here?"

"A few. You get the occasional sighting, and every ten years some unlucky hiker runs into one on the trails."

"You worried it will come back?"

"Only because I have someone to protect." He hooked his thumb at Will.

She turned around and admired the little boy. "What is he building in there?"

"He said it's a new remote control, but I think he's just taking apart his game console," Diaz laughed. "He's got part of a broken sensor in there. If you need it back—"

"Let him have it for now, I've got the worrisome part here." She held up the battery. "And I'm sure he'll get bored with that soon enough. When it's time to pack up, I'll grab it."

Diaz finished his beer and stood up. Stretched and eyed the glow of the fading sun painting the hills. "You still shoot straight?"

"Straighter than most."

He opened the refrigerator and came out with a plate of leftovers.

"Good. With two of us here, I feel more comfortable being stupid."

He scraped the leftovers into a plastic bucket and headed out the back door. He gave her a mischievous grin and motioned for her to follow.

In the back of his truck, he had a wire mesh cage. An animal trap with a gravity operated door.

"I see you're bandaged up. Are you healed enough to help me

with this cage? One of my Game and Wildlife buddies loaned it to me today. It's heavy, but between the two of us we can get it out."

"I specialize in heavy," she said.

She got into the bed of the truck and grabbed the cage. She then jumped down, still holding it level. No problem.

Diaz stared at her in disbelief. "You've been working out, I see."

"Something like that."

"It took two men to get that into the truck. How are you—?"

"Now you mention it, it is getting heavy. Where do you want it?"

Diaz shook himself out of his surprised daze and pointed at the fence. He guided Nicks to the place he remembered seeing the animal.

Nicks put the trap down. She hadn't even broken a sweat.

Diaz littered scraps inside the cage and around it. The grease from the food made a little stream in the dark soil, reminding him of the blood trails he'd found in the gopher hole. He eyeballed her as he set the trap door.

"Bait!"

BACK INSIDE, Nicks sent pictures of the sensors to the team at the Cage.

"You plan on offering me one of those?" She pocketed her phone and eyed his longneck.

"Oh, this was yours, but I thought you were working." He winked at her and headed back to the refrigerator. "Sorry, Nicks. My hosting skills are still pretty shitty. Usually it's just us boys. We live like savages."

"Divorce, huh? Sorry to hear that," she took the Corona. "Cheers. Here's to better times."

They clinked bottles to toast their reunion and then they both took a long pull.

He looked at her. "I'm so glad I made that call."

"I'm happy too," Nicks said. She reached out and gave him a hug. "It's good to see you."

They stared at each other again. There was something there, Nicks felt it. She sensed he felt the same way. But this was not the time or place. She stepped back, wishing it was.

"How about a home cooked meal?" He asked.

"Absolutely."

"I can roast a chicken and make mashed potatoes."

"Sounds good to me."

Will ran into the room. "Mashed potatoes! Heck yeah!" The little kid shook his butt and clapped his hands.

"So, you're a good student and a dancer too?"

"Oh, yeah!" he said. "I know how to shake my groove thing, yeah, yeah!"

"Okay, groove on over and help me." His father laughed.

Will danced over to the counter, picked up some napkins and silverware, and set the table in record time. As he returned to the kitchen, he zeroed in on Nicks's arm.

"Whoa!" Will stepped closer. "No way! Are you a robot?"

Nicks hadn't noticed, but the regenaderm had curled up, exposing a glimpse of her metal wrist joint. Must have happened when she lifted the cage.

"Hey, buddy, that's not—" Diaz tried to grab his son's attention.

"No, that's okay. I'd want to know too." She sat at the table and unwound the bandage up to her bicep. Will's eyes widened.

"A cybernetic prosthetic. Wow! Did DARPA make that?"

Nicks and Diaz looked at each other. Now, it was her turn to be shocked. How did this little kid know that? She stared at him in disbelief.

"Super-soldier program. I've watched a gazillion videos about it," he said. At a huff from Diaz, the kid threw him a face. "YouTube, Dad. Duhhhh."

Will stroked Nicks's arm until his father snapped his butt with a kitchen towel.

"Ow! What's that for?"

"No inappropriate touching, young man."

"But it's so cool."

"And it's attached to someone that's really hungry. Remove your grubby little fingers before she bites them off."

Nicks playfully snapped her teeth at Will.

After a bit of horseplay, she did her best to explain her bionic arm. For the first time in the longest time, she was happy to have that secret exposed.

When Will went back to the living room, flashes of playing house went through her mind. She imagined cooking dinner, something she'd never done. Folding laundry, something she was allergic to. Surprising Will with a plate of cookies and demanding the occasional bear hug from the little man.

Could she be a mother?

The doctors had told her it was impossible, and she'd tried to accept that even though a part of her wished they were wrong. But with all the changes, the upgrades, and the memory loss because of the constant use of her AI assistant Flux, was she still human enough to nurture a child?

"You okay?" Diaz asked.

"Yes," she lied. "Just admiring the life you've built here. I understand why you want to protect it. He's something special."

AFTER DINNER, Nicks and Diaz retreated to the back porch.

"You know, you were great with him in there. The way you handled his curiosity. I appreciate you letting him off easy. Sometimes that kid's mind seems to be miles ahead of his mouth."

They both peered through the window. Will was cutting wires and twisting them together.

"He has that feel, like the people I work with now—they don't realize how gifted they are." She patted Diaz on the shoulder. "You're doing a great job with him, don't worry."

He smiled, then turned away as if embarrassed. He told her it had been a long time since a woman complimented his parenting. Dates were exceedingly rare. He'd decided not to bring new women around the house, at least not for a long time.

She suppressed the impulse to lean over and kiss him. Instead, she put the Corona bottle to her mouth and took a big swig.

"Thanks for the compliment, but it's like the service. You're only as good as your last mission."

Yep, she understood that perfectly.

"So, you have mutilated bodies, a rabid cougar, and pieces of DARPA tech scattered across your ranch," she said, counting these things out on her fingers. "Definitely my kind of job."

"Guess it's a good thing I called you."

"Well, the great thing about calling me is that nowadays I come as a packaged deal," she said, reaching for the small radio clipped to a belt loop on her jeans.

"Cartwheel. This is Viper. Come in, over."

He raised an eyebrow. "Didn't know you brought anyone."

"She came earlier. To get the lay of the land, maybe do a little clandestine border crossing. But you didn't hear that from me."

The radio came to life.

Fatima had news.

ONE MILE AWAY, Fatima continued her reconnaissance. She scanned the ground with Mouse's device. A weak signal flashed across the screen.

"It's not much more than a radio tuned to a special frequency," Mouse had said. "As long as the batteries hold up, it should find any nearby sensors."

She'd been out hunting for most of the day, having started near the tunnel discussed in the deputy's report. From there, she headed south into Mexico for a few miles. There she'd found a string of loose sensors.

Nicks radioed for an update and asked if she'd had any luck. Fatima explained what she'd found. Then said, "But the trail is cold at the moment."

"Interesting. Where are you right now?" Nicks asked.

"Rather not say. But I sent coordinates of each find back to the Cage."

"Copy that."

"I'll search another half-mile, then head back to your location."

"What's your ETA?"

"Should arrive by nineteen hundred unless I find more of these things."

"Let me know if you need backup. Don't mind stretching my legs," Nicks said.

"You'll be the first one I call, believe me."

14

After an hour of reminiscing about their time in the Rangers, Diaz collected the empty beer bottles and the two of them stepped back into the house. He was about to dead-bolt the back door when she stopped him.

"Something's out there, I can hear it."

"You sure about that?" He strained to listen. "I don't hear a thing."

"My arm wasn't the only thing that got an upgrade." She squeezed past him and stepped off the porch. "I think your bait worked."

Diaz grabbed his shotgun and followed her. "Show me."

Nicks pointed past the fence line. The sound was coming from a grove of trees at the edge of his property, but neither of them could see anything.

After a minute or two, the sound was unmistakable. Something was coming through the woods. Diaz took aim with his rifle. The shapeless shadow finally took form, and it was larger than expected.

In fact, it was a horse. And the man leading it was Sheriff Chet Turner.

"Hold your fire!" he yelled.

The old cowboy emerged from the dark woods holding a shotgun. He held it tight against his shoulder, scanning the horizon as he walked. In the other hand, he held the reins of his palomino quarter horse, leading the big mare beside him.

Diaz and Nicks stepped off the porch and walked over to greet him.

"Chet, what the hell are you doing out here?" Diaz asked.

"Should've called, I guess."

"Chet's not that good with cell phones," Diaz said to Nicks.

"Too bad. It prevents death by friendly fire," she joked.

Sheriff Turner pushed his hat back on his head and gave Nicks a hard look. "This can't be who the Pentagon sent, can it? She's too much woman for that."

Nicks rolled her eyes. Diaz seemed embarrassed by the old man and rushed through the formal introduction.

"Captain Natalie Nicks, this is Sheriff Chet Turner. Our local lawman. My boss."

"Nice to meet you, Sheriff."

"Same, young lady, same," he said. "Honestly, you're too pretty to be a soldier."

She ignored the comment and shook his hand. But she squeezed hard enough to make a point. "What are you doing out here so late? Bit past your bedtime, isn't it?"

The sheriff grinned, acknowledging he got the point.

"Thought I'd do a little hunting before I turned in. Never know what's lurking 'round these parts."

"If you're hunting cougar, seems you just missed it," Diaz said.

"Funny, you'd say that."

The sheriff explained he'd had a few calls about animal sightings. Nothing definitive. All the callers had seen it at night but couldn't identify it. So he thought he'd check it out. Diaz filled his boss in on the prior night's events. The three of them walked the fence out to where Diaz had set up the trap.

"You can see it's been here," Diaz said. "Strange it didn't touch the bait."

"Not a paw print one," said the sheriff. He turned on a flashlight he'd been carrying and scanned the ground. "But it leaves a trail of sorts. Just one I can't make any damn sense of. I think it might be wounded."

The sheriff tied off his horse and moved off into the dark toward the river, following the tracks.

"Shouldn't he stay with us?" Nicks whispered.

"He's crusty as hell, but one of the best trackers I've ever met."

Nicks and Diaz waited and watched as the beam of his flashlight swung here and there like it was being carried by a ghost. After a few minutes, he came back, brow creased.

"I don't know what to make of this thing," he grunted. He switched off the flashlight, letting their eyes adjust to the starlight. "I think you ought to go on back to the house, young lady. This thing could be dangerous—"

Before Turner could finish his thought, a shadow leapt out of the darkness, grabbed the old man by the throat, and disappeared before he managed a scream.

"Holy shit!" Diaz yelled, grabbing Nicks by the arm. They both stumbled back, mouths agape.

The sheer horror of the animal's power was heart stopping. It was as if a great white shark had leapt out of the ocean and pulled someone under.

The sheriff was gone.

15

Nicks and Diaz frantically searched for the sheriff to no avail. The animal and the old man had completely disappeared.

At a movement to the west, Diaz turned and raised his rifle. Nicks grabbed the barrel and pushed it down.

"He may still be alive. You could hit him," she said.

Diaz turned to her. He was shaking. She wasn't. He seemed out of practice with this kind of action.

"Turner!" Nicks yelled. "Turner, are you out there?"

Diaz followed her lead, yelling for his boss, but there was no answer.

"Flux, sonify the target." She held out her right hand, palm flat. Her skin, as if melting, formed a cone-shaped well, honeycomb holes appeared within it. A stream of infrasonic sound waves detectable only to her bionic ears pulsed out into the dark.

Nicks moved her hand in a sweeping motion back and forth, hoping Flux would echolocate the animal.

Flux reported, *"One target moving along a north by northwest axis. Forty meters to your right. Rendering its profile now."*

"This way." Nicks grabbed Diaz by the arm and pulled him along after her. The path led back to the house. As they moved, they searched the ground.

"There's blood here," Diaz pointed at a dark stain a few feet ahead. The strange tracks of the animal cut through the dusty ground beside it.

"His hat," Nicks said. She pointed at it but didn't dare bend over to pick it up. They needed to be ready for anything at this point.

"Sheriff Turner, can you hear us? Yell out if you can," Nicks pleaded. But nothing came back from the inky black beyond them.

As they approached the house, Flux gave Nicks a warning.

"Target has changed direction. Closing from the south on your position."

Nicks turned around and faced the river. Her ears picked up a weird metallic sound, like a pair of scissors opening and closing. It sped up until it was a flurry of metal wings. The animal galloped past their position, ignoring them altogether, heading straight for the house.

She turned around to warn Diaz, but he'd already figured it out

"Will!" he yelled and took off running.

"Diaz, stay with me!" But it was too late. He was already in a full sprint. She heard the scissors again coming from the backyard. "Dammit!"

Diaz had slung the rifle over his shoulder. Using one hand, he hurdled over the fence. But with her enhanced speed, Nicks cleared the railing and powered past him like he was standing still.

Will had just stepped out onto the porch. He stood there like a statue, framed in soft, warm light emitting from the house.

"Dad ..."

The monster had beaten them home. It crouched in the darkness about eight feet away from the boy—ready to pounce.

16

Nicks skidded to a halt, an equal distance from the animal and Will. What she saw in the shadows confused her. It was familiar, yet alien. The outline in the faint light revealed a body of clean curves and odd rectangular elements. It was midnight black, and its eyes glowed like red Christmas lights. The strange mechanics mimicked an animal, but it was anything but.

"Flux, can you ID this thing?" She whispered.

"*Origin unknown. Please choose a name for this profile.*"

Nicks was at a loss. The only description that seemed to fit was *monster*. And it was living up to that name, stalking the most vulnerable victim it could choose.

It crouched and crept forward like a predatory cat, preparing to lunge at its prey. If it did, it would kill the boy. The animal was twice his size and had already taken down Sheriff Turner. Will had zero chance against it.

Brett Diaz stopped and took careful aim. "Son, I've got this thing in my sights. Don't make any sudden movements!"

Nicks, now shoulder-to-shoulder with Diaz, noticed Will was holding the remote control he'd built. She guessed he'd finished it and had come out on the porch to show it off, only to discover his father was gone. Now, he faced a monster right out of every child's nightmare.

Will pushed a button on the device he was holding.

The cat rotated its strange head as if listening. A purr, like the whirl of a motor, reverberated through the darkness. It stepped forward, still crouching, storing up energy to leap.

Diaz inched closer. "I'm coming for you, son."

"Do not shoot. At this angle, you could hit Will," Nicks whispered.

"That's my son, I'm not backing off—" His eyes were wild with fear.

Diaz took a few more steps. The cat slinked closer. Will stared at the creature, mesmerized and unaware of the danger he was in.

Nicks had to act now.

The cat beat her to it. It leapt toward the boy.

Nicks jumped forward bionically.

The boy screamed

KABAMMMMMM!

The unmistakable sound of a gunshot rang through the night, knocking the animal off course. It tumbled away from the porch and fell in a heap as if someone had swatted its hindquarters with a baseball bat.

Nicks landed next to Will, grabbed him, and leapt again, back to Diaz. She handed Will to him. Her superhuman agility shocked them, but she didn't have time to explain, because the monster rose from the dead. It stood in one fluid motion, rotated its head three sixty to get its bearings, and galloped toward the river.

Nicks took off after it. The scissor noise vibrated in her ears as it disappeared into the dark night at a speed that would put a real cougar to shame. She pushed herself to match its pace.

It reappeared, bounding out of the darkness. And when it leapt to clear the ranch's fence, it got hit again.

KABLAM!

It tumbled over itself and collapsed. This time the monster didn't get back up. Instead, its motors whirled in spurts and sputters.

When Nicks skidded to a halt next to it, the cat-machine raised its head, and snapped its jaws, as if it were trying to frighten Nicks away. In the starlight, the black fangs were slick, probably with blood.

To get control of it, Nicks side-stepped the snapping jaws and stamped a foot on the animal's neck. Putting her full weight on its frame, she grabbed its head and wrenched it off at the neck joint. She tossed the head to the side, and it rolled away into the darkness with its jaws still snapping.

Nicks then punched through the creature's side-plating and tore out part of the engine driving its core. In short order, the thing was dead.

Diaz and his son approached cautiously.

"Someone shot that thing, and it wasn't us." Diaz said.

"There's only one person I know who would've risked a shot like that." Nicks pointed over his shoulder to the west. "Her."

As if on cue, Fatima Nasrallah emerged from the shadows with a large rifle slung over her back. She was running as fast as she could. Nicks greeted her with a wave.

"What would you do without me?" She asked breathlessly. Her eyes widened when she saw the machine. "What the hell did I shoot?"

"That's what we want to know." Diaz stepped forward, holding Will.

Will clung to his father, sneaking glances at the machine while Nicks made the introductions.

Diaz eyed Fatima's rifle.

"Is that a .50-cal?"

"Close. 12.7mm. I built it myself. The base is a DsHK Russian heavy machine gun."

Diaz's eyebrows rose. "So, that's what took that damn thing down."

"Dad!" Will said. "*Language*—but I guess it's okay. I want to cuss too."

Everyone chuckled, breaking the tension momentarily.

"We should get in the house, lock up, and discuss this once we put Mr. Will to bed. Sound like a plan?" Nicks didn't want to take any chances.

"I won't go to bed without you guys," Will said. "Don't be crazy."

"That's fine, bud. But I bet you pass out soon, being that brave takes a lot out of you."

"I think the treasure I found belongs to that thing," Will said, holding out his remote. "It wanted it back!"

"Let's discuss that over pancakes in the morning?" Nicks suggested.

"Pancakes, really?"

"Heck yeah!" She said.

"Okay, that's a deal."

She gave the boy a fist bump and father and son headed back toward the house. She was happy the thoughts of breakfast comforted Will, but she knew the morning wouldn't be pleasant. The sheriff was still out there.

Fatima keyed in on her concern.

"I tagged his location with my GPS on the way in," she whispered. "Massive trauma to the neck. He was dead the second that thing attacked him. He's not going anywhere. We can recover his body in the morning."

Nicks didn't want to leave the Sheriff out there, her normal impulses chaffed against the idea of waiting, but it was the most sensible plan. She had no idea what this machine was or whether there were more of them lurking in the shadows. It would be safer for the others to continue their investigation at daylight.

They needed every advantage possible to find out what they were up against.

17

RAYLOCK INDUSTRIES HEADQUARTERS

D ylan Barnes yelled at Travis Raylock from across the
office. "You'll be the death of me, I swear it, Raylock!
Everything we built together will be destroyed with this
one idiotic misstep. I can't let that happen!"

The fit man paced in front of a conference table, running his
hand through his flaxen mane of stylish hair. Raylock turned briefly,
caught the desperate glance Barnes shot at the over-sized computer
monitor. A digital clock was ticking off the countdown and a dialog
box was flashing a message: *Enter Biometric Data To Confirm Bid.*

Raylock turned back, seemingly immune to Barnes's antics, and
put his sneaker-clad feet up on his massive desk, engrossing himself
in what appeared to be an elaborate flight simulator game. A swath of
desert landscape scrolled past in high-definition. He fine-tuned the
navigation controls. Moving the camera's crosshairs over his intended
target.

"I know you're here *somewhere*," he muttered.

"Are you even listening to me?" Barnes screamed.

No. He wasn't. Raylock endured Barnes's tantrums like a Zen
monk. A necessary coping mechanism from the early days of their

partnership. In that time of garage offices and wild idealism, Barnes had a softer edge. He controlled his anxiety with hourly marijuana smoke breaks and half-days at the beach surfing. As the money and responsibility mounted, so did these episodes.

Raylock Industries was now one of the most powerful conglomerates in the world. It had a bigger budget than entire countries, and its influence was ubiquitous, but somehow they flew under the radar. The company's name didn't have the panache of other larger organizations like Boeing, but that had been changing.

Dylan Barnes had always been annoying, but necessary to that success. From the beginning, Raylock used Barnes as a sounding board—a beta-tester of ideas and strategies. Barnes always found the flaw, the error in the plan, and fine-tuned it for the better. He was the governor on Raylock's brilliant racecar mind and suppressed his penchant for dangerously speeding ahead beyond what they could manage.

Dylan Barnes was also the silent, press-shy partner with a bankroll of life insurance money from his father's untimely death. He didn't want fame. He didn't want his name on the company logo. He wanted a safe stream of income from the initial seed money he handed over to Raylock.

His partnership agreement protected that, and only that. He had no visionary or creative role in the company. Responsibility to his family and employees and shareholders was more important than power. He only imposed his authority to buffer Raylock's risky schemes.

In short, Dylan Barnes was everything Travis Raylock was not and refused to be. Mostly, he was a sucker that had been marked and manipulated—not easily, though—for years by a genius-level conman. How shocked he'd be if he knew why his father had died at the exact moment Raylock had hatched the scheme to start a technology company. It had always surprised him that Barnes never suspected the timing of that insurance windfall—it had been too good to be true.

Today was different, though. The bid at hand, a potential

contract with Homeland Security, was the largest Raylock Industries had ever pursued. It risked everything they had built. Dylan Barnes saw the danger and intended to stop it. But he would not block Raylock this time, though he didn't know that yet.

A digital buzz broke through the tension, and the voice of Raylock's secretary made an announcement over the intercom. "Your new security hire is here, Mr. Raylock."

"Send him in," he muttered.

"Right away."

Raylock's efficient response to the secretary seemed to enrage Barnes more. He swatted a stack of documents off his desk. And hundreds of carefully created spreadsheets exploded against the wall.

"'Chill the fuck out, Barnes.'" Barnes said, doing a terrible impression of Raylock's surfer-bro accent. "Is that what you're trying to say? Because I've spent half a year making sure we were ready for this contract. And now you're underbidding? At the last minute? Have you gone insane?"

Raylock glanced at Barnes. He wasn't the one acting like a lunatic. Stomping around on the rejected budget like a child having a tantrum.

The door opened and a hulk of a man, easily the size of both Barnes and Raylock were they ever knit together, entered the room.

Raylock didn't look up to acknowledge the muscle-bound giant.

"Mr. Brightside, Dylan Barnes. Dylan, this is Brightside."

"Fuck you, Travis! Fuck you!" Barnes spat back.

Brightside said nothing to Barnes. He walked toward Raylock's desk and stopped in the center of the room as if hitting the mark on a stage. He adjusted the collar of his white dress shirt, pulling it up to obscure a chain of neck tattoos—leopard spots, perhaps. He buttoned the top button of his dark blue suit and settled into a soldierly parade rest.

"How sure are you about the coordinates of our friend's compound?" Raylock asked him.

"Absolutely sure," Brightside replied.

"Well, you can see for yourself. There is nothing here but undeveloped land. Blue skies and bronze desert. Granite and greenery. Not much else."

"The compound is there." His response was unfazed by Raylock's tone of doubt. "I led the scouting team myself."

Raylock fiddled with the game controller and the crosshairs stopped and hovered over a particularly dense section of the landscape.

"I actually believe you. It seems he's *borrowed* some of my technology to camouflage the area and forgot to send me a thank you note. I'll add this misappropriation to his next invoice."

"Why?" Barnes yelled. "Do you suddenly give a shit about our company's financial health? I sure as hell hope so because this bid needs to be changed right now. We've got about five minutes left."

Raylock once again ignored Barnes and continued talking to Brightside. "I will say it is good to see the system works under such *different* conditions. This is a massive operation, and its undetectable from the air and satellite imagery."

He toggled a joystick on the hand-held controller. A simulated female voice announced that the drone's auto-pilot feature had taken over. Raylock tapped a few more buttons to select the drone's recall flight path. Once it was engaged, he tossed the controller onto the desk and turned off the monitor.

"You were saying?" He swiveled his ergonomic desk chair around to face Barnes. He gave Brightside a cursory glance. "Like the suit."

Raylock appreciated style even if his was out of place in the defense contractor world. His hair, tied in a perfect man bun, was long and dark, which matched his beard, speckled with silver streaks. It was as if Merlin had been resurrected as a hipster. He wore skinny dark jeans, T-shirts with ironic slogans and groovy graphics, and long beaded necklaces and dharma beads. There were so many damn dharma beads on his wrist it had become a signature look that some of his younger employees imitated. If you knew nothing about the company, you would have thought the guy was the hip social media

manager. But this was Travis Raylock, a rockstar among celeb entre-
preneurs.

Everything he touched was instantly infused with his magic.
Everything except the dour naysayer on the other side of the room.

The monument of man-flesh didn't reply to Raylock's compliment, but turned to face Barnes as well.

Raylock got up and walked over to his partner's desk.

"Four minutes, Dylan. I've already verified. Now it's your turn."
He pushed the retina and thumb print scanners across the desk
toward Barnes.

"I told you, I'm not doing it. We have to raise the bid." He was all
but foaming at the mouth.

"The point is to win the contract." Raylock spoke calmly. A
slightly patronizing tone slipped out here and there. "We've been
over this already. I promise you it will work. Just like it always does."

Barnes softened momentarily.

"Travis, honestly. Is this best thing for our company, really?"

"Literally, it is the *best* thing."

Barnes rolled his eyes and threw up his hands. "We specialize in
the future and you want to build a wall? I just don't get it, man. We
got into this to build rockets and electric cars and date super-models.
And you want us to build a fucking fence? It doesn't make sense!"

"No, you misunderstand. I want to build a secure border. And I
also want to make billions of dollars for our company. Security is one
of our specialties, you know that don't you?"

"The contract is about building a wall, Travis. What the hell am I
missing here?"

Dylan Barnes was partially right. Senator Jason Snell's ambitious
plan, endorsed by the president, had promised to secure the entire
Mexico border. That was over two thousand miles. The contract
outlined the complexity of the goal. Barnes, like every other company
bidding on the project, had fixated on this section.

Raylock smirked. Barnes didn't know what he had planned. To
secure the border, as Barnes said he understood it, you needed a lot of

concrete and steel. The wall had to be at least thirty feet high. This was five feet higher than the infamously imposing Israeli West Bank Wall. It had to extend six feet from the base into the ground to deter tunneling.

It had to withstand penetration by all conventional construction tools for at least one hour. If some industrious vandal created a hole twelve inches in diameter before the one-hour mark, the wall was no good. It had to be unclimbable. And it had to be aesthetically pleasing, on one side. No guesswork was needed for which one. Even though the Mexicans "were paying for it," they would still get the shitty side.

Once finished, this would be the best border wall in the world.

Barnes rifled through the remaining files on his desk. He snatched out one particular document and read it like a Shakespearean actor.

"Our best estimate is that this project will cost seven million dollars per mile. That is a grand total of twenty-one billion dollars for the whole damn thing. It has a deadline too," said Barnes. "You have to have the first 1250 miles completed two years after acceptance of the contract. Ostensibly, so that the senator could attend the unveiling and record the monumental achievement. Assuring the most impressive twenty-first century photo ops of all time."

"We'll have it done in a few months," Raylock said.

Barnes snapped back, "Are you going complete Howard Hughes on me? Do I need to check your bedroom for bottles of piss?"

"So you won't do it?"

"Fuck no, and I'm sure as hell not going to discuss this any further while your new goon is in here. What is his function here, anyway?"

"Mr. Brightside, I think that's your cue. My partner's demands can't go unmet. Not today. Please, show him your function."

Brightside came to life like a robot given a command. He marched over to Dylan Barnes. Grabbed him roughly by his beautiful head of hair and smashed his face into the desk repeatedly. The last smack made a sickening wet thud. Brightside let go and stepped back.

Barnes lifted himself off the desk. His perfect nose was cocked to one side, already swelling and bleeding profusely. There was a nasty gash in his forehead.

"Damn! Brightside is as efficient as you, Barnes. He gets the job done, wouldn't you say?"

Barnes's mouth cracked open and blood dribbled out in a stream. He tried to reply but slurred his words. His jaw wasn't working properly. It appeared to be partially unhinged.

"What's that buddy? I can't hear you. Which is odd because you've been screaming and whining all morning. Don't tell me you're giving me the silent treatment now."

Raylock signaled Brightside to continue. Brightside grabbed Barnes by the neck and punched him several times in the face. His enormous fist slammed down with the force of a sledgehammer.

Raylock winced at the sound of fracturing facial bones. Eventually, Brightside let go and stepped back. Barnes collapsed back into his chair. His face was a bloody mess. Almost unrecognizable now.

"Damn, what a gruesome show this is, but it doesn't have to continue. Will you verify the bid now? Never mind talking. Just shake your head yes or no. We only have two minutes left."

Barnes's head wobbled back and forth. Whether he was agreeable or still defiant, didn't seem to matter to Raylock. This was one of the most entertaining moments he'd experienced in years.

"Not sure if that's a yes or no. Guess we have to do this the hard way. Use the thing—" Raylock said excitedly. Gesturing like he was swinging a sword. "I haven't seen it in action yet."

Brightside stepped closer. He flicked his wrist and was suddenly holding a solid black handle about six inches long. It looked like the hilt of a sword, but the blade was missing. He flicked his wrist again and that problem was solved. The centerpiece of the weapon telescoped out and, like a flower blooming, an array of small individual black razors sprouted around its length. It was a macuahuitl—a shortsword made of gnarly teeth instead of a solid blade.

Barnes saw it, gurgled in protest, and tried to stand up.

Brightside swung the weapon at Barnes and slashed him across the face. Upon impact, one blade embedded itself in his left eye. Brightside jerked back, ripping it out.

Barnes let out a blood-curdling scream.

Raylock winced at the gore.

"I would make a joke about not seeing eye-to-eye," Raylock said. "But we don't have the time."

Brightside held out the sword for inspection, and Raylock plucked the eye like he was being served an hors d'oeuvre. He held it up to the retina reader. The computer acknowledged identity confirmation.

"Good job, Brightside. The retina was still intact," Raylock said. "Now the right thumb."

Brightside was one step ahead. He'd already pinned Barnes's hand to the desk. He swung the macuahuitl down. In seconds, he'd severed Barnes's thumb with surgical skill. Barnes tried to scream, but Brightside had already muffled him with his massive hand.

Raylock took the thumb and placed it on the device's glass, activating the laser print scanner. The computer chimed, and the verification was complete.

"Fifteen seconds to spare. Damn, that was cutting it close. Pun intended."

The computer processed the verified bid for a few seconds until a confirmation screen appeared congratulating the firm on its successful submission.

"Excellent," Raylock said. "See, that wasn't so hard, was it?"

Barnes, who was obviously dying, looked at Raylock with his remaining eye and muttered an unintelligible plea for help. Raylock just smiled back as Brightside strangled him.

"I sense you understand," Raylock said over the gurgling death rattle. "Our partnership has run its course."

18

The next morning's pancake breakfast made Will happy, but it did little to change the bitter mood that had settled over the ranch.

Once Diaz had delivered his son to school, he returned with the county coroner and began the grim process of collecting Sheriff Turner's remains. Diaz didn't know what to do about the horse. Turner lived alone and had no family in the area. He called a neighbor who had horses, and she picked up the mare. Then he followed the coroner back to the station to file a report and deal with the problems associated with losing the most senior sheriff in the area.

While Diaz busied himself with things at the office, Nicks secured the bulk of the robotic animal in the barn. Fatima helped her lay out the minor components next to the larger pieces. The chunk that Nicks had torn out seemed to be part of the transmission. It was almost as amazing as her own bionics. Not as advanced, but eerily similar in sophistication.

Nicks held out her hand and Flux sonically scanned what was left of the machine. While Flux processed the data, they searched the ranch for more evidence. They found the first bit in a clump of grass near where the cat had fallen. Nicks picked up something like a metal straw. It reminded her of a bicycle spoke, but one part was larger in diameter, and the other piece moved up and down. It seemed to be a part of a hydraulic mechanism.

The closer she looked at the ground, the more pieces of metal she found. One seemed to be a cover or lid. It had a bullet hole right through it where Fatima had hit it. Fatima grabbed it from her and admired it.

"What is this thing made of," she wondered, "that it could take my specialized shell, lose a chunk of itself, and hardly miss a step?" She set it aside and found another metal plate with the exit wound.

Nicks noticed the shell was covered in small ceramic plates, armor perhaps. On closer inspection, they seemed to be solar cells. Or were they both?

"Well, that's something," Fatima said. "There can't be too many people making these things. Our first real clue."

"You'd think a large robotic cheetah was clue enough," Nicks said.

The absence of identifying information was the most interesting thing about these clues. There were no part numbers or codes on any piece of the robot.

The sudden text on her smartphone confirmed Nicks's midnight report had stirred the waters.

"We're coming down to see this thing," Byrne wrote.

The entire team was onboard the ARES, flying to the ranch— only a few minutes away.

"Do you know what this is?" Nicks typed back.

"One idea, and it's not good."

19

Nicks and Fatima climbed inside the ARES. Byrne, Quinn, and Mouse were there waiting, and they started the meeting. Nicks explained the events of the night before, including everything that Diaz had told her about the mutilated victims and the machine's stalking behavior.

Flux had sonically scanned the parts, but Nicks was unsure how to convey that to the team. Quinn helped her activate her new networking ability.

"All you have to do is ask Flux to patch you into the computer. In fact, you only have to imagine it happening. You should think of this as part of your body, like another finger."

She opted for the first choice.

"Flux, patch me into the DR-Ultra network."

A nanofiber wire grew from under her fingernail and threaded itself into the first available port on Quinn's computer. Flux sent the 3D model of the robot to the display, and everyone leaned in.

Byrne confirmed what Flux had already told Nicks the previous night. There was nothing like this in the DR-Ultra pipeline. Past or present. This was not a creation of DARPA or the United States Government.

"That may be, but it's pretty close to this." Quinn showed everyone an image of a robotic animal.

On the screen was the specs of a well-publicized DARPA project built by Boston Dynamics. It was one of the most popular DARPA videos on the internet.

"Big Dog was its name, oh," Mouse said in a sing-song voice.

"Come on, be serious; is this a joke?" Nicks had never heard of the program.

"Mouse is right. The name of the project was Big Dog. It was a four-legged robot that had a small car grill for a head, laser sensors, and two video cameras for eyes. It was a strange thing to look at, but it did the job they designed it for," Byrne said.

"Which was what?" Fatima asked.

Quinn explained, "DARPA built it as a pack mule for the military. It could carry up to three hundred fifty pounds and walked at about four miles per hour, faster than most marines can march. But it was loud as hell. If you used these things on a real battlefield, the enemy could hear you coming easily. So, despite of all its success, they scrapped it."

"Unsuitable for combat," Byrne said.

"They put Big Dog down like Old Yeller. Sad, even for a robot." Mouse grinned. "Unsuitable for combat is the stamp you never wanted to see on any of your project documents."

Mouse explained the process. He'd made the bulk of his fortune through government contracts.

"DARPA insists researchers shouldn't fear failure. Even on a project this big. They're good like that. But if you've spent a decade working on a new piece of hardware, and the Army deems it unsuitable for combat—well, that kind of project-killing rejection leaves a mark."

"Just one problem," Nicks said. "A mechanical mule didn't rip the sheriff's throat out."

She pointed back at the 3D model of the robot. It was almost identical to a cougar, or as its color suggested, a black panther.

"What we have in that barn is something very different from what you are showing me here."

"Yep, and that's why we came down. But, whatever this is, it isn't DARPA technology," Byrne said.

"So what are we going to do about it?"

"I ran this up the flagpole already, and they told us to stand down."

"Stand down? Are you kidding me?"

"That's what I was told. Maybe you've seen Senator Snell on the news? His Smart Wall project is moving ahead. In fact, the bidding process started today. That added attention has turned up the heat on our original mission."

"Are you sure about that? Because it seems this thing was acting autonomously. Don't we want to know who the hell built it and released it into the wild?" Quinn asked.

"Yeah! What she said!" Nicks's blood pressure was rising.

"It could be connected, but the Pentagon wants those stolen sensors recovered yesterday. So we follow orders and stay the course until the first job's done."

"I'm not setting this aside for some repo job, Byrne. A man died right in front of me. This thing killed him. This is a murder investigation, first and foremost."

"We'll let local law enforcement handle that angle."

"The man that lost his head to that machine *was* the local law enforcement. We're the only ones in a position to help. We've got to find out if there are more of these things before more people die."

"I understand the concern, but—"

"Follow orders, that's it? Have you forgotten Project Starfire already?" Nicks seethed.

Quinn grabbed Nicks by the shoulder. Fatima leaned in, probably thankful the boring part of the meeting was over. Mouse stared at his feet. Byrne didn't respond but worked his jaw side to side.

"I told Diaz I would brief him on our next move." Nicks stood up to leave.

How could her team overlook something like this? She'd seen this machine's power with her own eyes.

It had almost killed a child.

This was everything that people feared about future technology. Now, all of those fears had come true. She would find out who was behind this no matter what. Orders be damned.

20

N icks stormed down the gangplank of the ARES. Byrne caught her before she made it too far and pulled her aside. "Natalie, let's talk."

"Why the hell are you here?" she demanded. "I thought you were *taking time off*."

"What did you think? I was on a beach somewhere drinking beer and working on my non-existent tan? You think I would have gone somewhere like that without you? You know me better than that.

"They forced me to take the time. They moved the TALON lab to Granite Nine because of the breach at Blackwood Lodge. Penbrook insisted they finish tweaking my bionics. Upgrade a few things."

"Like your ability to tell the truth?"

"Like my *ability* to *stay alive*. That old TALON tech was slowly killing me. Now, I'm better and I can do more than just sit on my ass. Penbrook wants me back in the field."

"Great, so you *are* leaving," she sneered.

"Not right now. I'm still the leader of this team, goddamn it!"

"I'm pretty sure that needs immediate reevaluation—I assumed it was in process."

"Demote me? For what cause, Nat?"

"You know the reason, are you serious right now?"

A wildfire of anger and pain raged through Nicks. But something resisted digging the dirt back up, and honestly, what good would it do, here and now? But their last mission had exposed long hidden secrets. Ones almost too painful to bear. Especially her former lover confessing that he'd been part of the same covert operation that had nearly killed her.

He took a deep breath, then blew it out slowly. "Do you think the people that put me in this position didn't know about every minute detail of my past work?"

"*Work?* Is that what you call turning a sane man into a suicide bomber, who then blows my body to goddamn dust?"

"Are you ready to hear me out on that, or do you want to keep hating me for something I didn't do?"

"I heard you admit it." Her hands fisted on her hips.

"You heard part of the story. You heard a man trying to save the life of his team. His team that was being tortured by a *psychopathic child.* You heard me saying anything I could because you were dying right in front of me, and I thought ... I thought—"

"You thought, what? It would save your ass?"

He turned and roared at her. "I thought she was going to cut you up for parts like she did Vargas. I was freaking out!"

Nicks backed off. She knew about freaking out. She tried a softer tone. "What's the other part of the story?"

"What?" Byrne yelled.

She could see his mind had taken him back to that moment. He was reliving it right in front of her. She knew the look, she could feel the sickness of that mind-numbing fear, and how it oozes out of the dark corners of the heart and fills the bloodstream with its black tar.

She took a deep breath. "You said there was more to the story. Tell me."

She knew she was being unfair but couldn't help herself. They'd both pushed past their limits, no longer in the emotional place they needed to be to deal with the complexities of the truth. Nicks felt betrayed and was ready to rip his heart out if any of his confessions warranted it. And it was obvious to Nicks, Byrne was drained emotionally, unclear of how in the hell to repair what that little serial killer, Azmara, had done to his team—most tragically their relationship.

He shook his head. "I'll tell you the rest. All of it. But another time. Under better, *calmer* conditions."

She accepted that. They were both too worked up.

"There is something important, I need to tell you before I leave." He spoke slower, more deliberately as he laid it out. "There's intel. Enough to be relatively sure. The Dharmapala is still operating despite Starfire and Scorpio being dead."

Nicks had wondered if this was true, but had no proof other than her nagging intuition. He stared at her, saying nothing for the longest time.

"I'll find a way to get this investigation approved so you can stay down here. But you're on your own. Our team is on a short enough leash as it is."

Byrne walked away. Nicks was torn by her longing for him and her angry need to distance herself. All the time, all the trust, everything they had built together had crumbled. Didn't a soldier deserve more when they survived a battle? Or were they forever cursed—living casualties of war?

Another bad thought to bury with the rest. And another reason to find a bottle of tequila as soon as possible. She stormed back to the house as the ARES lifted off, climbed into the clouds, and disappeared.

21

After discussing it with Diaz, Nicks decided she would stay one more night, and at a minimum, meet with the Coroner about the Sheriff's death. That was going to be a tricky situation to navigate. If it yielded clues, she'd get a room at a nearby motel, use that as her local base, and widen her investigation. Surely, someone in the area knew something about the robotic cat. She'd dig quietly under the guise of looking for the sensors. Hopefully. Byrne would clear her to keep going if she found some leads. If nothing came of her efforts, she may have to return to Los Angeles with her tail tucked between her legs.

The thought of that made her want to get really, really drunk. But it was obvious she'd need to drive into town for that. Diaz only had two more Coronas and a bottle of Crown Royal that was so old, she couldn't twist the damn cap off without destroying the bottle.

Why the flood of feelings, now?

It was a terrible soup of terrible emotions. Her fight with Jack Byrne. The adrenaline of the night before. The murder of the sheriff. The near tragedy of what could've happened to her friend's son.

A child in danger.

That was one trigger.

Another child could've died because of you ...

That was the thought torturing her. Fighting with the other thought:

But you saved this one ...

There were flashes of herself as a kid—in danger—but she refused to go there. She needed to numb herself. Fall away into some manufactured oblivion, burn away the mind-numbing anxiety, and find a bit of peace.

She took one bottle of beer and excused herself to the hallway bathroom. Turned the sink on and, even though she shouldn't have done it, dug through the medicine cabinet.

Nothing of use here. Wait, what the hell am I doing? Stealing from a friend? Since when am I a pill popper? Try to calm down. No, don't try, do it.

She'd never been officially diagnosed with PTSD, but these moments made her wonder. Was there something wrong with her emotionally? Psychologically? She sat on the edge of the tub and took a few deep breaths.

I will not freak out. I will not freak out.

She repeated this mantra in her head. Breathing in and out. Gripping the tub. A small crack spider-webbed under her thumb. Dammit, she was gripping it too tight.

I will not freak out.

Flashes of the Jehanni Market flickered in her mind.

The beautiful fall day. The children running up to her. The explosion. The children running up to ... The suicide bomber. The children running ... The vest was a bomb. The children ...

"Hey, you okay in there?" Diaz tapped on the door.

"I'm good," she said. "I'm about to take a quick shower."

Tears weren't allowed. But that didn't stave off the pain forcing itself out one traumatic thought at a time—soldiers breaking into her castle. Sometimes all of your defenses fail, no matter how masterfully you've built the walls.

She opened the Corona. Drank half of it down and turned on the shower.

NICKS FINISHED in the bathroom and walked through the dark house. She peered out the window onto the ranch. No moving shadows tonight. Will's strange collection of small tools, computer and radio parts were sorted on the coffee table next to her.

Down the hall, the little boy was back in his own room, completely passed out, snuggled up with every stuffed animal and action figure he owned. Out of curiosity, she wandered into Diaz's bedroom. There was one picture of the Diaz family, most likely still there for Will's sake. She picked it up and admired it. Erin Diaz was stunningly beautiful. Diaz was an attractive man; it didn't surprise her.

Diaz came out of the bedroom bathroom in a towel, still drying his hair. He startled when he saw Nicks standing there. She was in her panties and one of his favorite classic rock t-shirts. He stared at the Van Halen logo stretched out by her firm breasts.

"You've been shopping in my closet?" he said.

"What? Fatima told me this was hers. I'm going to *kill* her." Nicks shook her head.

"Keep it, it looks so much better on you."

She noticed his eyes tracing over her exposed skin. His longing clear. Had it been a long time since a woman had undressed in his presence, in the intimate way a wife or girlfriend would, with no sense of self-consciousness—vulnerable?

Nicks was anything but vulnerable. It was an illusion helped by the moonlight, their loneliness, and the beer. He moved closer. She did the same. Both of them magnetized by their collective need. The heat radiating from their bodies was an immediate comfort. Awakening further desire.

She wrapped her hand around his neck and pushed herself into his body. Kissed him firmly on the lips and opened her mouth, inviting more.

His towel fell away as she pushed them both onto the bed.

He wasn't sure whether to touch her or where. Perhaps confused by the mysteries of her artificial limbs. She ripped her shirt off, grabbed his hands, and guided them to her breasts. His hands so warm, rough, and strong. It felt so good to be touched. They both needed this. So bad, in fact, it was obvious it wouldn't last long. But she didn't care.

She pulled her panties aside and pressed herself into him. When they finally found each other, she gave herself over to the pleasure. The rush of exhilaration overwhelmed her. She fell on top of him as he pushed in deeper. They found a perfect rhythm, moving in unison as if they'd done this a thousand times.

There was no time for creative positions, the pleasure was building too fast. His thrusts came faster and faster, and she welcomed them. Shifting her body, adjusting the way she joined his, until they were both swept up in a wave of passion that crashed over them, draining them of all their energy, and swirling all their combined longing into a whirlwind of ecstasy.

They collapsed into each other, and Nicks rolled over beside him. Breathlessly possessed by the lingering euphoria.

"Good job, soldier," she whispered.

He laughed and couldn't stop laughing.

But soon they were both on the edge of sleep.

He squeezed her hand warmly. She opened one eye, winked, and then rolled over, slipping into a long overdue sex coma she hoped she'd never wake up from.

22

When Nicks woke up the next morning, Diaz was already up and in the shower. Will was in the kitchen having cereal and watching a video on his father's phone. So Nicks got dressed and made coffee. When Diaz was ready for the day, they discussed next steps.

He would take Will to school. Check in at the office, then swing by and take her to meet the Coroner. Diaz was not looking forward to that part, but he knew it needed to be done.

Nicks had assumed she'd fare better at the morgue. But when they entered, she changed her mind. The mutilated corpse of Sheriff Chet Turner was front and center, laying on a stainless-steel exam table, partially covered by an ivory sheet speckled in crimson.

Nicks was shocked by how horrible the wounds looked. The machine had made deep ghastly tears in the muscles of his chest and neck. His right carotid artery, the primary route of blood to his brain, had been severed, and white bone was visible through the wine-colored wound.

His skin was a rainwater gray, and everything about the man that made him who he was, had disappeared. Now, he'd joined the border's numbered dead that filled the coroner's office on a regular basis.

His only distinguishing feature was he was still whole, at least mostly. Most of the bodies that accumulated in Dr. Sam Jackson's examination room were missing parts—the aftermath of cartel violence. The sheriff's last dignity was that they would bury him with all his limbs intact. Even Nicks couldn't claim that macabre victory.

She thought this gruesome thought while sipping a lukewarm cup of coffee, secretly hoping Dr. Jackson's autopsy would be over before she finished her drink. Diaz had explained Nicks was an old army friend from his Special Forces days. She was passing through the area and was interested in law enforcement. Tagging along. He'd said he wasn't sure she'd be able to stomach the work.

Nicks was playing the part very well.

"God bless the old man. What a terrible accident," Dr. Jackson said.

"It was over fast," said Diaz. "Too fast for us to save him, unfortunately."

"Long time since I've seen a mauling. I've only had one death by panther in these parts, and that was over thirty years ago, when I was just starting out."

"Believe me, it was a shock to us as well," said Diaz.

He turned to Nicks. She gave him an almost imperceptible nod. They'd rehearsed a bare bones cover story. Dr. Jackson was a possible leak that she had to make sure was plugged.

Reaper Force didn't want any public record documenting a death by the robotic animal. Diaz had agreed to keep things quiet, but they had to make sure nothing unusual landed in the doctor's report.

"There is one odd thing," Dr. Jackson said. He pulled the surgical light closer and used his forceps to point at the neck wound. "Right here, there's something embedded in his clavicle. Take a look, yourselves."

Dr. Jackson reached over to the side table and picked up a stainless steel specimen bowl and dropped the item in it for Diaz and Nicks to examine.

It was a jet-black, trapezoid-shaped object about the size of a matchbox.

"I know this," Diaz said. "It's obsidian."

"I believe you're right, son. You can find little balls of this on our hiking trails. Black stones that some people call Apache Tears. But this piece is very strange."

"Obsidian?" Nicks asked.

"Volcanic glass," Diaz clarified.

"Do you mind?" Nicks reached out to pick it up.

"Careful—" Dr. Jackson lunged to stop her, but Nicks registered the warning a second too late. The edge of the obsidian sliced right through her new fingertip, exposing the artificial bone underneath.

It was a split-second mistake, but impossible to hide. Nicks showed no pain. There was something like blood, but very different in color. And though she hid her wound as fast as possible, Dr. Jackson got a good view of her bionic finger.

Nicks noted the surprise and confusion in his eyes.

"I'm fine," she said, almost apologetically.

"Yes, I see you are," he marveled. "Were you injured in the war?"

She knew he was reaching for an explanation for what he'd seen.

"Something like that ..." Nicks said. Hiding her hand from view.

"I don't mean to overstep my boundaries, but that's the most life-like prosthetic I've ever laid my eyes on. Remarkable."

He seemed eager for her to allow another glimpse. But she flashed her prettiest smile and did her best to steer him back on course.

"I'm just so curious—you said there was something *strange* about this piece of obsidian. What did you mean?"

"Yes, well, like the Deputy guessed. It is obsidian. But it's not in its natural form. It's been *worked* into this shape."

Dr. Jackson walked over to his computer. Typed a few words into the search engine and pulled up a page of text and images. He spun the laptop around to show Nicks and Diaz. An enhanced image of a crude drawing filled one half of the screen. It depicted a man dressed in a leopard costume, holding a club. Other pictures showed close-up diagrams of his strange weapon.

"There are many fossil collectors in these parts, and they'd consider this a find of a lifetime. Obsidian blades were a favorite tool of the Aztecs," he said.

"The Aztecs had a strong warrior culture. Their army even had its own special forces." He glanced at Nicks. "They called themselves Jaguar Warriors. They were notoriously brutal killers who used a weapon called the macuahuitl."

He clicked the cursor and a larger, more defined image of the weapon appeared on the screen. It was a long flat club like a cricket bat studded with small black blades encircling it like the teeth on a chainsaw.

"The macuahuitl served two purposes: the Jaguar Warriors could bludgeon you to death or cut you in half if they swung it like a sword."

"You think this piece of obsidian came from one of these weapons?" Nicks asked.

This was a leap that Nicks knew didn't fit the situation, but she was interested in the connection.

"Very doubtful," said Dr. Jackson. "But this piece is shaped the same way the Aztecs did it. It's called flint-knapping. There are a few old-timers in the area that make these things. Real artisans. Sell their stuff at flea markets and local hunting stores."

"Makes sense. There must be tons of these scattered on my ranch. Like arrowheads," Diaz said.

Dr. Jackson stared at Diaz like he was crazy. "You aren't suggesting the Sheriff was attacked by a panther and then fell down on this by accident?"

"I don't know how else you'd explain it." Diaz gave a quick side-glance at Nicks. He'd backed himself into a corner.

The doctor's tone shifted.

"You two don't have to tell me what's really going on, but please don't play me for a fool," said the old doctor. He closed the laptop and set it aside.

The old man's forthrightness embarrassed Nicks, and from the color seeping into Diaz's cheeks, he felt the same.

"We don't mean to disrespect you," Nicks said.

"Let me put it this way, I can control my tongue. And even do my part to help. But it'll be a lot easier if some of my curiosity was laid to rest."

Nicks decided he was worth the risk. She outlined the broad strokes of who she was and what had happened. To his credit, Dr. Jackson took it in stride. He was a man of science, after all.

"To sum it up, a machine we've never seen before killed Sheriff Turner. And whoever made the thing seems to appreciate obsidian."

Dr. Jackson stared at the ceiling. Then he got up and walked over to the sink, turning his back on his two visitors.

"You need to keep this on the down low, Doc. All of it—including me."

"I didn't hear a word of what you said. Sorry my hearing gets a bit worse every day." He pumped soap into his hands and washed up.

"If you're asking my opinion on this case. I think it's obvious that wounds sustained in an animal attack caused the Sheriff's death. If memory serves, this will trigger the Game and Fish boys to start an investigation of their own, but my guess is they'll be searching for the wrong thing."

He turned around to face Nicks as he dried his hands. Then sealed the obsidian in an evidence bag.

"Obsidian is twelve times sharper than surgical steel. Dangerous even for someone like you, Ms. Nicks."

He handed her the bag.

"Best you and yours find whoever made this machine—and do it fast."

23

Diaz dropped Nicks back at the ranch, and they agreed to meet up later. She imagined it might be time for a motel, but he offered her another free night at his place. They didn't discuss the sex, and Nicks was happy about that.

Diaz then spent the rest of the day handling the details of Sheriff Turner's burial and memorial service. There was also the regular police work and the sudden influx of minor requests that went along with becoming the acting sheriff.

Back in Diaz's barn, Nicks compared Dr. Jackson's sample to the robot's parts. The jaw of the animal was full of similar blades—meaning its teeth were all made of obsidian.

Nicks discussed the new clue with Maggie Quinn by phone. Quinn was helping Byrne with the sensor investigation. But said she had no qualms about recruiting Mouse to help with a little research. An hour later, the two of them called back with some information.

"It wasn't hard to track your man down," Mouse said. "There are only a handful of knife makers in North America that make professional prismatic blades. Only a few that work in obsidian. And, fewer still that recently accepted six figure payouts for a massive order of such blades. In fact, there is only one. An eccentric knife maker named Vegas Santos who fancies himself a reincarnated shaman. I've seen some of his work. It's extraordinary."

"So where can I find Mr. Santos?" Nicks asked.

"We're making arrangements for you now," Quinn said. "Appears you'll get to spend a little time in Tijuana."

"Is that safe?" Nicks asked sarcastically.

"Not if you show up!" Quinn joked.

"Seems Santos has a lot of patrons in the cartels. Specifically, the Sinaloa Cartel, many of the sicarios from that outfit carry his knives. They treat him like a king. Apparently, shamans love hookers and booze," Mouse said.

"We created credentials for you. You're a freelance journalist who writes for travel magazines. You want to do a cover story on Santos. We'll have someone on our end arrange the meeting," Quinn said.

"Who made these big payments?" Nicks asked.

"The DIA says the money is flowing through a string of shell corporations. The accounting magician behind this transaction is superb," Mouse said. "So they haven't traced it to a legitimate source yet. But I'll send you the info, anyway."

"I'm including a background check as well," Quinn said. "On your friend. Byrne insisted."

"That figures." Nicks rolled her eyes. "What does it say?"

"He's essentially clean, but it's complicated."

Wasn't it always? Nicks thought.

"We're also compiling a list of every known DARPA scientist that might have a connection to this type of work," Quinn said. "But I'm hoping that Santos gives you something better than we have."

"Unfortunately, he's my only lead right now." Nicks said.

Tijuana was the next stop. One of the most dangerous cities in the world. Was it the key to finding the person behind the machine? She was about to find out.

PART V

ENTRE NOUS

24

Many hours later, Nicks was stuck in a traffic jam crossing the US-Mexico border. It was a nightmare most of the time, but this moment seemed especially bad. The sea of humanity moved at glacial speed.

She was glad Diaz had found a babysitter for Will and come with her. He knew the town well, or did, back in the day. It was a place he'd frequented in his youth, and again while on leave from the Army searching for the pleasures it offered. But he also knew it as a lawman —it was the source of some of the worst crime he'd ever known.

Through her window, she could see the primary hub for Senator Jason Snell's Smart Wall project. Some of the biggest government contractors in the world had built sentry stations there to demonstrate their ability to fulfill the contract. The variation in design was stunning and made Nicks curious about who might get the job. The winner would become one of the wealthiest companies in the world.

"So, if this is a clandestine op, what identity are you using?" Diaz mused.

"I meant to ask you the same thing." Nicks tilted her head.

He gave her a hard look. She stared back blankly, making sure she struck the appropriate tone. This was an impromptu confrontation.

"Your team checked me out—is that what you're getting at?" Diaz narrowed his eyes.

"Of course they did. Before I flew down, they were digging."

"So you know about my family's past, and you still trust me?"

"Of course, I do. I served with you. I *know* you. But the team is another story."

To the west, Nicks could see San Diego. Diaz pointed to a section of town as they approached.

"That's Barrio Logan. I spent a lot of my early years in that hood. My father made the wise decision to pull us out when my cousins joined the Logan Heights Gang. I'm sure they would've recruited me."

"How do your cousins feel about you being on the other side of the law?"

"Most of them are dead or in prison, so I think they would agree it was the right move."

"And what about the ones that aren't?"

"Doing what your team already suspects. They're caught up with the narcos."

"Were you ever tempted?"

"Tempted? With that kind of money? Hell yes! But it's *wrong* and destroys people's lives. Plus, it would've crushed my parents and disrespected all the sacrifices they made to get me out. Now I'm a father myself. Can you imagine a kid like Will in the center of that? I want him as far from that violence as possible."

Nicks agreed. That was the only sane choice.

Diaz continued, "Maybe I should have gone farther, because now I'm back in it again."

"I just had to put the cards on the table before we get any deeper. The truth. Trust. In my world, those are in short supply."

"You can trust me. For Will's sake and yours, I'll make sure nothing happens to any of us."

When they finally made it into the heart of Tijuana, night was setting in. Diaz warned Nicks. There were plenty of politicians who declared Tijuana safe, but he didn't share their opinion. His central evidence was the murder stats, and that data was clear. Over twenty-five hundred bodies dropped in one year. Mass graves had to be approved for the coroner's offices. Blood was in the streets, and he didn't want it to be theirs.

But you couldn't deny the attraction of the cheap thrills. Cheap being the key word. Vendors galore hawked delicious-smelling street food and handheld racks of knock-off toys. Strip clubs offered the thrill of sin, and preachers proffered salvation in rented store fronts.

Tijuana was trying to shake off the bad reputation, but it couldn't decide what it wanted to be. A new cultural scene had taken root. Gourmet restaurants, hipster art galleries, and fancier nightclubs had popped up in the better parts of town. But head north through the infamous arch, and you were in questionable territory. Everything Senator Snell wanted to keep out with his Smart Wall lived in Zona Norte. The very place they were going.

NICKS WALKED PAST A ZEBRA. Its owner waved her down.

"Selfie? Si! Bueno, selfie! One dolla."

The poor donkey had thick stripes of black and white house paint up and down its hide. Eyeing Nicks, it gave a disgruntled snort, and went back to chewing the bridle in its mouth and eyeing its owner with contempt. It seemed to hate its job.

"Some advice, the quickest way to cause trouble around here is to make jokes about the red-light district, the cartel, or the donkeys. So don't. This town has a huge chip on its shoulder," Diaz explained.

"Duly noted." Nicks gave a quick nod.

They walked on until they hit the main strip, past a line of prostitutes hovering near a narrow alleyway that lead up to a row of hotel rooms. These women were the parad001tas, or standing girls. Each one had their own dress code. Some wore colorful spandex or black yoga pants. Others had squeezed into short skirts and push-up bras.

Only a handful looked like they were old enough to be there. The youngest dressed in schoolgirl uniforms. The women all gave off an aura of wishing they were anywhere but on the street, unless a customer approached. Then the charm switched on.

Farther down, a neon sign read *The Tai Pei*. It was one of the most popular strip clubs. Nicks stepped through the blackout curtains and into the darkened lair of the establishment. Crazy neon colors, lit by the purple glow of black lights, illuminated the circus inside. Half-nude women gyrated on several stages throughout the main room. A bar adorned one wall and customer tables lined the opposite.

Diaz paid the cover and tipped the doorman, who then flagged a hostess, and she escorted them past most of the drunken tourists, into a more exclusive part of the club.

They sat at a corner table and ordered shots of Tequila, frozen margaritas, and some bar food. Here, they were shielded from the relentless techno beat. Nicks watched the action. It was a true den of inequity.

While nursing their drinks, they waited, hoping their target would make an appearance. They kissed and pawed each other like teenagers, for cover purposes of course, while Diaz explained the neighborhood's economy.

Zona Norte was the *zona de tolerancia*, a protected zone where the sex trade was allowed. Prostitutes had to get a permit and agree to monthly checkups. The Tai Pei was a club that funneled men to the prostitutes who operated in the small hotel rooms attached to the building out in the alley. They had passed that on the way in.

There were other kinds of prostitutes down darker alleys and hidden in special brothels. Nothing about the trade was empowering or good for anyone other than the gangsters who profited from them. But it seemed to have been going on forever, and it showed no signs of changing.

The average daily wage for Mexicans couldn't buy them a value meal at an American fast-food joint. So the money earned in the sex trade was life changing and standardized. The women negotiated a price—something less than a hundred dollars—then took the man to get a room. The room was another twenty. Customers ordered sex like sides off a menu. If you wanted something more advanced, you paid an up-charge. All of this took place in an efficient fifteen minutes, at which time the girl would escort the man back down to the street and do it all again.

Hearing this put some of Nicks's worst experiences in perspective. No matter how much she'd suffered, things could've been worse.

Having covered that vice, Diaz explained the rules of the drug trade. The narcos divided the city into retail zones. You could buy anything in Tijuana. Marijuana was plentiful, and you could find heroin with a little work. But there were two main staples: cheap crystal methamphetamine for the locals and cocaine for the gringos. Drugs were sold in little plastic bags called wraps, and they were available everywhere.

Diaz subtlety pointed at some of the bar patrons that were doing these kinds of deals. This fairy dust kept the nightlife magically alive. But its magic had dark consequences.

"Last night some rivals dumped two corner sellers out back *emtambado*."

"Emtambado?"

"Stuffed in fifty-gallon drums."

That detail disgusted Nicks.

"There's been a turf battle going on for several years now. There's so much poverty and greed in this town, people will fight over scraps the dogs ignore."

Nicks recalled how the DIA target package on El Draco had discussed the Tijuana market. The Draco cartel was gaining ground, but the US government wasn't sure how.

Nicks took another sip of her drink. As she set the glass down, she saw her target moving through the crowd. He headed for a table near them.

"I think that's our man," she said.

As he drew closer, they made a positive ID. An obvious regular, he took a table in the back.

Vegas Santos maintained a regal air that few of the other men in the club had. He wasn't rushing to the stages to stuff bills in the strippers' bikini bottoms. Or taking ten-dollar selfies with his head between a dancer's breasts—or worse. Vegas Santos didn't partake in any of that; he held court instead.

His hands were never empty, though. He was either holding a drink or a young woman's hand. *The fish*—the inexperienced girls who encouraged patrons to buy expensive drinks—stayed away. They allowed only the most expensive girls, along with the most expensive Tequila, into his orbit. It was the only thing Nicks admired about him.

After some time, they noticed one side-effect of the old man's drinking and it didn't seem to be intoxication. He held his liquor, but he hit the restroom every thirty minutes like clockwork. And for whatever reason, he enjoyed pissing in the alley instead of the crowded bathrooms. Maybe because he smoked while he was relieving himself.

Nicks decided that would be the best place to confront him.

When she finally made her move, and spoke to him in the alley, the old man's jovial mood soured.

"No sex, young lady. Drinking and drinking only. Excuse me."

Nicks pitched her cover story. Explaining she was a journalist from Los Angeles who wanted to write about him for a special story on important Baja artisans. She said her office had called and left messages. But Santos didn't seem interested in the opportunity, something most in his position would have thought a godsend. Nicks pushed it politely.

"Come to the shop tomorrow, noon, no earlier. Maybe we'll talk then. Excuse me now, I have at least another half-bottle to finish."

He tried to push past her, but Diaz stepped in his way.

He scowled at the old man. "Tomorrow won't do."

"Take your girlfriend and go, amigo."

"We need to talk now, Santos," Nicks said.

"I said no. Now get out of my way!"

Nicks stood her ground. Then pulled out the tiny evidence bag and discretely showed him the obsidian tooth.

He blanched and glanced over his shoulder as if he were being watched.

"Not here, not now—*maybe never!*" he hissed.

Nicks grabbed him roughly and shoved him hard against the brick wall. To make her point, she lifted him off his feet. "Maybe not here, but we talk tonight. So you pick the place."

He stared at Nicks as if he was seeing her for the first time, confused and amazed by her strength.

"My shop is a ten-minute walk from here. But make sure you're not followed," he whispered. They agreed to meet in one hour. She let him go, and Santos slipped back into the bar.

They watched him for a bit longer. Santos was downing the rest of his tequila like it was water. Nicks had sobered him up and he was compensating.

"That old man is a snake. I can sense it. We need to be careful."

Diaz agreed. The night was still young and Tijuana had a body count to maintain. They needed to avoid being added to it.

25

When Santos finished drinking and stumbled out of the strip club, Nicks and Diaz followed from a distance, arm-and-arm, playing the part of tipsy lovers enjoying Avenida Revolución. They passed Hotel Garcia and a Kentucky Fried Buches stand crowded with raucous patrons.

When Santos took an unexpected turn down a side street, Nicks realized other people were following him. He was right to worry about surveillance. She wondered if it had been a mistake to confront him in the alley?

"I see the tail. Blue baseball hat and ugly jean jacket walking together, four o'clock." Diaz whispered.

He grabbed Nicks by the hand and they crossed the street so she could get a better look at them.

"We'll need to split up so we can shake these guys," she whispered back.

Diaz wasn't on board. "Did you hear anything I said about this city? I don't think that's a good idea."

"Don't worry, I'm sure you'll be okay," she said. "I can take care of little ole me."

"That's not what I—" Diaz stopped himself. "I get it. You don't need a white knight, but still—let's not be stupid."

"Here. Take this." She handed him the small radio she'd used to communicate with Fatima. "If you get in over your head, call my team. They'll respond immediately." Like all of her team's toys, this was more than what it seemed. "The red button on the bottom turns on an encrypted distress beacon."

He had to laugh. She was full of surprises.

"Okay," he agreed. "But I don't like it."

"See if you can buy me a little time," she said, patting him on the shoulder. "I'll take care of Santos."

Minutes later, when Santos took another corner, they split up. Diaz double-backed to an alleyway they'd passed and hid in the shadows to ambush the two men following them.

Nicks, satisfied that Santos was headed to his studio, took a quicker route. By the time the old man made it to his door, she was already there waiting. As he fumbled for his keys, she stepped out of the shadows and greeted him.

"Hello, Vegas," she said, and smiled.

He didn't return the smile, but he invited her inside.

While he turned on a few lights, she perused his collection of knives, laid out in a few modest display cases.

"I'm not the man you're looking for," he said.

"How do you know who I'm looking for?" she asked.

"Beautiful women like you, only chase old men like me, if they are crazy. Or want money. You don't seem crazy, and I don't have any money."

"That's not what I've heard. I understand you're doing quite well."

"Success never hangs around me long. I'm nothing but a piss-poor knife-maker peddling his wares for drinking money. Sometimes when the spirits plug me into the right channel, I make something beautiful. That's it."

He moved a few tools around his work bench nervously while he talked. Nicks took a closer look, trying to understand his process. The bench was covered in leather mats and large chunks of flint. Pieces of deer antler and round hammer stones of various sizes were laid out. Nicks picked up one of his unfinished prismatic blades and examined it. It was thin as a razor. Almost transparent.

"Did you make all of these?"

"Get me drunk enough, I'll make whatever you want, dear."

"I'd like an obsidian tooth," she said. "How drunk do I need to get you for that?"

He growled at her and turned away. His lack of response said everything. He reached into a drawer and pulled out another bottle. His anxiety more apparent.

"Not drunk enough, huh?" she said.

Nicks gravitated to a display case filled with his largest work. More elaborate blades. She noticed several pieces identical to the Aztec images Dr. Jackson had shown her during the Sheriff's autopsy.

"These are weapons for warriors. Do you consider yourself one?"

"I'm a simple artist, nothing more, nothing less."

"A spiritual man—but you make things this brutal?" She pointed back at the macuahuitl. Santos walked over to the case and admired the weapon.

"A museum piece, really," he said. "But in times of crisis, some people return to the old ways. That thing may be one of the most deadly weapons ever devised, but you need to know how to use it."

She moved on past the weapons and hovered over a stone carving in the center of the last case. It was an animal sculpture. She admired it while flashes of recent events danced along the walls of her mind.

"What is that?" She pointed at it. "It's beautiful!"

"Panthera Onca."

Santos explained that the black panther motif was a favorite of his. An homage to one of his favorite childhood stories. "Mi abeula would tell it. The myth of the evil brujo, or wizard, who uses the

souls of the dead to transform himself into a powerful black jaguar—
the Pantherix."

Nicks laid out the evidence bag again. This time, Santos picked it
up and looked it over.

"Is that blood?" he asked, then quickly corrected himself. "Never
mind, I don't want to know."

"It's blood." she said.

"I have my customers and hard-core collectors. No matter who
my patrons are, they come here, buy the work, and leave. I don't have
control over what comes next."

"So you can confirm this is your work?"

"It looks like they made it according to my specs."

Nicks raised an eyebrow. "Elaborate, please."

"One of my collectors, with a connection to an even bigger
patron, offered me a small fortune for the secrets to my process. I
confess I sold out."

Nicks heard a concerning sound. Something behind one wall.
She wanted to investigate, but Santos was finally talking.

"Poverty drains the soul of creativity if it lingers too long. And it
has lingered too long around here. The deal was too good to pass up. I
have simple pleasures. My cigarillos. My tequila. But one needs
money even for those. My only extravagance—an electric sports car,
but I rarely drive. As you know, I walked tonight. Modesty keeps the
wolves away."

He took a sip of his tequila and moved closer.

"You know, you are a very beautiful woman. Let's stop this and
focus on you."

"Who paid you?" Nicks whispered in her most sultry voice, an
attempt to play into his flirtation.

"I never discuss my customers. Especially in this town; that's why
I've stayed alive for so long. I have the city's respect."

"*Respect?* Is that why they watch you?" Nicks asked.

"Who knows who watches who?" he shrugged.

Nicks stepped closer to the wall. Listened. Then punched through the flimsy sheetrock. A puff of white dust billowed out, along with a flash of sparks, as she wrenched the small video camera from its hiding place.

"I'm guessing this isn't your equipment? It's hard-wired into your electrical system. Pretty unnecessary for a piss-poor knife-maker."

It was obvious from the shocked expression on his face he was just as surprised by the video camera as he was Nicks's display of strength.

Within minutes, a Mercedes Escalade SUV screeched to a halt in front of the shop. A group of men got out. Gathered around the back of the vehicle, talking in hushed tones, sorting something among them.

"Flux, what's going on out there?" She held out her hand, pointing it at the storefront window, allowing it to sonify the group of men. "Are those weapons I hear with my little ears?"

"*Four men, all armed,*" Flux reported.

"Goddamn it," Santos sputtered. He reached for a switch and turned off the main lights. "This is your fault, woman."

"Give me your door key," Nicks demanded.

He fished it out of his pocket, and she rushed to lock the front door. Santos turned off the remaining lights. They then retreated behind the largest counter, ducked down, waited, and watched to see what the gunmen would do.

That's when they were surprised by a man who had already slipped inside through the back entrance. He cursed at them in Spanish, chambered a round, and aimed his handgun squarely at Santos.

Nicks threw herself into the intruder, tackling him against the wall, and knocking his gun away. She kicked his leg, shattering at least one bone, maybe more. When he doubled-over, she kneed him in the head, sending him down for good.

The rest of the gunmen had lined up in front with their automatic rifles at the ready.

"We have to get out of here!" she yelled.

"The Quantum," he said. "It's parked in the back."

An onslaught of gunfire tore through the storefront, shattering the plate glass. Nicks grabbed Vegas Santos by the arm and they ran.

26

Nicks floored the Quantum. It skidded around the corner, then roared down the street. Raylock Industries made a sleek electric sports car. But would it be powerful enough to outrun the gunmen she knew were only minutes behind her? They had the advantage of knowing the city, friends to call for backup, and a helluva a lot of guns. She couldn't let them catch her.

"They, they would've killed me back there!" Santos screamed at her until his face turned so red, she thought he was having a heart attack. "What the hell have you done, woman?"

She looked in the rearview mirror and saw the black Escalade was doggedly trying to close the gap. What she had done, unfortunately, was start a car chase.

Nicks gunned the engine and headed southeast on the Vía Rápida Oriente. The highway was clear, allowing her to take advantage of the straightaway.

"If you are trying to get us to the border, you're going the wrong way," Santos yelled.

"I'm trying to stay alive. We'll worry about the border later. Now, tell me who you're working for, or I'm stopping the car and throwing you to those wolves." She hooked her thumb, pointing behind her at the SUV.

"I only dealt with one man, and I didn't ask questions like you. No names. You have to believe me. He arranged the big work. I don't know who was paying, or where the money came from."

"You're lying, Santos. You're a smart man. You know something."

"Okay, I did lie about one thing."

"One thing?"

"Okay, I lie all the time. It's part of my mystique," he said, throwing his hands up in surrender. "Truth is, I didn't buy this car. It was part of the payment. So don't fuck it up."

"This car is the last thing you need to worry about."

The gunmen were coming. One was hanging out of the Escalades's rear window, trying to line up a shot with his automatic rifle.

Nicks fumbled through the center console. "Please tell me you have something better than a knife in here."

Santos's eyes filled with sudden recognition. "Under the seat."

Nicks felt around and found it. A small caliber pistol in a beat-up leather holster. The gun looked like an antique.

She rolled down the front window to create a draft. Slowed the car a bit, so they'd catch up. Then swiveled in her seat and shot out the Quantum's back window.

The glass shattered and flew out. It blanketed the Escalade and the man trying to shoot them. He screamed, dropped his gun on the road, and groped desperately at the shrapnel embedded in his face.

One of the other men in the Escalade opened the door and kicked his comrade out. The glass-covered man hit the road headfirst and rolled away like so much roadkill.

Nicks, who had one eye on the action, couldn't believe it. "Damn, these guys are brutal."

"They're just getting started," Santos said, anxiously. "Get us the hell out of here!'

In the next curve, Nicks noticed a ravine running along the road.

They passed a junkyard and what appeared to be a small industrial park. As they approached the gates of a cemetery, two men holding automatic rifles stepped out of the darkness onto the shoulder of the highway.

"Get down!" Nicks screamed while swerving into the other lane.

A hail of bullets tore through the side window. Nicks winced at the breaking glass. And Santos groaned and clawed at his side.

She surged ahead, straddling the center line, trying to keep their pursuers boxed in behind her.

"I'm hit," Santos wheezed.

He showed her his hand. It was covered in blood—way too much blood.

"Don't die on me, old man! You haven't even given me a name!"

He looked at her blissfully, smiled, then spoke in a theatrical tone as if he were telling a ghost story. "Beware the shaman in the Jaguar Mask."

He laughed at himself, but the laughter turned to wheezing. Then he coughed and sprayed blood all over the Quantum's control panels. He needed help, fast. She had to get them away from these animals.

"Stay with me, Vegas!" Nicks shouted.

Santos slumped over. His head hung limp against his chest. The seatbelt was the only thing holding him up. Nicks pressed her fingers against his neck, checking for a pulse but couldn't find one.

The Escalade surged forward, ramming into them. Nicks swerved but recovered swiftly.

Another long burst of automatic gunfire followed. She could hear the *plink-plink* of it hitting the back of the car. No gas tank, she reassured herself. This was an electric car. It could take a few shots to the rear.

But then one of the back tires blew, and she lost her ability to steer as she approached another curve. More gunfire peppered the back of the car. She ducked. Pulled the wheel too much to the left and skidded into the gravelly shoulder.

That's when something caught the wheel. The Quantum fish-tailed uncontrollably. Nicks couldn't correct it. Then she was airborne. The car sailed forward, rolling several times. Then crashed upside down in the muddy ravine.

Everything smashed to black.

PART VI

RED SECTOR A

27

Natalie Nicks thought she was dreaming. A dream right out of her childhood. She smelled hay. Heard strange animal noises, rumbling deep and low. The creaking of metal cages, and the drip of water splattering in the corner, as she lay her head on the cold concrete.

No, that wasn't right. She'd never laid down like this. She'd never been on the wrong side of the bars or chained to the wall. It couldn't be real.

She strained against the hypnotic grogginess, keeping her eyes at half-mast. Her head—a hundred times its regular weight—wouldn't budge without an immense effort.

It had to be a nightmare. Yet the concrete felt real enough, leeching away all her body heat. And the fetid smell of the animals was disturbingly authentic. She forced herself up on one elbow, trying to get a better look.

My God, it was real. She was a prisoner ... in a zoo.

Her leather jacket was gone, and her blouse torn. Her black bra hung by one strap. Her jeans were ripped, and she was missing one of her boots. There were too many scratches to count and a throbbing gash across her stomach. Dried blood here and there. Most of it from Santos, the poor bastard, or so she guessed because there were no major wounds except—

My hand! My God, where the hell is my hand?

Her new hand was gone. Missing from the wrist down. The strange thing, she wasn't suffering. She theorized Flux had somehow turned down the pain receptors in her cybernetic limbs.

"Flux?" No response. "Flux!?" Nothing.

It was as if the AI assistant had checked out of Hotel Nicks. The thing had always annoyed her, but now its absence made her feel strangely alone.

Her regular human memory seemed to be on the fritz too. Flashes of the prior night danced in her mind. She'd been pulled from the wreck by the gunmen. Fallen in and out of consciousness as they traveled by car to who knows where. Then her half-assed attempt to resist as they dragged her from their SUV into this cage. Their shock at her power and the regenaderm ripping away, exposing her new bionic hand.

That's when the tactics became more brutal. A new gang of men held her down, chained her, while someone—a younger man—different from the rest of the gang—activated the locking mechanism as easily as Mouse had back at the Cage.

Her memory was blank after that. But she was definitely chained to the wall inside a zoo.

She could see she was in some kind of two-story structure because a set of stairs was in view. Her cage along with the others formed a semi-circle around an animal enclosure. Guillotine doors made of galvanized steel connected the cages. Thick, black fencing composed of four-by-six wire panels stood about two stories high, forming barriers on all sides. They'd welded the same panels together to create a roof over the top. Right outside her cage, a gangplank led to a steel hatch in the center of the roof.

Two men in green jumpsuits worked on the gangplank. One

stood guard with a high-powered rifle while the other managed a large plastic container filled with marbled slabs of raw meat.

An adjacent cage door opened, and a beautiful black panther slinked out of its holding pin into the enclosure. It jogged around enjoying its morning exercise. Sniffing the air, aware now that breakfast was served.

A lanky third man shuffled by Nicks's cage, pushing a heavy wheelbarrow full of more raw meat. He seemed devilishly pleased when he caught her watching.

"Maybe it's your friend, heh? You don't know, do you?" He picked up a hunk of the bloody meat and swung it obscenely in his boney hands. "That him there, all choppy chopped? Well, you'll find out soon enough."

The zookeeper proved not all the animals were locked up.

"They'll take care of you, real good. Yeah, you'll see, won't you? After this one."

He pointed at a man in the corner of the adjacent cage. Nicks hadn't noticed him until now. He'd been beaten to a bloody pulp, stripped to his underwear, and thrown in a bed of hay like an extra from a Planet of the Apes movie—chillingly barbaric.

"You're next. Yeah, I hope so real bad. You hurt my friends, bitch!"

The zookeeper filled a plastic bin from his wheelbarrow of bloody meat, and panic crawled up her spine as she tried to get a better look at her fellow prisoner.

Diaz! Where was Diaz?

She called to the man sprawled in the hay. Was that him?

"Hey! Shut your trap." The zookeeper hit the cage with his electric cattle prod. The voltage rattled the bars. Sparks flashed, ionizing the foul air. "That's Denada, you dumb bitch. Not no Diaz. You so stupid."

Not Diaz! Thank God, she thought. But then wondered where he was? She hoped he'd reconnected with her team and was safe.

The zookeeper looked around, unlocked her cage and slipped inside. He watched Nicks and edged closer, his eyes tracing her body.

"Dumb whore, that's you, right? Maybe I get a taste before those big cats do. Eh, whatta you think?"

He muffled his own laugh like a devious child. Then unzipped his jumper down to the waist, wrestled his arms out, and lowered the uniform to his ankles.

"I think you like what you see, eh? I know you do."

She made her move the moment he exposed himself.

She ripped the chain from the wall. It was a shock to both of them. She hadn't known if she could do it. They both stared at the broken chain dangling from her good wrist.

The zookeeper panicked and stumbled toward the cage door, frantically trying to dress himself.

Nicks lunged to grab him but forgot she was missing a hand. Her bare wrist slashed through the air. Luck was not on her side. The zookeeper raised his cattle prod at the perfect moment. By sheer accident, Nicks fell into it. Electricity surged through her, and she collapsed at his feet.

The zookeeper sadistically continued zapping her until she had no choice but to curl up in a fetal position and pray the man would stop.

28

"There's no sign of Viper or Vegas Santos in the wreckage."
Fatima was very worried, which made her angry. She had climbed down into the ravine and scoured the perimeter of the wreck at least ten times now. There was no trace of Natalie Nicks, but the interior of the car was covered in blood.

Where the hell are you, Natalie?

She circled one more time, searching for any clue. But it was dark and almost impossible to see anything of significance.

"She gave her tracker to Diaz," Quinn said, over the radio.

"Why would she do that?"

"She knew there was a backup in her new hand."

"Any signal from that?"

"No. None. Total radio silence."

"What good is this high-tech shit, if it doesn't work?"

"It could be disabled," Quinn said.

"What would cause that?"

"Several things. Damage. Loss of power. Or—" Quinn stopped herself from speculating any further.

Fatima was glad. She wasn't ready to count Nicks out, or worse—count her among the dead.

A massive truck tricked out narco-style stopped on the side of the road.

"I've got contact, stand by," Fatima said, as she took cover.

The truck backed up, swung the front end in the wreck's direction, and parked. The driver got out and unreeled a cable from a winch bolted to the front.

A van sped up to the crash site and parked next to the truck. Two men got out, talking. They moved with purpose down the embankment.

"If you get Viper's signal, let me know. Going dark." Fatima whispered as she faded into the ravine's overgrowth.

She quietly unholstered her pistol. Ever the weapon connoisseur, Fatima carried a vintage High Standard .22 HDM semi-automatic pistol with integral suppression. It was a weapon she'd bought off a crafty arms dealer overseas. He claimed it came from the American U2 pilot shot down by the Russians.

Though it was true, the CIA had outfitted such pilots with those pistols, and even preferred them in the field, Fatima didn't believe a word of her gun's provenance. But she was convinced the extra panache made her aim more true.

She watched the three men work. They lacked the cold, calculating professionalism she expected from ruthless cartel gangsters. As they swarmed around the wreck, she understood why. They were the cleanup crew.

The first man gave the interior of the wrecked car a rough wipe down. The rags went into a black trash bag. The second man carried down several bottles of liquid. He cracked the seal and poured it all over the Quantum's seats and dashboard. The strong smell of chlorine bleach floated by on the breeze.

After finishing the interior, the two men helped the truck owner hook his winch cable to the chassis of the car.

Slowly but surely, the winch pulled the car out of the ditch. Fatima ducked low and made her move.

The truck owner lit a small cigar and pointed at his winch. "This beast was worth every bit of money I paid for it."

They watched it work like fishermen reeling in a line. But when their catch came into view, their calm expressions turned to shock. Fatima, wearing black tactical gear and holding a long-barreled pistol, was sitting calmly cross-legged on the trunk of the wrecked Quantum.

She fired four times before any of the men could react. The cleaners on the right and left fell dead. Two expertly placed bullet holes tattooed their foreheads.

The lone survivor stood frozen his mouth agape in horror. His smoldering cigarillo tumbled down into the sand next to his boot.

"You should put that out very carefully, dumbass. This area is covered in gasoline," she said. "There are many *better* ways to die."

29

The two men in green jumpsuits dragged Nicks onto the gangplank. She tried to speak but was too punch drunk to form a complete sentence. Surely every million-dollar circuit in her brain was fried.

The zookeeper gave her another shock even though she wasn't resisting.

Below her, in one tree, she could see the most beautiful animal—a midnight-black panther—Vegas's obsidian carving come to life. But the panther wasn't alone. At least half a dozen more similar cats skulked about, staking their own claim of the enclosure.

All of them watched Nicks with eager eyes.

The green jumpsuits dropped her and pushed her toward the edge of the open hatch, like they were rolling up a carpet. A severe flash of panic gripped her and she resisted one last time by clinging to the gangplank's lattice with her one good hand.

"Those cats will get sick trying to eat me."

She got another shock and a kick in the gut, forcing her to let go. They rolled her to within an inch of the fall.

"Stop!" a man screamed. "You goddamned imbeciles!"

The men stiffened like soldiers snapping to attention. The screaming man marched right down the gangplank, muttering blistering curses under his breath. The men's bravado melted as they inspected their feet like scolded schoolboys.

When the man reached Nicks he stopped, took a deep breath, and composed himself. His tone cheerful but forced.

"Good morning, Ms. Nicks," he said.

"Good morning ... *I think?*" she groaned.

"Ms. Nicks, My name is Alejandro. The Don's estate manager. You have my most sincere apologies. It's *obvious* there's been a *terrible mistake.*"

The men cowered as Alejandro chided them with another scalding tirade of Spanish curses.

"Help me get her to her feet," he demanded.

The men looked incensed.

"Damn you all, I'd throw you in that hole myself if it wouldn't spoil their appetite."

They obeyed, not being too gentle while helping Nicks get up. She could barely stand without their assistance.

"Ms. Nicks, I see you are having trouble. Please take my arm and I'll escort you out of here myself."

Alejandro snapped his fingers and pointed back to her original cage.

"Make sure Ms. Nicks's belongings are brought to me at once —*all of them!*"

With Alejandro's help, she made her way off the gangplank, every fiber in her body aching.

"You must forgive them, Ms. Nicks. Our employer believes in giving everyone an opportunity to embrace a new future despite their past. But these ignorant men cling to their superstitions. Some worship Santa Meurta and mistake your *unique* abilities with ... well ... witchcraft."

With her body so numb, and her mind on the edge of shutting down, the man's calming tone provided a minor source of relief. He took her down a flight of stairs and into a tunnel leading under the enclosure. It connected the zoo with the main compound.

"Don Miguel has arranged one of his best rooms for you. After all, where would the world be if we can't show a stranger simple hospitality." He smiled and looked her in the eye. "As long as the stranger means the host no harm. Do you mean your host harm, Ms. Nicks?"

"Wasn't on my agenda this morning."

"Oh, wonderful!" Alejandro beamed, another weight lifted.

They passed through the kitchen and up a flight of stairs to the second level, then down a hallway to a wing of tastefully decorated suites. Through an open bay window, she saw an entrancing landscape reminiscent of a French winery. It surrounded the mansion.

"Here we are. This is your room." Alejandro escorted her to the bed and swept through the suite, apparently making sure it was to his standards.

"You're invited to lunch at two. For now, I will send up coffee, pastries, and some medical supplies. Please use the rest of the day to rest and recuperate."

Alejandro disappeared into the bathroom and returned with a silk robe he laid on the bed.

"If you'd like, I can make sure your clothing is washed and repaired while you rest."

Nicks allowed him to help her out of her tattered, bloody clothes, and into the robe. He seemed delighted to assist. He then turned back the sheets, poured her a glass of ice water, and placed it near the bed.

"Shall I draw you a bath?"

"No thank you, I can take it from here."

"As you wish." He walked to the door but paused and turned before stepping through. "Again, I apologize for the inhospitable behavior of our staff."

He smiled, bowed, and slipped out of the room, closing the door behind him. After a moment of silence came the unmistakable metallic clang of a magnetic bolt. For her own protection, she was sure.

"Flux? Are you with me?"

Nicks lay back on the bed, waiting for a response. As she drifted away, she made a different connection.

Don Miguel.

She'd heard the name before. It had been in the DIA targeting package, but under a name much more recognizable.

Miguel Solis—one of the most dangerous men in Mexico—better known as El Draco.

30

Half-past eleven, Nicks woke to the sound of the magnetic bolt in her door—this time sliding open. A female servant delivering her clothes entered. Just as Alejandro had promised, they were washed and stitched back together, but her rough night had left its mark.

The servant apologized. "We did our best, ma'am. But the damage was too much. Mr. Alejandro insists we make up for your loss."

She snapped her fingers and two large men pushed an elaborately carved wardrobe, on a rolling dolly, into the room. Once they positioned it against the wall, the woman opened it to show Nicks it was full of clothing.

"Take your pick. They're all in your size."

Nicks thanked the young woman and escorted her out. Then she showered. She was covered in red welts from the cattle prod and bruises galore. The car wreck had banged her up, but the men had done worse. At least she was alive, something she couldn't say about poor Santos.

Doctoring and bandaging her wounds proved difficult. Despite being an amputee, she'd never dealt with the challenges of being without her arms and legs. They'd fitted her with bionics right after the bombing, and rehab had focused on living with the new limbs, not living without them.

Reflecting on her bionics reminded her to check her internal systems. "Flux?"

"How may I assist you, Captain Nicks?"

"Where have you been?"

"Emergency protocol required all resources divert to life support."

"What does that even mean?"

"Your systems were critically overloaded."

"No joke. Okay. Since you're back online, tell me where we are."

"I'm unable to pinpoint our location."

"Why not?"

"Interference from a nearby signal blocking transmitter."

"Will the distress beacon in my new arm work?"

"Negative."

Nicks considered this predicament while looking through the wardrobe. The selection was breathtaking, and she immediately wished she could have all the clothes packed up and shipped back to Los Angeles. Everything was high-end, gorgeous, and as the woman had said, tailored to fit her.

She chose a floral mesh top with scalloped sleeves. Black linen slacks. And an ivory hooded cardigan with extra-long sleeves to distract from her missing hand. For shoes, she took a pair of short leather boots with a flat heel, mindful running for her life might be required at any moment.

From her window, she could see El Draco's compound was reminiscent of a resort. But the perimeter suggested a fortress. High walls and well-armed guards who watched vigilantly from strategic vantage points surrounded it.

On the grounds, beauty reigned. A rainbow of gorgeous shrubbery swayed in the cool breeze. Purple jacaranda trees lined the tiled walkways. She heard birdsongs and the soft rainfall of a water feature in the courtyard below her.

Beyond the buildings were rows of grapevines, hinting this might be a vineyard. But upon closer consideration, there wasn't enough to make this a commercial wine operation.

Past the manicured landscape and high walls was a massive farm, lush with its maturing bounty. This was the dominant crop. Whatever it was seemed to be the central concern.

The bell in the bell tower rang. It was time for lunch. Nicks walked into the courtyard just as her host arrived. He waited for her across the garden.

"Good afternoon, Ms. Nicks."

El Draco was both handsome and short. Tan and reasonably fit with a slight potbelly. His dark hair was accented with silver around the temples. Thick black eyebrows added a certain intensity to his chestnut eyes. But that was tempered by his expressive face and warm smile.

He shook her hand while caressing her shoulder warmly. His natural charisma on full display.

"It's a pleasure to meet you," he said.

"Likewise. What an unexpected surprise." She flashed her teeth.

"I hope Alejandro took good care of you?"

"Yes, he's been very attentive. As have all your staff."

El Draco laughed with the ease of a politician.

"Such an exquisite woman with an amazing taste for adventure. I hope you'll share some of your exploits at lunch."

El Draco was dressed casually but wore a mariachi jacket detailed in decorative fabric and beadwork. It was an unexpected contrast considering his reputation and profession. One might mistake it for a joke if he hadn't worn it with such sincerity.

When he turned to lead her through the mansion, Nicks caught sight of the decoration on the back of his jacket. Fashioned like a dragon, it glittered as if beaded in gemstones. He noticed her studying it.

"My father wore this jacket. I so admired it as a child. It filled me with pride then, and now. I can be very sentimental about my past, Ms. Nicks, and not always in a good way. But I must tell you, I refuse to dwell there. No, I am a man of the future. I set my sights on the horizon. But that's why you are here, of course. My commitment to the future is a commitment to the use of technology—the *best* technology. This is something I believe we have in common. I can't wait to show you."

He led her through an elegant archway and into the main house. They strolled through the great hall which served as a kind of lobby for the compound. Then up the stairs to the second level and out onto the main balcony. Here, they had the best view of the farm.

"I'm not your average business man. I strive to defy expectations and limitations. Let me show you what I mean."

He pointed to the farm.

"Coca as far as the eye can see."

"Out in the open like this? How's that possible?"

"Innovation, of course."

A corner of the balcony was covered in electronic equipment, computers, and monitors. One man stood in the center of these machines, like a DJ spinning vinyl, touching screens and typing commands into a keyboard.

"You see, the fundamental challenge with coca farming is labor. You need so much of it. The second challenge is secrecy. You can't employ half a village and expect them to keep quiet about their work. This leads to continual crop failure through confiscation and seizures. To avoid those losses, one must take extreme measures. Threaten the entire village. Murder a quarter to ensure the silence of the rest. Oh, I hate thinking about it, it gets so messy. But even with this level of violence, only five percent of all coca farms are successful."

El Draco led her over to the corner. He introduced her to the young man in the center of the control pod. His name was Tomas. The man looked like he was in his early twenties. His finger nails were painted black, one side of his head shaved, and the rest was dyed green and fell over his sullen eyes. He turned and nodded at Nicks, only briefly, and went back to his work.

"This is the future! Only myself, and a few others know exactly what is going on here. Most of my staff are gloriously ignorant of what we are doing. And, you can see, there is one thing facilitating this."

El Draco directed her to watch the monitors.

"Technology! Ms. Nicks. Wondrous technology!"

NICKS HAD NOTICED the farm was a very busy place, but she hadn't noticed who worked it until now. El Draco was using *drones* to tend his crop.

He pointed at the video feed. Automated microtanks rolled between the plants.

"Those are weeding robots. They can scan the beds for invasive species and remove them with the precision of a surgeon. They can also apply herbicides or insecticides."

Aerial drones the size of toasters flew down the rows, taking readings as they went.

"These drones measure moisture levels."

Behind them, larger water-carrying robots either misted the plants or rained on them, careful to preserve their resource for those plants in the most need.

In the more mature fields, driverless tractors pulled harvesting machines, picking leaves from the coca plants and sucking them into vacuum tube canisters. Those cans were flown to the production warehouses next to the fields.

In the center of the farm was a giant structure similar to a grain silo. Drones flew in and out like bees.

"What is that?" Nicks asked.

"The drone hive is the central hub for our operations. It's the primary power source and interconnected with our wells. Drones nest there when they are unused. The servers running the algorithms are stored there too and cooled by the well water as it's drawn from the ground."

She watched as several smaller machines emerged from the hive, hovered, and then joined together into a much larger configuration.

"All the machines are built from a few basic droid units. They combine in different patterns to create the tools necessary for that phase of farming. Using 3D printers, we've automated the repair process."

Small plates covered the outside of the hive. Nicks thought they were shingles until they moved.

"Those are greenhouse drones," El Draco said.

The clear octagonal discs flew by means of a central rotor, made of the same translucent plastic. She watched as they lifted off the hive in a swarm and joined themselves to each other like puzzle pieces. This created one massive panel hovering in the sky. Tomas toggled some of his controls and the interior of the panel darkened. A shadow fell over the coca plants below.

"These greenhouse drones allow us to increase the temperature by raising and lowering the panels during early stages of growth, and as the plants mature, we control the sunlight by toggling the opacity of the panels."

El Draco walked up behind his farm DJ.

"They also serve another important function. Give her the satellite view of our property, Tomas."

Tomas tapped a few keys and brought up an image of the farm. The time-stamp proved it had been captured only minutes before. The entire operation and compound was missing. The landscape appeared to be an undeveloped wilderness.

Nicks raised her eyebrows. "How's that possible?"

"We captured the raw footage prior to clearing the land and starting construction. Using those images, and a little Hollywood magic, we project the illusion you see now. How the electronic camouflage fools the satellites is a trade secret borrowed from one of my partners."

"You've thought of everything," Nicks said.

El Draco seemed pleased to have impressed her. They walked up to the edge of the balcony to look at the farm. Tomas followed behind.

"You may notice, one thing is missing from the fields—*people*. Without people, all you have is the product. The violence, chaos, and conflict ravaging the industry is gone. Replaced by pure profit."

Tomas was continuing to control everything from a computer tablet about the size of a magazine.

Next to them was a piece of equipment like a metal telephone pole sprouting a web of cords connecting to other devices. About nine feet high, it narrowed at its top, ending in several antennae.

Nicks noticed it had a unique ultra-sonic sound. It pulsed in a rhythmic pattern which changed every thirty seconds. She guessed this was the signal blocker Flux had detected.

"So you control the entire farm from here?" she asked.

"Yes, isn't it efficient?"

"I have to agree, it's amazing."

"Not as amazing as your hand," Tomas responded. "We have it in our lab right now."

He held out the tablet, showing her a video feed. Her hand was being examined by two technicians in lab coats. Drones buzzed in the background. They were in a clean room, most likely in the drone hive.

"This is not your only cybernetic prosthetic. I scanned you earlier."

He tapped the tablet and played a video of Nicks taking a shower.

It was the first grin she'd seen on Tomas's face and proof he was a pervert. He had no qualms about admitting to the violation of her privacy. Hidden cameras and instruments had analyzed her body composition and the TALON technology hidden within. Data spilled onto his screen, and Tomas explained it to El Draco.

"Most of her body is cybernetic. Not the tits though, those seem to be real."

Nicks wanted to rip the tablet from his hands and reinstall it up his—but she restrained herself. She needed that hand back.

"I'm very fond of all my body parts," she said.

"I can see why. They're beyond anything I've read about." Tomas said, excitedly. "Senor, if we can examine more of her cybernetic systems, well—"

El Draco interrupted, waving him away. "Thank you, Tomas, we'll leave you to your work now. Lunch is served."

Lunch at a time like this seemed absurd, but it would give her time to think. She saw a way out of her dilemma, and if it worked, she'd be able to escape and take care of El Draco at the same time. But she had to play it smart—timing would be everything.

31

Despite getting to kill two awful human beings, Fatima was in a dark mood. She wasn't sure why. Then she considered the fact she hadn't slept or eaten in over twenty-four hours. She was probably *hangry*. An American sentiment she'd learned watching reality TV.

Her Kurdish family or friends didn't have a similar term. Perhaps she could make it up and add to her native language.

There was another word she needed. A new codename. Something like Butt-Saver. Or Ass-Cover-*er*. It had to celebrate her new job as Viper's number one guardian angel.

Guardian Angel ... that's a good one!

Did Natalie Nicks have any idea how lucky it was she'd joined the team permanently?

Fatima continued thinking about this as she watched through her riflescope, from underneath the big monster truck she'd taken from the man with the winch.

The good news was he ended up being cooperative. He'd been defiant when she shot him in the kneecap with her High Standard, but he melted like butter when she threatened to burn his new truck.

That's all it took to get him to hand over his keys and spill the location of El Draco's secret compound.

Men could be so ridiculous about their toys.

He'd even offered to give her specific directions, an offer she accepted. Once they arrived, she tied him up and scouted the compound from a distance. When she confirmed Viper was on site, she returned to dig more information out of the man, but found he'd already bled out. That put her in the unfortunate position of having to gather intel the sniper way—hiding, waiting, and watching.

Speaking of men and their toys—El Draco's compound was like a Narco Disneyland. Everywhere she looked she saw advanced machines. That rubbed her the wrong way. Here was a rich criminal with the technology that could end famine, but he was using it to grow illicit drugs.

Her *hangriness* reached its zenith when her eyes landed on Viper. Dressed like a fashion model, she strolled onto the mansion's main balcony escorted by the imitation Pablo Escobar. They acted like they were on a date in Napa Valley.

"Cartwheel, it's Mouse, over."

"Go for Ass-saver," she said.

"I *love* your attitude!" he chuckled. "I have a new image of El Draco that might help you make a positive ID."

The image came through and Fatima confirmed it.

"Definitely a positive match."

"Damn, you've hit the jackpot. Every law enforcement agency worth their salt is looking for him, and you found him without breaking a sweat."

"I broke a sweat."

He laughed. "Stand by. I'll try to verify your location."

Quinn came online. "Maybe Viper's found the sensors. Any sign of those?"

Fatima had wondered the same thing.

"That's possible, but I can't get any closer to confirm. It's acres of farmland. There's no cover, and they have drones everywhere."

Mouse asked, "Did you say, farmland? Because the satellite imagery of that area shows it's undeveloped."

"My eyeballs say otherwise. There's a small army bunkered down in that compound. I'll need help with her extraction."

"Is she okay?"

"Fine."

"What's she doing?"

Fatima grumbled. She couldn't believe this one.

"Fucking mothers ... she's having lunch!"

32

E l Draco escorted Nicks to the other side of the balcony where they sat down at a table set for two.

"I understand you are an American war hero, Ms. Nicks." He pulled the chair out and helped her settle in.

Nicks deflected the question as she sat down. "Did you serve in the military?"

"No, but my father served. He was always bitter about his treatment in the army. Full of corruption, he said. He made me swear never to join. However, there are days it feels like I have betrayed that promise."

They continued to talk as the staff served the food. Grilled shrimp dressed with tomatillo salsa on a bed of salad greens. Sliced avocado. Margaritas.

"I'm fascinated. You were injured in the war and yet as Tomas says, they rebuilt you like one of my machines—completely whole."

"Not completely," Nicks raised her arm, flashing her bare wrist. "I consider my hand on loan from the United States government. It's important that I get that back before I leave."

"Leave? But you just arrived. I hope I'm not keeping you from more important matters."

"This is an unexpected detour. As delightful as it is, I'm afraid I can't stay long."

"On the contrary, I think you'll want to stay long enough for me to show you the most interesting way I've been using your government's technology. I've saved the best for last."

Nicks smiled and took a drink of her margarita.

"This wouldn't be *sensor* technology, would it?"

This time El Draco deflected. He signaled his bodyguard, who approached the table.

"No. Something much more extraordinary."

He smiled at her and whispered to the bodyguard. The guard strolled off, giving her the opening she needed. She picked up her steak knife.

"I need my hand, I won't ask again," she said.

"You can ask all you want but—"

Nicks stabbed El Draco in his hand. The blade hit him with such force and speed it pinned his hand in place before he even realized what had happened.

"How about a hand for a hand?" She twisted the blade ever-so-slightly.

El Draco howled. Then swallowed hard and laughed. A deep, disturbing laugh that made her wonder about the man's sanity.

Two of El Draco's largest guards jogged from around the corner and took up positions near their lunch table. They pointed their weapons at Nicks.

El Draco gestured to them with his free hand. "Please bring Ms. Nicks what she wants."

One man turned and disappeared around the corner and El Draco said, "You have more balls than *any* of my men. How much to hire you? I need new sicarios after you eliminated so many last night."

Several more guards appeared and lined up along the north wall. Each with a machine gun.

"So many guards and guns. Is the great El Draco frightened of little ole me?"

She twisted the knife again. El Draco grimaced trying hard not to show any weakness.

"No, Ms. Nicks. It's not you we're afraid of ..."

He gestured for her to turn around, which she did. What she saw walking their way justified everyone's concern.

Nicks was speechless. A robotic animal like the one she'd faced on Diaz's ranch slinked toward her, carrying *her hand* in its mouth.

She pulled the steak knife out of El Draco. He grimaced and let out a groan and wrapped his white dinner napkin around his wound.

The animal walked up and stopped. Its camera eyes analyzed her. She stood up and inched her way, carefully, closer to the machine.

"The Pantherix, Model II," El Draco said. "Amazing, is it not?"

Images of the machine leaping up and ripping the Sheriff Turner's throat out flashed through her mind as she reached down into its open mouth. She took her hand and stepped back. It followed her. She continued to edge back. It stepped closer again.

"It senses you are one of its kind," El Draco said.

Nicks activated the reattachment protocol and her hand rejoined her wrist.

"Flux, can you clone this thing's hard drive?" she whispered.

"Cloning system's code. Stand by."

Nicks walked around the Pantherix, inspecting it. This version was much more realistic than the one on the ranch.

"Source code is encrypted. The operator could detect breaching. Confirm to proceed."

"Confirm," she whispered. It was a risk worth taking. Hopefully, Tomas wouldn't notice.

"Proceeding ... stay in range of target."

"What was that, Ms. Nicks?" El Draco asked.

"Just making sure my hand is back in place," she said, as she rubbed her wrist.

Waiting for its next command, the Pantherix stared at Nicks.

"Where did you get this technology?"

"Would you believe me if I told you it's our own innovation?"

"Do they offer robotics courses at Narcos University?"

El Draco chuckled. "Let us continue our lunch, and I'll be happy to tell you."

Flux needed more time, so Nicks agreed and sat back down.

One of El Draco's underlings skittered over and offered a proper bandage and alcohol to clean his wound. While he dressed his hand, he lectured Nicks as if nothing had happened between them.

"Earlier, we discussed the challenges inherent in my business. Competition is another one. The Pantherix Project is an investment in security," he said. "One unit can patrol an area up to thirty square miles for over twelve hours before it has to recharge. This one runs at over fifty miles per hour and is equipped with offensive capabilities."

"The *teeth*, you mean?"

"Yes, obsidian blades based on the work of our mutual friend Vegas Santos. I appreciated his contribution. He will be *missed*."

Nicks played along, but El Draco was proving more dangerous by the minute. She had to get word to her team. But that was impossible unless she could disable the signal blocker.

As they finished their lunch, Tomas rushed to El Draco's side. He watched Nicks out of the corner of his eye as he gave his boss what seemed to be troubling news.

"Sir, there's been a breach."

Nicks stiffened. Had he detected Flux's intrusion?

"A breach? Where?"

Tomas passed his control pad to El Draco. It showed the thermal image of a woman on a hillside overlooking the compound.

"A sniper," El Draco decided.

Fatima? Nicks wondered. *It had to be.*

"What do you want us to do?" Tomas asked.

"The only logical thing," El Draco said. "Kill her!"

33

El Draco insisted on showing Nicks one more thing while his men searched for the sniper. He escorted her to the edge of the balcony overlooking a special corral. Several black panthers were in the pen. They trotted in circles, sniffing the air.

"Such magnificent creatures. I considered myself a collector, a protector of the species, if you will. They're so fierce and majestic. They thrilled me for the longest time."

"Has that changed?"

"Yes, I'm afraid so," he said. "The panthers make me feel like a king. But the *Pantherix* make me feel like a *god!*"

A guillotine door rose, releasing several pristine Pantherix units into the corral. The real panthers, becoming nervous, growled, and cowered as their robotic cousins encroached on their space. At the first opening, the panthers bolted back into the enclosure and the guillotine door slammed shut.

"I imagine that's how your fellow soldiers feel around you, Ms. Nicks. They know you are different—*a true threat.*"

Nicks ignored the comparison while she watched the Pantherix trot around the pen. They fell into a coordinated pattern, each equally spaced behind the other. She marveled at how lifelike they seemed.

"I can't allow these to fall into the hands of the other cartels," he said.

"I understand the problem, but why are you telling me?" she asked.

"Because one of my units went rogue. And you know something about it."

He snapped his fingers, and the zookeeper and his green-suited coworkers dragged a man across the balcony and dropped him at El Draco's feet.

"This is my nephew, Denada. He handled one of these units with complete disrespect."

Denada shook his head, which he could barely lift, and pleaded through his swollen lips. "We were drunk, Uncle. Having fun. Please forgive me. I meant no harm."

"One of his drivers stole part of an important shipment. This idiot reprogrammed the Pantherix to find the man without my permission," El Draco explained.

He grabbed a handful of Denada's hair and twisted his head so he was staring at Nicks.

"You see this woman? She found your toy, Denada. Thank her for doing that."

"Thank you," he sputtered.

Without warning, El Draco shoved Denada off the balcony into the corral. He hit the ground with a dull smack and rolled over screaming. His arm dangled beside him, broken.

"Please, I beg you. Don't do this!"

"Don't worry, boy, we're just having *fun*."

Denada's cries for mercy were cut short when the first Pantherix swiped him with its teeth. Blood sprayed from the young man's neck like water from a fountain. Then the rest of the pack joined in, attacking him from every side. In seconds, it looked like they had dropped Denada into a wood chipper.

El Draco turned on Nicks. "I want my Pantherix back, Ms. Nicks. And if I don't get it, there will be terrible consequences."

"Are you threatening me?"

"Most certainly," he said. "Not only you, but your sniper friend. She'll die like Denada. Except I'll make sure it lasts longer, so you can enjoy every second of it."

Show and tell was over, and El Draco's ruthlessness was in full bloom. He turned to watch Tomas, who was tracking Fatima on one of his monitors. A truck full of men were headed straight for her.

El Draco wanted his lost machine, and Nicks wasn't about to give that up. But she was also surrounded, and her luck wouldn't hold out much longer. If they cornered or captured Fatima, it would be game over for both of them.

Only one man stood next to El Draco while the rest of the gunmen paced around the edge of the terrace. The men were alert, but thanks to Fatima, their attention was on protecting the compound from outside threats. Nicks was only getting the occasional suspicious glance. It seemed to be her only advantage.

She sized up El Draco's nearest guard, and at the right moment lunged. She grabbed the barrel of his rifle and kicked the man in the chest. He flew off the balcony, leaving Nicks with his weapon.

She turned it in El Draco's direction and opened fire.

34

Fatima saw a truck kicking up dirt as it sped toward her position. She eased her rifle a few degrees to the left, sighted in the driver, and fired. The front windshield exploded in a shower of glass and red mist. The truck careened off the road into a drainage ditch and crashed.

That temporarily took care of that problem, but it also revealed her position. The rescue window was closing. Time to move.

Gunfire erupted on the balcony as Fatima refocused to check Viper's position. She found her teammate in the middle of the firefight. She was shooting everything around her with an FX-05 Xiuhcoatl, an assault rifle used by the Mexican Armed Forces. It seemed El Draco had his own cache, and Viper had found it.

"Might as well join her," she said.

She scoped the most threatening target and fired.

35

El Draco was adept at saving his own ass. He dove behind another guard as Nicks opened fire. Her volley of bullets hit the man in the chest, and he went down. El Draco grabbed the dead guard's handgun and darted across the terrace. Nicks opened up again, forcing El Draco down behind a giant terra cotta planter.

The compound was in a panic. Distraught servants were screaming, running, and hiding. Draco's men were confused and yelling contradictory commands to one another. El Draco had lost control. Exactly what Nicks had hoped.

Another gunman sprinted around the corner. Nicks knelt, aimed, and shot him dead. She advanced on El Draco's position and was surprised by a servant who appeared out of thin air. He defiantly blocked her path.

"Ms. Nicks, you gave your word. No harm, you said! Remember? You promised!" Alejandro scolded.

"Move Alejandro! Damn you!"

She pushed him out of the way and discovered the planter was a fake. It swayed back and forth on its hinge, revealing a hidden escape tunnel. Alejandro had let his boss through. El Draco was gone.

For a split second, she considered following him. But she'd thought this through—the key here was *survival*—and she wasn't getting out of here without some help.

She headed for the control pod.

36

Nicks's gunfire emptied the terrace, clearing a path to Tomas, who was in the middle of his equipment, furiously tapping commands into his control pad. Nicks ignored him and hit the transmitter tower like a linebacker. The tower quaked from the impact.

"No, stay away from that!" Tomas screamed.

Nicks ignored him and rammed it again with her shoulder, but it wasn't enough. She extended her arms, locked her elbows, and pushed with all the power she could muster. Slowly but surely, the tower tilted to one side. She shoved it one more time, and the whole thing toppled over, ripping away its power lines. Falling like a tree across the balcony, it crushed most of Tomas's equipment.

Tomas's face flushed with rage. "You've exposed the compound to god knows who!"

"That was the plan," Nicks said. "Cartwheel, do you read? Over."

There was a crackle of interference, then the response she'd hoped for.

"Loud and clear!" Fatima said. She was upbeat but out of breath.

"Watch your six. El Draco's men are coming for you."

"Too late. They've already found me!"

Now that they knew her position, Fatima had lost her key advantage. Despite killing the driver, the rest of the search team had survived the wreck and radioed for backup. A truck full of fresh men and guns arrived minutes later.

The new group had driven up the rugged hill and parked close enough to shower Fatima in bullets. It was almost impossible to return fire. She had to find new cover.

She aimed at the man barking orders. The top of his head bobbed up and down behind the truck frame until she fired and removed it. His squad cried out in panic. She fired a few more times to cover herself and scurried up the hill to a new location.

This put her in a better position, but it was temporary. She was outnumbered and nearly out of ammunition. She couldn't hold these men off for long.

Nicks wanted the control pad to access El Draco's network, but Tomas wasn't cooperating.

"I don't have time for this. Don't make me shoot you!" she said.

"Go ahead, see what that gets you."

He crawled out on the fallen signal tower. It dangled out over the Pantherix pit like a tree limb. "Shoot me, and we both go in. Good luck getting it after that."

He smirked at Nicks like he'd won a game of chess.

Nicks dropped her gun and stepped out onto the tower. It tilted under the added weight.

"Hey! What ... what the hell are you doing?"

"I'm coming to get the controller," she said.

"Are you crazy? You're throwing us off balance."

"Don't worry, I'm sure your pets won't attack their programmer." Nicks stepped closer. "Or would they?"

The giant piece of steel teetered Tomas's way. The Pantherix units turned their heads in unison. A new threat was entering their target area.

"Stop, please, stop!" Tomas pleaded.

"Hand it over."

"Okay, here." Tomas held out the controller. "Just back up."

Nicks took a step back. Tomas crawled forward, holding out his prize. When Nicks reached for it, he wouldn't let go. Then he raised his other hand—he was holding a gun.

"You stupid bitch! Back up, or I'll shoot you in the face."

"You're calling *me* stupid? I'm not the one playing tug of war with a bionic woman."

Nicks wrenched the controller so hard she heard Tomas's shoulder pop. He twisted over, trying to keep his balance. Nicks jerked the opposite way, and Tomas followed suit. The controller came free in Nicks's hand, but Tomas kept going, tumbling with a yell into the pit.

He hit the ground with a sickening thud. The handgun fell beside him. He reached for it just as the first Pantherix attacked.

"My hand!" he screamed. "It has my *hand*!"

"Believe me, I know the feeling." Nicks said and turned away as the carnage began.

Tomas hadn't reprogrammed the units to torture their victims slowly like El Draco had requested. So they ripped him apart with their normal efficiency, shredding him without mercy.

Nicks used her new upgrade to network into the controller. "Flux, we have to find a way out of here. A truck. Another sports car. Anything that moves."

In a few seconds, Flux discovered the solution. It was logical, but would it work? It better, she thought. Two lives depended on it.

37

F lux took control of the hive. A swarm of greenhouse drones
swooped out and flew toward the mansion. As they whizzed
forward, they self-assembled, creating a giant megadrone.

"*I've commandeered the system*," Flux reported.

"Can you navigate it as well?"

"*Affirmative.*"

Nicks backed up to get a running start, burst into bionic speed,
and leapt skyward for the massive panel sailing toward her. Having
underestimated its height, she slammed into it and collapsed over the
edge. She began to slide back off, but quickly dug her fingertips into
the metal lip of one drone to anchor herself.

"Go, Flux, go!"

Flux revved the megadrone's rotors. They tilted in unison, lifting
away from the mansion and spinning into overdrive. The big mother-
ship sailed out over the farm with Nicks dangling from it.

She looked back with concern. The good news was she was
getting away. The bad news was she was completely exposed, and
one of El Draco's sentries had figured that out. He raised the sights on
his Russian RPG-30 rocket launcher to center Nicks in his crosshairs.

"Cartwheel, guard tower, six o'clock. Take him out!"

THE PLEA from Nicks came in loud and clear, but Fatima couldn't help. She was on the run.

She had just emptied her last clip into the men chasing her. It bought her some time because she'd killed the lead pursuer, but they weren't giving up.

One remaining trail lead straight up the hill at a steep angle. She struggled up the incline and over a pair of large boulders. Draco's men scrambled up the rocky path right behind her.

One man fired, and she hit the dirt. Several bullets whizzed over her head. She got back on her feet, dug deep, and hauled ass up the trail.

"Broken arrow. Broken arrow." Fatima shouted into her radio. "I'm overrun."

As she made the summit, the path disappeared. She skidded to a halt. And found herself on the edge of a sheer drop-off.

There was nowhere else to go except down.

"Nat, if you have any tricks left up your sleeve, it's time to use them."

"FLUX, target Fatima's radio signal. And punch it!"

Flux recalibrated their heading and banked the megadrone toward Fatima's position.

Nicks looked back. The man with the RPG was taking care to get the trajectory right. She was still in range. Even if he missed, the blast-wave might knock her out of the air. This was it. She dug her fingers in deeper, praying she could hold on.

Kabam!

The bullet hit the sentry in the head, and he fell over dead. The

RPG clattered down the wall. Nicks scanned the horizon for the shooter. No one was in range. Then Alejandro stepped forward with a rifle. He regarded her with a solemn stare, then nodded his goodbye, as the floating panel sailed away to safety.

Up ahead, Nicks could see Fatima pacing the edge of the cliff as the megadrone streaked toward it. She was searching for a way to climb down. But it was impossible without a rope. She held out her hand and sonified the cliff.

"Get as close as you can, Flux."

Nicks radioed Fatima. "We're coming in hard and fast. Be ready!"

The megadrone throttled up and sped toward Fatima. At the exact right moment, Flux cut the power to the rotors, and the drone plummeted, rocketing down, nose-first toward Fatima's precarious perch.

"Jump!" Nicks shouted as they zoomed past.

Fatima hurled herself off the cliff. Nicks stretched out and they locked arms. With her momentum, Nicks swung Fatima up and over the edge. She landed on top of the megadrone with a hard smack.

"Go Flux!" Nicks yelled.

Flux engaged all the rotors, and the megadrone made a jarring course correction. Rapidly gaining altitude and passing over the cliff. Nicks crawled up beside Fatima as they climbed higher.

El Draco's men stood on the lip of the cliff, swearing and firing their guns to no avail. They were quickly out of range. Fatima shot back with rude hand gestures, the only ammo she had left.

"You are so lucky, I'm always saving your ass," Nicks said.

Fatima grinned. "Yeah, what would I do without you?"

They embraced for a moment, then rolled over on their backs, exhausted. Nicks took a deep breath and sighed as all the pent-up stress drained from her body.

They were alive but so was El Draco. Disrupting drug cartels and arresting drug lords was not in her regular job description, but this one was too dangerous to ignore. A retreat was in order for now, but the hunt for El Draco, and those supplying his tech, would have to continue.

PART VII

TOM SAWYER

38

US ARMY CAMP NORTHSTAR, US-MEXICO BORDER

About twenty-four hours later, Natalie Nicks stood with Jack Byrne on a hill overlooking Camp Northstar. The small army base stretched out before him. Beyond the camp, Senator Snell's Smart Wall project loomed.

Nearby, a group of Delta Force operators prepared for deployment. Three prototype Sikorsky-Boeing Defiant helicopters, candidates to replace the famous Black Hawk, rolled out onto the camp's helipad. Natalie Nicks stood next to Byrne, watching the air crews get the birds ready for flight.

One of the unit's leaders rushed up the hill.

"Colonel, the teams are good to go. We can start the meeting whenever you're ready."

"Thanks, Sergeant. Give me another thirty minutes."

The soldier saluted and headed down to continue the preparations.

"So you're briefing them on the operation?" Nicks asked.

"Yes, and I'm quarterbacking this one," Byrne said.

"From here?"

"From the field."

"That's *different*," she said, giving him a hard look.

He ignored her. "What you and Diaz found in Mexico has changed things. The Pentagon wants our team leading on this one. The orders are to clean out Draco's tech cache before we turn over the location to the State Department. The analysis is that the Mexican government is too unstable to secure this kind of weaponry effectively."

"That farming equipment could change things for a country like Mexico if they used it correctly."

"Yes, it could. But Penbrook believes what you discovered is a case-in-point why all of it needs to be under our control." He smiled at her. "Good job, by the way."

Nicks looked at him, surprised by the compliment. It was so hard to stay angry with the man.

"Thanks," she said. "Diaz was a big help. I appreciate the team picking him up when things went sideways. And making the effort to get him back home safe."

"When we got the signal, we were wary of him. Wondered if he'd set you up. But without his help, Fatima wouldn't have found you. He's proven himself a good ally," he said, then added. "I see why you like him."

She ignored the probing comment. Byrne had never been jealous or possessive, but their relationship was on such thin ice at the moment, she didn't want to say anything to make it worse.

But he was not being as cautious. "You need to think twice about involving Diaz and his family any further. I don't think it's smart, or safe."

Nicks flashed him a look that said it was none of his business. Byrne glanced away, and she said, "He's smart and he knows how to protect himself."

"This is a dangerous business, Nat. Keep his family out of it. That's the safest play. They're no match for the people we're up against."

She buried the impulse to argue, nodded, and changed the subject.

"So... you're back in the field, huh? Are you ready for that? It's been awhile for you, hasn't it?"

"Is that genuine concern I detect, Captain Nicks?" He regarded her with a smirk.

"Possibly."

"You want to test that concern?" He gave her some serious side-eye. "Get some real data and see if it's valid or not?"

The challenge piqued her interest. "What do you have in mind?"

Byrne leaned over and touched his toes. A few bones cracked as he stretched.

"Easy old man, don't break something," she joked.

Byrne laughed and straightened. Pointing at the horizon, he said, "You see the first section of Snell's demo wall? It's about three miles due south."

"Yeah, I see it."

He crouched in a runner's stance.

"Ready, set, go!"

BYRNE BURST FORWARD with bionic speed. Hammering his feet into the soft desert clay as fast as his first-generation TALON legs would allow him to run. Nicks stood on the hill, amazed at what she saw.

"I know you can hear me with those ears of yours, Nat." Byrne was a blur, racing toward the camp's southern perimeter. "First one to the wall and back wins. Better catch up!"

She exploded off the hill and chased after him.

In all her time with DR-Ultra, she'd never seen another cybernetic soldier with her speed. She'd heard rumors. Even suspected that Byrne might be the first TALON soldier. Yet, when they had met, he hid his secret convincingly. The entire time she'd known him, the man could barely walk. He'd worn leg braces. Disabled by a faulty battery that had been turned down to its minimum power to save his life from its toxic effect.

The contrast to that man and the one she was chasing was miraculous. But she didn't want him to win, so she pushed her legs to capacity and powered on.

Byrne approached the perimeter fence without stopping. He leapt just when it seemed he might crash and hurled himself over. He hit the other side hard and tumbled on the sandy ground before righting himself and racing onward.

Nicks matched his jump but stuck her landing, giving herself a boost. They were running through open desert now. Byrne seemed delighted to hurdle over the various obstacles in his way. Nicks wove around them, concentrating on increasing her speed. As they approached the sentry station, she'd caught up.

Byrne looked back and frowned. He circled around the construction site, disappearing from Nicks's line of sight.

"Nat, hopefully you can hear me. There's a group of guards on break. Best if we slow down."

Nicks mindful that their bionics were still top secret skidded to a halt and jogged around the corner, expecting to see Byrne doing the same. Instead, she saw he had never stopped. In fact, he'd increased his tempo and was half a mile ahead, having regained his lead and then some.

"What the hell?" She could hear Byrne laughing.

She raced after him, cursing under her breath. Pushing herself, she tore through the desert after him. But Byrne kept his lead. When she reached the hill, he was waiting for her, wearing a smile wide as the moon.

"Cheater!" Nicks jeered.

"Come on, don't be a sore loser," he chuckled.

"I'm impressed," she said. "You pass inspection."

Byrne pulled out his silver flask and offered it. "Drink?"

"Sure." She took a pull and handed it back to him.

"What you discovered puts the Draco Cartel on track to becoming an FTO."

Nicks perked up. She knew the DoD was reluctant to classify drug cartels as Foreign Terrorist Organizations. To do so would make the world a much messier place.

Byrne continued, "Project Pantherix violates the prohibition on autonomous weapons. So, El Draco may have just graduated from drug kingpin to war criminal."

"If that's true, he's not the only one that should be on that list. Draco was worried about losing his *supplier*. That's why he demanded I return the Pantherix we found on Diaz's ranch."

"Did he give you any hints to who that might be?"

Nicks shook her head. "No, but Quinn is exploiting all the information she can from the controller I brought back. She even swabbed me for biometric data, hoping to get DNA samples."

He took another swig from his flask. "I hope that will give us some clues to the whereabouts of the sensors as well."

They began walking down the hill. Byrne needed to start his briefing. "What will you do with the Pantherix units? There were a helluva lot of them."

"Mouse is coming down here to oversee their analysis. We'll set up a contained lab in the camp. Seal it off just like we do the Cage and catalog the machines. I'll make sure he keeps you updated about what he finds."

That reminded Nicks of her own specialist. She needed to check in on his progress. And check on Diaz. They'd only talked briefly after the rescue. She was sure he was overwhelmed after what happened in Tijuana. Single dad. Acting Sheriff. Random covert op that almost gets you killed. She needed to get back down there.

They made their way to the operations tent and Byrne said, "You were right to pursue the Pantherix angle. So I'm putting you in charge of that part of our investigation. I'll continue hunting for the sensors, and you follow your leads."

She nodded. "Okay, I'll start with El Draco's supplier."

As they approached the entrance of the tent, Quinn stepped out, fuming. "That herd of meatheads is ready for you, Colonel. Blunt instruments all of 'em, hope you've got more patience than me."

"Thanks, for warming them up," Byrne said, and gave Quinn a fist bump as he stepped past her and entered the tent. "See you soon, Nat. And good luck."

Nicks said goodbye to Byrne and greeted Quinn.

"Got the ARES programmed for you," Quinn said. "It'll drop you off at the Diaz ranch, turn around, and fly back."

"Good, I'm ready to head out."

They walked over to the hanger where the ARES was waiting. And after a few quick preparations, it was ready to go.

As Nicks stepped on board, Quinn said, "Mouse wants to know when you're delivering the robocat?"

"Not any time soon, I turned it over to my own specialist."

"Who would that be?" Quinn smirked.

"Someone DR-Ultra hasn't heard of, but he's good."

"Oh, really?" Quinn eyed her suspiciously.

"Hey, this is my rogue mission, right? I can recruit my own team if needed."

"Aye, aye, Captain." Quinn gave her a mock salute. "Has your *specialist* found anything yet?"

"I'm about to get an update. I'll let you know."

39

Nicks read the sign made of red construction paper.

Diaz Robotics Lab. Please Do Not Disturb!

She knocked on the bedroom door anyway, but no one answered. Peeking inside, she found the room was littered with bits of copper wire and small machine parts. It looked like one of the workbenches in the Cage.

A little hand tugged on her shirt. "I had to move outside."

Nicks turned around to find Will Diaz smiling at her. It seemed her new robotics engineer was returning from his lunch break. He was wearing an old Minecraft T-shirt, a milk mustache, and pieces of an Oreo cookie all over his face. The crumbs had blackened the corners of his mouth.

"If I turn this thing on in my bedroom, it won't have any place to move," he said. He grabbed her by the hand and led her down the hall. "And if the barn burns down, Dad will be less pissed."

"Makes sense," she agreed.

"Yep," he said. "Want some cookies?"

Nicks accepted his offer of three Oreos but declined the milk. She followed him out to the barn while breaking down the cookies.

She ate the white stuffing first, then snapped each individual cookie in halves and ate them one at a time.

Will watched her ritual with a grin and asked. "Why do you do that?"

"Habit from when I was your age," she shrugged.

He smiled. "What's it feel like being bionic?"

"Sometimes it's strange," she said.

"Strange like tingly or strange like you feel weird 'cause you're different?"

"Weird 'cause I'm different."

"Yeah, I feel that at school all the time."

"Well, now you know you're not alone. There's a lot of us weirdos out there." She tussled his hair while he polished off his last cookie.

When they stepped into the barn, Nicks couldn't believe what she saw. The Pantherix One was restored. The kid had repaired all the damage she'd done. The machine was a patchwork quilt of brightly colored spare parts. Will had somehow infused some of his own warm personality into the robot, as if he'd domesticated the monster and turned it into a pet.

"Will, this is amazing!"

"He's ready for a test run."

"You're being super careful, right?" Nicks raised an eyebrow.

"Of course. I've got this thing under control," he said.

He led her to his parts table and rummaged through his tools for a small screwdriver. He had a dented laptop connected to a dirty CRT monitor. The screen had a chip in the glass and a crack that ran across it.

"Where'd you get all this stuff?"

"The garage, Goodwill, and the trash. Ethan's mom was throwing this laptop out and gave it to me."

"What's all this for?"

"It's a maintenance terminal. You need it to upload the software and tweak the computer code."

He ran a long ethernet cable from his terminal to the Pantherix. The Pantherix turned and looked at Will.

"Don't worry, I'm just showing Natalie how cool you are."

The Pantherix swung its head back to its normal position as if satisfied.

Will rummaged through his tools again and picked up another piece of equipment. He handed it to Nicks. "It's an old iPhone. First generation. I made it the controller."

Nicks marveled at what the kid had done.

"There's just one problem."

Computer code scrolled past on the maintenance terminal.

"You see right here? This is where I'm stuck." Will pointed at a particular block of information. "There's a bug in the code. It was corrupted. That's why it was doing all the strange things around our house. I haven't figured out the original code. Still working on that."

"I may have a solution for you," Nicks said. "I brought you something."

Nicks reached out and touched Will's terminal. Nanofibers from her hand snaked into a crack in the old laptop's bent frame.

"Wow! That's so cool!" Will said.

"Flux, download the code."

The maintenance terminal came to life as Flux transferred the file. Brightly colored lines of new information spooled down the screen.

Will perked up and read along.

"Hey this is the source code. How'd you get it?"

"One perk of being a weirdo."

He typed manically. After a few minutes of very animated hacking, he was beaming with pride.

"That worked. I fixed Shadow."

"Shadow?"

"Yeah, I named her that."

"Her?"

"Well, I wish it was a *he,* but it doesn't have boy parts." Will walked behind the robot and pointed. "See, nothing's there."

"Hold on, I can help with that too."

Nicks ran into the house, and a minute later returned with her solution. She held it out for Will to inspect, and the kid laughed hysterically.

"What is *that?*"

"Truck nuts."

"Truck nuts?" Will doubled over. "I'm about to pee myself."

"Well, don't do that." Nicks found a piece of copper wire and a pair of pliers and performed an impromptu gender reassignment surgery.

"I can't believe this. Dad is going to love it."

When she finished twisting the wire together, she let the balls drop. "Okay, give Mr. Shadow a walk around."

Will tapped in a few commands and activated the Pantherix. The machine trotted in a circular path, scanning its environment as it went. The gaudy truck nuts swung indecently under the robotic cat's carriage.

"That's the best thing I've ever seen!" he said.

The Pantherix appreciated his sex change. There was more bravado in his step. Most importantly, Shadow obeyed every command Will gave it. The machine seemed to be completely under his control. Nicks was impressed, and Will couldn't be happier.

It delighted her to see the little guy so radiant. She tussled his hair again.

"I'm pretty sure you're the smartest kid I've ever met."

Will looked up at her and smiled. "So ... will you let me keep him?"

"I sure wish you could, kiddo. But I'm not the one that makes the final call on that. What's important is that you have figured out how it works and how to control it. That is so helpful to me and my team. We'll have to talk about who keeps Shadow later, okay?"

"Okay," he said. "I'm starving, anyway."

"Should we order pizza?"

"Heck, yeah!"

"Done! Let's go find your father."

Will powered Shadow down. Before shutting down the terminal, he hesitated. "Hey Natalie, I want to show you something. You were wondering who made Shadow, right?"

"Yeah, that's right."

A long flood of computer code scrolled down the screen. Will paused the scrolling in intervals as he searched for something.

"Okay, here it is," he said. He pointed at a section of text set apart from the rest.

Nicks couldn't read any of the code, but she could read this. It was a series of numbered notes about changes to the software. Under the notes, Nicks read the project's name: Pantherix Fatalis.

"I'm pretty sure that's the guy that made Shadow. There aren't any other names in the code. Most code monkeys leave a signature."

"Where do you see a name?"

"Right here." He pointed at the last block of text.

The kid was right. Nicks finally had the clue she needed.

"His name is Dr. Milton Gardner."

PART VIII

LIMELIGHT

40

MEXICO CITY, MEXICO

As the car drove through Mexico City and down Avenue Juarez, the urban park known as Alameda Central came into view. One of the oldest parts of the city, it was a beautiful collection of gardens, statues, fountains, and paved paths teeming with people enjoying the pleasant afternoon sun.

"That's the Palacio," her driver said. "Muy hermosa!"

At the head of the park, across the many blocks of green lawns, sat the Palacio de Bellas Artes. Nicks agreed the museum was stunning. The host of tonight's gala was known for making an impression; it made perfect sense why he'd chosen the museum for his event.

Her car pulled up to the Hilton Mexico City Reforma and stopped. Even though she didn't need the help, she let the driver get out and handle her bags. She thanked him with a cash tip and proceeded into the hotel.

She was in Mexico City to find Dr. Milton Gardner. He'd been a hard man to track down. But once they had, the plan came together. Gardner was a US citizen who had lived in Mexico for over a year. He was known for secluding himself months at a time to further his research, then emerging for long weekends of hard partying and socializing. Tonight, he was a special guest at the Palacio's gala. When they'd found his name on the guest list, they'd immediately worked to get Nicks into the event. Now she had to get situated and ready for the evening.

The hostess at the front desk was all smiles while checking her in. "You have the penthouse suite, Ms. Nicks. Courtesy of one of our favorite patrons."

"Sounds lovely. Which patron are you referring to? I'd like to thank them."

"Mr. Travis Raylock, ma'am."

Nicks was surprised, but she hid it under a forced smile. She'd weaseled her way onto the guest list under false pretenses—using her cover as a journalist again. Was Raylock sending a signal he knew about that, or had he given all the press upgrades? She had to assume it was the latter. Raylock had connections, but he didn't know about Reaper Force. Or did he?

The receptionist slid a small package across the desk to Nicks.

"Here are your credentials and your ticket to tonight's gala. I'll let Mr. Raylock's team know you were pleased with the accommodations."

"I'd appreciate that."

The receptionist waved at the nearest porter, who hurried over to help with Nicks's bags. "Arman will escort you to your room."

"Thank you," Nicks said.

"Yes, ma'am. Enjoy your stay."

As Nicks stepped into the elevator, she heard the hostess's cheery tone shift while speaking into her telephone. "Natalie Nicks just checked in," she said, and hung up.

From across the lobby, the hostess flashed her practiced smile, oblivious to the fact Nicks's cybernetic ears heard it all.

Nicks smiled back, and the elevator door closed.

Something was up.

Arman used his special access key, and they rode the elevator to the penthouse level where they disembarked into a small foyer.

"The other members of your party are already here."

Nicks looked at him with a puzzled expression. Byrne had insisted she'd have to pursue these leads alone. Arman opened the door and stepped aside.

"You first, please," she said, wary of what may be waiting.

"No, ma'am. I insist. You are our guest."

Nicks gave in and entered the room cautiously. She did indeed have visitors.

"Nat, what's up, baby!" Mouse yelled. Then to Fatima and Quinn in the adjoining room: "She's here, ladies. Now the party can get started!"

Nicks laughed as Mouse strutted her way. He was wearing one of the hotel's fluffy terrycloth robes and drinking a cocktail. "What the hell are you doing here?"

"Nice to see you too." He sneered playfully and tipped Arman, sending the kid on his way.

Nicks gave Mouse a quick hug, and they wandered deeper into the suite. Quinn and Fatima lay sprawled out on the living room couches, reviewing video surveillance of the Palacio.

"Seriously, why are you guys here?"

"Byrne called after his operation. They secured all of El Draco's tech at the compound, but they didn't find any new leads. You have the hottest intel at the moment. So he sent us to help," Quinn said.

Nicks didn't say it, but it secretly relieved her.

"We're setting up surveillance. We'll have eyes on you during the gala," Fatima said.

"And we brought you this," Quinn said. She held out a bottle of El Tesoro Blanco.

"You sure know how to make a girl feel at home."

ONE TEQUILA on the rocks later, Nicks hunkered over Mouse as he scrolled through the Pantherix code.

"Wow, and you said this kid is nine years old?"

"Yes, he's amazing."

"We should hire him!"

"I was thinking the same thing. Hey, what time is it?"

"Six thirty, why?"

"Damn, I have to get ready."

Nicks jumped up and made a beeline for the shower, disrobing as she went. "Quinn, Fatima, are you going to help me? You know, the hair and makeup?"

"No!" they shouted simultaneously. Then they gave each other a high five.

Nicks rolled her eyes and threw her jeans at them.

"Why are you asking those two for fashion advice, when I'm the only one with style on this team?" Mouse said. "Check your closet and prepare to be blown away."

Mouse had come through for her. Hanging on the closet door was a black and white Christian Dior jumpsuit with long sleeves and embellished detailing. A pair of matching Dior pumps lay in a box. And on the dresser, the finishing touch, a diamond necklace so spectacular she was sure it came with its own security detail.

"Mouse, you're incredible. Thank you!" she yelled.

"No problem. Glad to do it," Mouse yelled back. "Hey, Nat, one last thing. I found something in this code. I think the kid missed it. We need to take a harder look at this. Because it—"

"Save it, I have to get ready." She turned on the shower and stepped in.

"Okay but—"

"Later, Mouse, later!" she shouted over the sound of the hot water. The spray hit her bruised back, soothing away the tension. She didn't have the mental bandwidth for more technical discussions. There was only one thing on her mind. One person, really—Dr. Milton Gardner.

Nicks was confident by the end of the night the mysteries of the Pantherix's origins would be solved. She'd make sure Gardner helped her do that, one way or the other.

41

The Museo del Palacio de Bellas Artes was considered one of the most prominent cultural centers in Mexico City. But tonight it proved why—its opulence was on full display. Floodlights lit up its grand sculptures and flashed over its architectural majesty. The scene buzzed with interested onlookers, dignitaries, celebrities, and press from all corners of Mexico.

As Nicks's driver pulled ahead in the car line, she found herself very impressed. At over three grand a pop, this was reported to be one of the most coveted tickets of the year. Now she saw why.

Several cars ahead, a young Mexican actor and his gorgeous date exited their vehicle and stepped onto the red carpet. The paparazzi went into a frenzy. Nicks took advantage of the distraction. She thanked her driver and stepped out of the black SUV. Then skirted the red carpet crowd and headed to the museum entrance.

"Com check," she whispered. "Are we ready to mingle?"

"I think I could do this better from the event," Mouse begged. "Is there still time?"

"Shut it. You're locked in a penthouse with two sexy women. Try to enjoy it," Nicks said.

"Yeah, stop complaining and hack into the security feed," Quinn said. "As soon as we spot Gardner, we'll let you know."

"Copy that," Nicks whispered, as she joined a line of ticket holders.

A large poster bearing the face of the celebrity entrepreneur, Travis Raylock, greeted her as she approached the entrance. In fact, his face and name seemed to be everywhere. His marketing team had taken advantage of his role as host to showcase their wares by staging several displays of Raylock Industries' technology along the plaza's pathway.

First, there was a new prototype of the Quantum electric sports car. Nicks admired the car from afar; she wasn't eager to get back in one. Dreadful memories of Vegas Santos dying next to her flashed through her mind.

Next to the Quantum stood a pair of futuristic motorcycles. Nicks gave them a curious glance as she strolled by. Upon closer inspection, she saw the Voltants, as they were named, were space-age hoverbikes, not motorcycles. One of the many side projects Travis Raylock spent his company's resources on, thrilling his social media fans, irritating his boardroom, and worrying his investors.

A woman in a green eagle mask greeted Nicks and took her ticket as she stepped past the white marble columns and continued under the portico. Once inside the museum, she noticed all the serving staff and security wore similar masks. A nod to the key event of the evening, the donation to the museum of a newly discovered artifact.

The art déco interior was stunning and comprised a main hall flanked by black marble stairways on either side. From the center of the room, she could look up and see all three floors of the main building. Starlight filtered through the iron and crystal dome above. Everywhere, decorative touches depicted Mexican plant and animal life and Aztec art.

Near the west stairway, a hulking man the size of an NFL linebacker conferred with a team of similarly buff men. He clocked her and stared for a few seconds through his green animal mask. Nicks looked past him and gave a polite wave to an approaching server with a tray of drinks.

"Security is tight here. I'll need somewhere private to talk to Gardner, if I can ever find him." Nicks took a glass of champagne and wove deeper into the crowd.

As she approached the center of the main hall, the museum director, a tanned, silver-haired man, stepped up on the first floor dais and spoke to the crowd gathered below him.

"Ladies and gentlemen, thank you for coming this evening. Before the Bellas Artes was home to this impressive collection of art, or the ballet, or the exquisite sounds of Maria Callas—this was a sacred site. I'm not referring to the convent and the church that once stood here. No, I'm talking about the first people who worshipped here. The warrior priests known as the Aztecs. Today, we bring home a piece of that history, recently discovered by Raylock Industries during an excavation of their regional facilities."

The director gestured to his right, and a black drapery rose off a small illuminated display case. Inside was a carved piece of green stone, similar in color to the masks the staff wore.

"This is such a delight and a veritable treasure for our institution. I'm happy to announce this pre-Hispanic treasure will become part of our permanent exhibit, thanks to our generous donor, Mr. Travis Raylock."

The crowd broke out in applause as the director searched for his honored guest. But after several moments of awkward clapping and murmuring, no one could find the man, and the director improvised.

"I'm afraid Mr. Raylock is playing the part of an anonymous donor this evening."

The crowd laughed politely.

"But I assure you he is here tonight. So, on behalf of the museum and all of our esteemed guests, I thank him again for his generosity."

There was another raucous round of applause as the director ended the brief ceremony and rejoined the party. Nicks followed the crowd as it milled closer to the stairs.

"Found Gardner. He's headed to the east foyer," Quinn said.

Nicks spotted him.

Gardner was making a beeline to one of the many bars set up throughout the museum. He parked himself there long enough to get a fresh drink and attract the attention of two very curvy women.

Nicks weaved through the boisterous crowd to get a closer look.

Gardner made quick work of the ladies. In five minutes' time, he'd turned them into his new best friends. Suggesting Dr. Milton Gardner was good with both computer code and women. Two skills commonly thought to be at odds with one another.

But why judge? Here was the proof. Gardner headed up the east stairwell with a drink in one hand and two beautiful women on each arm.

Nicks followed.

42

With one eye on Dr. Milton Gardner, Natalie Nicks stood at the west end of the third floor, admiring a painting titled *El Hombre Controlador del Universo.* Translated it was *Man, Controller of the Universe*, one of Diego Rivera's most famous pieces.

The original version, commissioned in 1933 by J.D. Rockefeller for the lobby of 30 Rockefeller Plaza, had been painted on three enormous plaster panels to depict man's mastery of machines. But when a firestorm erupted over Rivera's inclusion of supposed communist propaganda, the painter was fired, and his creation plastered over.

Using his sketches and photographs of the original, Rivera had created a new version of the masterpiece in all its glory for the Palacio. The painting featured a kaleidoscope of brightly colored images. The infinity of outer and inner space. Swirls of galaxies and atomic particles intermixed with scenes of a farmer's harvest. A magnetic induction coil loomed like a copper sun over the dominant figure, a square-jawed laborer.

But it was the center of the painting that fascinated Nicks. It depicted a disembodied hand—half human, half machine—holding an orb of light that seemed to project energy from the center of its palm. It was as if the painter had been inspired by a premonition of Nicks's new bionic upgrade. She studied the painting while glancing at her own hand. The symbolism felt personal.

"His work is stunning, isn't it? Makes me question my own motives." A voice said from behind Nicks. "Will we use our advanced technology for the good of mankind or—"

"—will its power corrupt us?" Nicks turned to greet her new friend.

"Yes, exactly," Travis Raylock said. "You read my mind."

Raylock was dressed in a suit that blended traditional formal wear with stylish athletic clothing; it was neither a tux nor a track suit, but some modern hybrid. It complimented his dark hair that was pulled back into a well-groomed topknot.

He was attractive, but not to Nicks's taste. He reeked of inauthenticity—manufactured glamour that diminished him in her eyes.

"Ms. Nicks?" He held out his hand, which she ignored. "Natalie, am I right?"

She feigned surprise, offering a seductive smile.

"And *you* are?"

Raylock laughed. "Well, talk about catching a man off guard. Are you telling me the most beautiful woman at this party doesn't know who I am? That's a knife in the old ego."

He gripped his chest to pull out the imaginary dagger.

"Let me do this formally, then." He offered his hand again "Hi, I'm Travis Raylock."

"Oh ... I had no idea. You must forgive me. Yes, I'm Natalie Nicks."

They finally shook hands and continued chatting about Rivera's painting. Nicks did her best to keep an eye on Gardner, shooting occasional glances over Raylock's shoulder, hoping he wouldn't notice.

Avoiding Raylock had been part of tonight's plan. Nicks calculated it took all of fifteen minutes for them to run into each other.

And now she felt he might be hard to shake. Also, he somehow knew her name. So much for keeping a low profile.

"May I offer you a drink?"

"Yes, that would be wonderful. Thank you."

Nicks noticed Gardner, and his escorts were on the move again.

"Friend of yours?" Raylock asked. He peered over his shoulder and scanned the crowd.

"What? Oh, I thought, perhaps it was. Sure looked like *her*." Nicks lied.

Raylock waved over a server.

"Martini?"

"Sounds lovely," Nicks said. "Vodka, please."

"Dirty?"

"Always."

While Raylock gave the drink order, Nicks snuck another glance. Gardner had disappeared around the corner. This wasn't good. She couldn't lose him, no matter who her company might be.

"You know what, while we're waiting on those drinks, I'll visit the ladies' room."

"Of course, but please don't stay away too long."

Nicks smiled and excused herself.

As she walked away, someone, somewhere nearby, expressed a similar interest in Gardner. It was clear as a whisper to her enhanced ears.

"Milton Gardner is attracting *attention*. Take care of him."

She suddenly realized she wasn't the only spider weaving a web. But who else was after Gardner? Where the hell was all of this leading? For the moment, it was leading around the corner and down the hall. The direction Gardner had headed seconds before. She followed her prey deeper into the museum, hoping she found him first.

43

D r. Milton Gardner was no longer enjoying his time at the gala. That was the first thing Natalie Nicks noticed when she twisted open the locked handle on the storage closet.

"Excuse me, I thought this was the ladies' room," she said, her eyes wide with excitement.

She didn't know who had suggested the closet, but she could see it had started as fun. The blonde's blouse was off, revealing her ample bosom heaving against her sheer lingerie. The brunette's hair was a mess, her panty hose ripped. Gardner had lipstick smears on his face and white dress shirt.

Unfortunately, the fun had taken a dark turn. Gardner's hands and feet were zip-tied. He was gagged and laid out on a thick plastic sheet. One of his sleeves was rolled up to the elbow, exposing his arm. The redhead was filling a syringe and searching for a vein while the brunette held a small caliber handgun next to Gardner's head.

"Oh wow, this is the real party, huh?" Nicks stepped in and shut the door behind her. "Mind if I join you?"

The brunette turned her gun on Nicks, who immediately kicked it out of her hand. It fell into the corner amid a group of cleaning supplies.

The blonde threw a solid haymaker, hitting Nicks in the side of the head and knocking her backward into the door she'd just come through.

Nicks returned the gesture with a punch of her own. It landed perfectly on the blonde's chin. Her head whiplashed into the wall, and it was lights out.

The brunette dove for the corner, scrambling for the gun. Nicks grabbed her by the ankle and jerked her backward. Unable to retrieve her gun, she grabbed the syringe and stabbed Nicks in her thigh. Confident she'd struck a winning blow, the brunette stood up and stepped back to watch the drug take effect. "Should've stayed home tonight, sweetie. Curiosity just killed the bitch."

Nicks grimaced and pulled the syringe free. She lunged forward and grabbed the brunette by the throat and pinned her to the wall. "Who the hell do you work for?"

The woman panicked. Her eyes searching for a reason the injection hadn't worked. "But ... how are you still standing?"

A group of people shuffled by outside the storage closet, and the brunette attempted to scream. Nicks muffled her mouth with her hand, and the brunette bit down. She squeezed her throat harder, more strategically; in seconds, she was unconscious, and Nicks dropped her beside the blonde.

She then zip-tied and gagged the two women just as they had Gardner.

"Come on, I'm getting you out of here." Nicks helped Gardner back on his feet, tidied him up, and stepped carefully back through the door. As she closed it, she broke off the handle, and they hurried down the hallway.

Quinn broke radio silence. There was concern in her voice when she asked for an update.

Nicks was short on details. "I need that private spot right now."

"Back stairwell straight ahead, leads down to a service hall, and that gets you into the theater wing. It's closed for the night. You should be all alone."

Nicks moved as fast as possible. It wouldn't be long before the team supporting the two female assassins discovered they'd been thwarted. She and Gardner didn't have much time.

44

Natalie Nicks and Dr. Milton Gardner made their way into the theater wing of the Museo del Palacio de Bellas Artes and then backstage. She pushed the man into the nearest dark corner.

"What is this all about? I hardly touched those women. And I'm not into drugs. If you want money, it's yours, okay?" Gardner was bewildered and panicked. His eyes searched Nicks's face as she leaned closer. He took a deep breath and asked, "Who are you?"

"The one who just saved your skinny ass," Nicks said, her head on a swivel making sure they were alone.

"They almost killed me back there," he sputtered.

"Yeah, the plastic tarp wasn't for Jell-O shots, I can guarantee you that."

"I don't understand ... What is happening?"

"No use sugar-coating it. You have a target on your back."

"Me? But why would anyone want to kill me?"

"Didn't you consider it might end this way when you worked for one of the most dangerous cartels in Mexico?"

"Cartel? I'm not working for a cartel. I would never do that."

"El Draco. That name doesn't ring a bell?"

"No! Who the hell is that, and what does he have to do with any of this?"

Nicks wasn't sure if the man was losing his mind or just lying to cover his ass. "Cut the bullshit, Gardner. I know you built those *things*."

"Built what?"

"The Pantherix Project?"

"How did you—" Gardner's face paled. His mind seemed to go into overdrive as he pieced things together. He stiffened and said, "I can't talk about that."

He pulled away from Nicks like he would leave. She jerked him backward hard enough to make a point.

"No, you will talk about this right now. I've seen your pets in action. They're savage murderers. I have no qualms about feeding you to one. So let's hear it."

"But ... I don't even know where to begin."

"Start with something simple. A name or the place you worked. But tell me the truth, Gardner. That's the only way you stay alive. If you don't then—"

"Rook."

"What?"

"Mr. Rook, that's who recruited me."

"How did you meet him?"

"When he approached me, I thought it was a godsend. They fired me from my last DARPA project when they deemed our robotics project unsuitable for combat. I was upset and felt blindsided. Yes, there had been disagreements, some nasty arguments, but normal stuff that happens on a project with that big of a budget. Then the ax came down, and they escorted me out of the building like a criminal. I sat in a bar down the street, in shock, drinking, trying to figure out what the hell happened. That's when he approached me. He knew who I was and everything about my research. He flattered me. He said he represented an anonymous tech investor, someone who would fund any project I wanted to pursue."

"Did he know about the DARPA contract you were working on? Was it Big Dog?"

"Big Dog? Hell no. This was way more advanced than that. Our device was meant to be autonomous, you understand. I'd made a breakthrough."

"And he knew about it?"

"Yes, he did."

"So, he had classified information?"

"I'm not sure about that. It seemed the investor had extrapolated the details from several sources. He was most interested in exploring how autonomous systems could evolve. He wanted me to keep that line of inquiry open. Said the budget was unlimited if I agreed to work exclusively for him. He had contracts already drawn up."

"Already drawn up? Like he knew they would fire you?" Nicks asked.

His eyebrows rose, and he said, "I've never thought about that."

"So, he could've been behind your dismissal?"

"Damn, do you think that's possible?"

"Anything is nowadays, Dr. Gardner. You of all people should know that."

Nicks heard something. A person inside the theater. A straggler from the party, perhaps. She lowered her voice.

"Where did you build the Pantherix units?"

"A secret location with more layers of security than any DARPA project ever had. They housed me at an exclusive resort under an assumed name. They shuffled me around in vehicles with blacked-out windows. Every day they flew me to my lab's location. I had no outside communication. It was unorthodox, but I had a complete team, any tool I wanted, any supply, nothing was denied me. We'd work for weeks at a time. Then took long weekends. During those breaks, they flew me to exotic vacation spots I'd never been. Allowed to run the town, have dinner, go to a bar, meet women. I know they followed me. Frankly, I didn't care. My work has always been my main priority. And this was the most exciting work I've ever done."

"Do you realize your exciting work has killed people?"

He shrugged. "I've worked for DARPA most of my adult life. That isn't surprising."

"But, this wasn't DARPA, was it? In fact, you don't know who the hell was funding this research, do you?"

"As I told you, I only had one point of contact."

"Mr. Rook?"

"Yes."

"How often did you meet him? And how were the meetings set?"

"They weren't set. He just appeared, randomly. It was rather disarming. The man was unique."

"As in ... distinguishing features?"

"No, I mean he was missing ... Well, it sounds silly to say this, but it was like the man had no soul. He was a machine."

"Aren't we all," Nicks said, under her breath. Then asked, "How were you paid?"

"They deposited funds in an overseas bank account. Paid to an LLC set up under my name. I drew a generous salary from it. Occasional bonuses, but nothing outrageous."

"What about security at the lab?"

He held out his arm and rubbed the skin below his left wrist. "Geo-tracker and entry key embedded below my skin. I found it ridiculous, but they insisted it was state-of-the-art security."

"I'll need that key," Nicks said and ran her finger over the slight bump.

"What? Are you crazy? Right now? That's not possible." He tried to jerk his arm back, but Nicks wouldn't let go. She pulled him closer. Squeezing his wrist in her vise-like grip.

"I'm sorry this is going to hurt." She flicked open a small pocketknife and Gardner yelled.

If he had accepted the quick surgery like a good soldier, Nicks would have heard the man pull the pin on the flashbang. Instead, she didn't notice it until it wobbled across the stage—seconds before it exploded.

45

Natalie Nicks rolled over, coughing, and cradling her head in her hands. It felt as if the blast had split her skull in two. Her aching head, the temporary blindness, and the complete lack of sound gave her the feeling she was underwater. Then she realized the blast had temporarily overwhelmed her cochlear implants. She guessed the tiny processors were running diagnostics while they recalibrated. She'd be deaf until they were back online.

She got up on her knees and waved her hand to clear the smoke pluming around her, then scanned the area for Gardner. A few feet away, a man too big for his dark blue suit stood over the shell-shocked researcher. Nicks groaned as she tried to get back on her feet.

The man turned toward her—he was wearing a green animal mask. A flash of recognition reminded her he was part of the security team she passed earlier. He pointed at her, and held up his hand, as if telling her to stay down. But she couldn't hear what he was saying.

The man turned back to Gardner and flicked his wrist, producing a long black handle. As if opening a butterfly knife, he flicked it again, and the strange device unfolded. Black blades arranged themselves around the weapon like teeth. Nicks recognized it immediately. It was some of Vegas Santos's best work.

Then Flux confirmed her hearing had been restored. Just in time to catch Gardner speaking to the man standing over him.

"Mr. Brightside?" Gardner said. "Thank God! Help me!"

The man Gardner called Brightside ignored the plea and raised his weapon over his head.

"Nooooo!" Nicks yelled.

But it was too late. The macuahuitl swung down like an ax and decapitated Gardner with one brutal stroke. Blood sprayed the nearby curtain. The head rolled across the stage floor, came to rest right-side up, and stared at Nicks with Gardner's final expression frozen in a macabre mask of shock.

Brightside then hacked into the man's arm and removed what Nicks had wanted—the small implant that served as an entry key.

The smoke from the flashbang wafted higher and triggered the fire alarms for the entire Palacio, and all hell broke loose. A crowd of distressed patrons rushed into the theater from the back, searching for the nearest exit. Brightside regarded Nicks one last time, then disappeared down the dark service hall.

Nicks held out her hand. "Flux sonify that sonofabitch!"

Flux tagged Mr. Brightside as she struggled to her feet and chased after him. She explained the new situation to her team as she ran.

"We're watching the security feed, but it's chaos. We can't see him," Quinn said. "They're moving everyone out of the building."

"Where is he, Flux?" Nicks growled.

Her systems scanned the environment as she neared the end of the hallway. Sonic waves were cast out and at certain frequencies even passed through the walls then bounced back, returning with the data they captured. Flux processed it for Nicks to use. It was like x-ray vision for the ears. She could hear Brightside's distinct pattern, or *earcon*, through the chaos of the crowd.

Brightside tried to lose Nicks in the panic, but it was no use. She had his sonic scent and wouldn't be thrown off. She relentlessly tailed him, forcing him to break out in a run, knocking over shocked guests and bewildered staff.

Finally, she cornered him in the sculpture room overlooking the rotund portico where she had entered the museum. He cracked open his strange weapon and swung it at her.

Remembering Dr. Jackson's warning about obsidian, Nicks tried to box him in without getting hit by the blades. After several expert swings and one too many near misses, Nicks pivoted on her back foot, picked up a bronze abstract that made no sense except as an effective weapon, and hurled it at him.

Proving he was quick on his feet, Brightside ducked and rolled out of the way, but not quick enough. One jagged end of the sculpture caught him, gashing him across the cheek before crashing through the French doors leading to the terrace. Glass and wood shattered as the bronze sailed out in a wide arc, ultimately landing on the brand new Quantum, flattening its beautifully curved roof and windshield. That made two she'd destroyed in a matter of days.

Brightside dove out through the ruined doors, climbed down to the lower level, and jumped on one of Raylock's hoverbikes, fired it up, and sped away like he'd driven one a thousand times before.

"Are you kidding me?" Nicks yelled.

She backed up, ran, and leapt through the hole she'd made in Mexico's treasured building. She landed next to the second hoverbike, climbed on, cranked the engine, and sped after Brightside. Because, honestly, what else was she going to do? He was the new clue that would solve this mystery, and she'd be damned if he was getting away.

46

Nicks slammed her foot into the Voltant's pedal and the hoverbike lifted off the ground and rocketed down the street on a self-generated river of air. Mr. Brightside, as Gardner had called him, was already thirty seconds ahead of her. She lay close to the body of the flying motorcycle and floored the accelerator.

Once she caught up, she saw the husky assassin had discarded his suit jacket, revealing a space-age looking motorcycle vest with extra protective plates running down his spine.

The bastard had obviously planned this.

Nicks zoomed in closer, smashing into the back of the other Voltant. Brightside turned around. He looked surprised to see Nicks behind him. He swung his macuahuitl out in one hand and aimed the tip at her.

Fawoosh, woosh, woosh!

Three of the obsidian blades shot from the weapon. They whizzed past her head like bullets, proving Mr. Brightside's toy was full of nasty surprises.

When he aimed it at her again, Nicks tilted the hoverbike and swung wide, then back-and-forth, trying hard to make herself a more difficult target.

Fawoosh, woosh, woosh!

Three more blades shot out. One ripped into a front rotor, breaking off the tip of that propeller. The broken part clattered around, threatening a jam. Nicks cut the engine momentarily, and the loose piece fell away.

But that gave Brightside time to zoom ahead. Now she was losing the race.

She did everything possible to speed up the machine, but her inexperience with the controls proved a disadvantage. Brightside, on the other hand, seemed to have no problems. He sped across the lawn of Alameda Central, forcing amazed pedestrians to scatter as he barreled through.

Where the hell was he going? Nicks wondered, as she followed after him. They were quickly running out of park with no sign of Brightside slowing. This meant he might try to lose her in the streets.

"Nicks, where are you?" Mouse shouted over the coms.

"Chasing the big guy on the hoverbike," she yelled back.

"Damn! Raylock's Voltant? What's that like?"

She titled the controls and zoomed forward into a busy street. "Like trying not to die!"

"Uh ... yeah. Right. Be careful," Mouse stuttered. Nicks could hear him typing furiously as Fatima and Quinn whispered in the background. "Listen, if you can plug into its system. I'll hack it and help you catch that bastard."

Nicks scanned the controls. But where to plug in? She didn't know.

Brightside swung wide to the left. Nicks did the same, barely missing a line of parked cars. There was a straight away coming up and Brightside was getting ready for it, trying to aim that damn toy of his at her again. Nicks backed off a bit and tried to stay in his blind spot.

"Where the hell do I network in?" Nicks shouted. "Help me out."

"Pulling up the schematics right now. There should be a panel cover near your right foot. Do you see it?"

Nicks quickly glanced down. "Yeah. But not how to open it."

Quinn chimed in. "Smash it with your fist."

Nicks did that, and it dented down the middle. She gave it another whack and one edge bent out. She kicked it and the thing fell into the street below her.

"It's off. Now what?"

"There should be a cable port in there."

Nicks saw it, leaned down, and held her hand over the opening. "Flux, do your thing!"

Her strange upgrade snaked its way into the machine. Mouse acknowledged receipt of the connection on his end. Quinn reported they now had her location through the bike's navigation system. There was even video from tiny cameras embedded in the Voltant's fenders. That was good, but all of this was slowing her down even more. Brightside was getting away.

Fatima cussed, acknowledging she saw how big Brightside was. "Easy target," she said. "Force him back toward the hotel, I'll shoot the bastard from here."

Nicks wished she could do that, but the chase was leading her further away by the second. She wanted to end this now. "Talk to me, Mouse."

Mouse cleared his throat and said, "The Voltant maxes out at fifty miles per hour and hovers at twenty feet off the ground. But that's because Raylock's engineers put a governor on the throttles. I'm about to bypass that and boost your power. Hold on."

"Can you pilot this thing too?"

"Oh shit, I hadn't thought about that. But, yeah, I think I can."

"Hell no, don't even try that," Quinn was yelling in the background.

Fatima agreed. "The video feed is shit. You'd be flying blind."

"Do it, Mouse!" Nicks demanded. "On the next straightaway,

send me as fast as possible into the back of that meathead. Here comes the turn. You've got about ten seconds. Go!"

Like an old cowboy stuntman on a horse, Nicks dangled over the right side of her hoverbike. Mouse disabled the governor and accelerated straight toward Brightside. He was aiming his weapon again, but Nicks had taken cover and was coming in too fast.

Bang! She rammed the other hoverbike hard and leaned forward over the handlebars, grabbing the back of Brightside's machine. She squeezed down, anchoring the two bikes together.

Brightside was furious. He spun around and hit Nicks in the face with a wild backhand.

She fell, losing her grip and her balance. She grabbed the handle with the accelerator to save herself, and that overrode Mouse's control. Her hoverbike flew in a wide arc toward a city bus. Everyone started cussing. Mouse course-corrected and brought it back in line with the other bike.

"Hold it there, Mouse!" Nicks yelled.

She angled herself to kick Brightside off his bike, but the man had other plans. He flashed a venomous look and, using his macuahuitl like a hammer, began smashing her front rotor.

Shbang! Shbang!

He hit it again and again. Until the blades bent and distorted, ripping it apart. The hoverbike smoked and sputtered and tilted at the wrong angle.

"Oh shit, you've lost an engine," said Mouse.

"He's trying to take me down. Keep the speed up," Nicks said.

They zoomed past an outdoor café, upending dishes, glassware, tables, and even patrons in their powerful rotor wash.

It was harder now to keep her Voltant stable. Nicks swung the bike out and then brought it back hard. A worrying crack and clang of machine parts sounded as her damaged rotor became entangled with its twin on Brightside's bike.

A small jam of cars lined the road ahead, but Brightside wasn't able to steer away. The hoverbikes were now fused together.

"Pull up, Mouse! Pull up!"

Mouse boosted the engines in the nick of time, and the rotors revved, allowing the hoverbikes to climb up and over the vehicles. Floating like hockey pucks on ice, they slid down the line of car roofs —to the horror of the owners and passengers.

Nicks hit Brightside in the face, busting open his bottom lip. He smiled with his blood-smeared teeth and swung the macuahuitl like a sickle. Nicks ducked in time to avoid the swipe.

She was tired of the damn thing and cursed Vegas Santos for making it. She kicked Brightside in the ribs and felt one crack on impact. She kicked again for good measure, but Brightside was ready, grabbed her ankle, and jerked her from her saddle.

She slid backward on the bike clawing for a handhold and ended up dangling precariously from the back.

Brightside jammed his throttle down, pointed the fused bikes toward his target, then hacked off the entire steering mechanism with the macuahuitl. Without warning, he then dove off his hoverbike, tumbling onto the hood of a parked taxi, and rolling off it onto the sidewalk.

Nicks was tempted to do the same, but the Voltants were headed straight for a crowded night market full of pedestrians and vendors. There was no time for her or Mouse to slow the bikes down.

Instead of abandoning ship, she climbed back onto her side of the fused machinery and used all her strength and body weight to make a hard left, off course, and into a narrow alleyway. The two machines scraped and skidded against the alley's walls, ping-ponging toward a collection of dumpsters.

She had no option but to ditch. She jumped, and the hoverbikes barreled toward their smashing end. The crash was tremendous.

After the smoke cleared, it looked like an alien spacecraft had exploded. Huge chunks of the futuristic vehicles littered the alleyway, but there was only one clue to the madness that caused all the damage—Brightside's discarded green mask—a jaguar frozen in a perpetual rage.

PART IX

DISTANT EARLY WARNING

47

El Draco held a gold-plated AK-47 against the head of Carlos Garza and cursed him. Garza, one of Draco's chief lieutenants, was a big burly man who'd always commanded the respect of his crew. He was a serious but jovial leader, full of crazy energy, that filled a room with good vibes. It was evident all of that had changed.

This room—a secret bank vault—was full of death. And Garza was barely clinging to life. He was tied to a chair pushed into one corner. Loose bills and empty safe deposit boxes cluttered the floor.

"How are you still alive?" El Draco snarled.

Bloodstains slowly inched across Garza's sweat-drenched shirt as he tried to respond. "I fell when it started. Blacked out. Woke up with Ramon on top of me. Covered in his blood."

"All of my vaults robbed at the same time. The Pantherix units gone. Everyone dead except *you*." He pressed the barrel of his rifle into the man's forehead. "And I'm supposed to believe you know *nothing* about what happened?"

"Please. Señor Solis. Believe me. I'd *never* steal from you. I swear it!"

A young man rushed into the vault. Loose American dollar bills swirled in the air as he skidded to a stop. El Draco's main bodyguard, the one who wore the black skull mask, grabbed the young man by the shirt and threw him up against the wall.

"I said stay out, you fucking imbecile," Black Skull yelled.

El Draco turned and pointed the AK-47 at the young man. "What the hell do you want, Alvaro?"

"The tracking code has come online. We've found the location of Denada's missing Pantherix."

El Draco raised an eyebrow. "Are you sure?"

"Si, Don Miguel. Absolutely sure," Alvaro swore. "The ping came from the American side of the border."

"Any word the police have reported it?"

"No sign of that. It must've malfunctioned. Gone offline temporarily. But now the signal is there. If we recover it, we can set up a new production facility of our own. Cut out the supplier. Start fresh."

El Draco signaled Black Skull to let Alvaro go. Then he asked. "Where is it?"

"Looks like a private ranch. Your men could be there before dark."

El Draco thought about that for a moment, saying nothing. He then turned around and aimed the rifle back at Garza and opened fire. A burst of bullets tore into his face and chest, killing him brutally. Stray bullets ricocheted off the interior of the steel vault. Everyone except El Draco ducked for cover.

"If you're wrong, Alvaro, you'll end up like Garza! Another sacrifice to Saint Muerte."

The nerdy computer engineer glanced at the dead man and immediately turned green. He rushed out.

El Draco handed the spent AK-47 to Black Skull.

"Go get my Pantherix. And this time, *no mistakes*!"

48

The ARES lifted off and followed its flight path back to Los Angeles. When it reached cruising altitude, Natalie Nicks and the rest of the Reaper Team gathered behind the cockpit and discussed their intel.

They reviewed the Museo del Palacio's security footage for the hundredth time, trying to follow the movements of Mr. Brightside prior to the attack on Nicks and Dr. Milton Gardner.

"He was stalking you when you went upstairs. I can't believe we missed it," Fatima said.

Brightside had avoided most of the security cameras. But one captured the flashbang rolling down the backstage corridor toward Nicks and Gardner.

"He's good. Has tactical training, spec ops maybe," Quinn said.

"I heard him approaching and ignored it," Nicks confessed. "Dammit."

"Do we have any clue who he's working for?" Fatima wondered.

"You've seen the footage. Nothing other than the audio Nicks overheard. But we can't pinpoint the source," Quinn said.

"Here's something we do have. A hidden tracer subroutine," Mouse said.

"A what?" Nicks asked.

"I tried to tell you about this in Mexico City." Mouse swung his monitor around to show her.

She stared at the screen. "None of that makes sense. Translate."

"There was a hidden program in the Pantherix source code you copied at El Draco's estate—it's a Trojan horse that only activates when it's connected to the internet. It worried me, but it made little sense until now."

Nicks gave him a hard stare. Hoping he'd get to the point.

Mouse took a breath and tried again. "It's a small program, but it sends coordinates back to the code writer so they know the location of the machine."

Nicks paled and quickly jumped on the communication panel to place a video call. "That means El Draco may know about Diaz's ranch."

She paced as the call rang through.

Bret Diaz finally picked up. His face filled the camera frame, but he didn't say hello. He held his finger to his mouth in the universal sign for silence. He then turned the camera toward the house, giving the team a terrifying vantage point.

A group of El Draco's men in tactical gear crept methodically toward his back porch. The angle of the shot told her Diaz was hiding in the barn.

The leader of the assault team suddenly stopped and gazed in the camera's direction, as if Diaz had revealed himself. Nicks saw the gunman was wearing a black skull mask.

The video call dropped, and Nicks received a single text.

"SOS."

She shuddered, thinking about what that meant. They had to act now.

"Reprogram our flight path," She gave the team a desperate look. "Diaz is in trouble!"

49

After texting Natalie Nicks, Brett Diaz turned the phone off so as not to give away their hiding place. He hunkered down behind the rusty freezer and squeezed Will close. Will hugged him back as tight as possible.

"You're doing great, son. We just need to keep hidden. No sounds," he whispered.

The gunmen advanced across the backyard and formed a perimeter about a hundred meters from the back door.

"Deputy Diaz, we know you're here. All we want is the Pantherix unit. Give that up and we'll leave. No one has to get hurt."

Diaz didn't believe a word Black Skull said. He knew the rules of the cartel. They'd have to make examples out of him and his family so El Draco could save face.

Will carefully lifted the edge of a nearby canvas tarp. Shadow lay hidden beneath it. The robot animal looked like it was asleep. All the tests had drained his battery, but he was plugged into one of the barn's outlets recharging.

"Dad, don't let them take Shadow," he whispered. "He doesn't want to go back."

"Don't worry. They're not taking anything from us." Diaz unhol-stered his Glock. He checked his belt. He had two full magazines. That was it.

His Colt CAR-15 patrol rifle was in his vehicle. He hadn't had time to reach it. Diaz peeked around the old Frigidaire to get a better look. The gunmen had moved closer to the back porch. No way to make it to his truck and the rifle without leaving Will. He wouldn't risk it.

Black Skull was now near the back door of the house. His men had the place surrounded, luckily they were ignoring the barn. "Last chance, Sheriff. Come out and bring the device, or we're coming in."

No way was he going to respond.

After a moment's silence, the man gave his crew a hand signal, and they opened fire. Bullets ripped into the screened porch and the picture window. Then the kill team moved in with Black Skull in the lead. He looked like the grim reaper intent on harvesting souls with his band of devils.

Diaz prayed God was sending a response. Angels with automatic weapons would be great. Or perhaps something even more miracu-lous—a bionic woman.

50

The ARES descended from the clouds in stealth mode and hovered over Diaz's ranch. Quinn engaged the cameras on the undercarriage and turned on the thermal imaging as they eased down over the house.

"Two people are in the barn. They're right on top of each other," Quinn said.

"That's Will and Brett. They're hiding there. Smart!" Nicks said. "Let's get these bastards before they find them."

"The largest group of hostiles is inside the house," Mouse said.

"You're up, Cartwheel." Nicks hit a lever, opening the hatch.

Fatima, who was screwing on the modified projectile, secured her monkey harness to the fuselage, flipped down her thermal imaging lenses attached to her Gentex helmet, and leaned out of the airship, aiming her rifle at the roof of the house.

She fired and the shape charge projectile whistled through the air and impaled itself into the roof's shingles.

"Your turn, Viper." Fatima said.

"Roger that." Nicks pulled on a filter mask, leaned out of the ARES, and listened for Quinn's count.

"On my mark, three, two, one, mark!"

Quinn pulled the pin on a smoke grenade and dropped it. Nicks leapt, feet-first, chasing after it. Fatima triggered the shape charge, and it exploded, opening a massive hole in the roof. Seconds later, the smoke grenade and Nicks dropped through the opening—a testament to perfect timing and countless hours of training.

The grenade detonated and filled the room with thick white smoke. Nicks landed right next to the canister amid a heap of roofing debris.

The gunmen were stunned from the explosion and didn't seem to comprehend Nicks meant them harm. They eyed her in amazement as she appeared like an apparition materializing from the swirling smoke.

Looks of wonder gave way to looks of terror as soon as she took out the first man with a perfect double-tap to the head.

Using her enhanced speed, she pivoted and shot the man to his left, then the next. Three men down in three seconds. Then she rolled into cover behind a couch, vanishing as quickly as she had appeared.

One of the remaining men fired as she moved and strafed one of his own team members. That man fell dead. Now two hostiles were left.

Nicks watched as they positioned themselves back-to-back. They peered around in the heavy cloud of smoke and cautiously moved toward the back door.

"Behind you!" Nicks yelled.

The men turned as a flying couch smashed into them and knocked them down. Nicks advanced out of the fog and shot them dead. Then she swept the house for stragglers but found none.

"House is clear," she reported.

Then Quinn said, "Outside, Viper. The barn!"

Nicks ran out of the house and around the corner. Brett Diaz was single-handedly holding off another group of assassins. One of them blasted the barn with a barrage of automatic gunfire. Diaz disappeared and didn't get back up.

Dread filled every corner of her heart and mind. Had she led El Draco here? Could she stop this madness in time? Or was it already too late?

The remaining group of armed men were closing in on the barn. Nicks feared she wouldn't get there in time. Thankfully, Diaz popped back up and continued shooting at the men as they tried to set up a perimeter.

One bad guy went down and the others retreated behind Diaz's police vehicle. The man in the black skull mask was there too, pointing and yelling orders as he put a new clip in his rifle. When Nicks sprinted closer, the nearest gunman strafed the barn, Diaz cussed, and Will called out.

"Dad! Dad! Are you okay?" The little boy screamed.

"I'm okay, son. Stay down!" Diaz shouted.

Nicks zeroed in on their voices. Through the open barn doors, she saw a huge metal toolbox. That's where Diaz was pinned down. It wasn't much cover. Will was behind an old freezer. They wouldn't last long against automatic weapons. She had to stop the assault fast, so she leapt bionically in the direction of the nearest gunman.

When she landed, she tackled him hard. He fell back on his ass, banged his head on the ground, and his rifle spun away out of reach. Nicks got to her knees, thinking he was down for good. But the stupidly brave man sat up, brandishing a long serrated tactical dagger. He lunged with the blade. She dodged it, grabbed his knife hand, and broke his wrist while twisting the blade up into his face. The dagger sank into an eye socket with a sickening squish, and the man went limp.

Nicks looked back at the barn and saw Will lunge from his hiding place and fish under a tarp. A large shape loomed into view at his side.

"Shadow, save Dad, okay? Go get 'em!"

The Pantherix sprung from the barn and galloped into the fray. It leapt onto the hood of Diaz's truck and scanned the horrified men with its camera eyes. Will tapped the controls as Shadow chose its first target. The boy was totally unaware he'd stepped out of hiding and exposed himself. Diaz was yelling at him to get down.

Shadow killed one bad guy instantly, then chased down another and tore into him. The gunman's stomach was gruesomely ripped open. He dropped his rifle to push parts of himself back into the gaping wound.

Nicks spun into the brawl and came face-to-face with Shadow. His black fangs snarling mechanically. She froze, waiting for his next move.

The robot regarded her blankly, turned its head and retargeted, pouncing on the nearest gunman with vicious efficiency. It appeared to be working its way toward their leader.

Black Skull sprayed Shadow with bullets as it bobbed and weaved, tearing through his team. But there was no stopping the machine's deadly rampage. In a matter of minutes, the rest of the sicarios were dead or dying, including Black Skull. He lay on his back, choking on his own blood—it looked as if Death himself was giving up the ghost.

Nicks heard Diaz cry out from within the barn.

As the smoke cleared, the reason was obvious and gut-wrenching.

Nicks joined in his anguish.

"No, God, no!"

51

Nicks engaged every ounce of power to get to Will Diaz. Outside the barn, she had to step over a gunman who appeared to be dead. He grabbed her by the ankle and begged for help. She had no mercy for him. Not now. She picked him up by the throat like he was a bag of trash and hurled him against the barn wall. He crashed through it and fell silent in a heap of shattered wood and splinters.

She rushed over to Will and stopped, horrified by what she saw. The little boy was covered in his own blood. Brett Diaz had wrapped his torn shirt sleeve around the child's head as a makeshift bandage.

When she stepped closer to help, Shadow lunged at her and bared his black teeth, as if he was protecting his own cub. He then growled a mechanical growl—a sound effect Will had programmed into the machine.

Maggie Quinn stepped into the barn and blasted Shadow with her EMP rifle. Like a prop from a Star Trek movie, the gun flared with blinding light and shot a pulse of electrical energy at the robot. Shadow stiffened as if he had been flash-frozen. Quinn nudged him with her boot and he tipped over, dead as a doornail.

The two women fell on their knees in front of Diaz and checked Will's wounds. The little boy groaned and muttered something unintelligible. Nicks leaned over to listen.

"Is Shadow okay?" he whispered.

"He's okay, I promise. Just sleeping. But you're not, buddy. We need to get you patched up," Nicks said.

Will's little chest heaved up and down as he struggled to breathe. Suddenly he convulsed.

"Quick, get him on the ARES," Quinn said. "We landed in front yard."

Nicks helped Diaz up and rushed them both to the airship.

Mouse had radioed Colonel Jack Byrne. As everyone climbed aboard, Byrne's voice boomed over the intercom. "I'm prepping the MASH unit at Camp Northstar. It's the boy's best chance. Move now!"

Seconds later, the team had Diaz and his son strapped in, ready for transport. Nicks jumped from the ship and waved them off. Quinn looked at her with concern.

"You're not coming with us?"

"I'll tie up loose ends here. You save that little boy."

She watched as her friends ascended like a spirit and disappeared into the moonless sky. A sky as black as her thoughts, where no light of leniency remained.

Her rage was at its peak. Soon, everyone and anyone responsible for this madness would find their world darker still.

52

Nicks wandered back toward the barn as the ARES flew off. Fatima radioed to confirm Diaz had diverted local law enforcement. Nicks would be alone until Byrne's Delta response teams arrived to sort the evidence and the bodies. Fatima said they were thirty minutes out.

Near the barn, she saw dead men, guns, and blood everywhere. Spent bullet casings covered the ground like brass seeds. There was more of the same inside the house. She searched the men and their vehicles. Perhaps she'd find some clues to where the sensors were or where El Draco was hiding.

She focused on the bodies littering the yard. Gruesome work, but a sensible starting point. At a minimum, she hoped to find some form of identification, but she came up short. The men were clean, a sign they had more training than your average gun-toting mafioso. Soon she realized the effort wouldn't yield anything new, and she made her way into the barn.

Next to Will's collection of homemade equipment, she found a second-hand video camera sitting on a tripod. Will had created a poster-board backdrop and pinned images of real panthers on it. The camera's battery icon flashed red, indicating it was out of power. Nicks picked up the camera.

"Flux, can you play the video?"

Flux networked into the camera, using Nicks's internal power to juice it just enough to turn it back on. The video rewound, and she watched it from the beginning in the camcorder's view screen.

Will started his presentation with a brief lesson on biomimicry that Mouse would've appreciated. Then he explained how the Pantherix One was designed. How its larger components fit together, and how those parts powered the finer mechanics, allowing it to move like a real panther.

He then discussed the computer code and how the machine could be paired with other devices that emitted radio signals like the ground sensors. Part of Shadow's old code had programmed the robot to patrol areas protected by those devices. But the code was flawed and made the robot unpredictable. So he shut down its machine-learning functions, ending its ability to act by itself. He insisted a machine this dangerous had to be on a leash. And he explained how he had repurposed the old smartphone to control it.

"The black panther is a melanistic jaguar. Many cultures consider it a really cool animal that protects people. So bad guys shouldn't use Shadow for bad things. This kind of machine should help people, not kill 'em. Duh!"

Will's words filled Nicks with pride. Then struck her as inspired. One might even say prophetic. He sounded like—

Vegas Santos.

Both Santos and Will thought the image of the jaguar was significant. What had Santos said about it?

Beware the shaman in the jaguar mask.

Mystical babble, really. Nothing of real significance. Still, it was intriguing. Who was Santos talking about? El Draco, maybe, because of his fascination with the animal? Or Brightside, perhaps? He'd worn a jaguar mask. Along with most of the staff at the museum's gala. Brightside was no shaman, that was for sure, but he had a taste for Aztec culture. Just like the host of the gala ...

Travis Raylock.

Impossible. He wouldn't be involved in this. It was crazy. He had too much to lose. He was a social media celebrity, obscenely rich, and already had everything a young tech executive could want.

Yet, Raylock was the tech wizard of Silicon Valley. A modern-day shaman of sorts. And there was the donation to the museum.

"Flux, pull up the promo for the gala and give me the description of the artifact donated by Travis Raylock."

"Researching ... the pre-Hispanic artifact is a hand-carved mask used in Aztec blood-letting ceremonies made from a single piece of jade dated to 1000-600 BCE. The forehead features a prominent cleft, suggesting the were-jaguar motif, a popular theme in Aztec art."

So it was a jaguar mask. Was Raylock the shaman Santos warned her about? It seemed far-fetched. Plus, Santos had sworn he didn't know his patron. He didn't know where the money was coming from. He swore he wasn't lying. Except about one thing—the Quantum. A car made by Raylock's company. Part of his payment, he'd said.

Beware the shaman in the jaguar mask.

That phrase danced in her head. The mask was the key to her next clue. The mask *was* the clue. She recalled what the museum director had said in his speech. "... recently discovered by Raylock Industries during an excavation at one of their regional facilities."

"Flux, give me the locations of all Raylock Industries facilities in Mexico."

"There are no listings for that company in Mexico."

No listings? Or no *public* listings? If he was building Pantherix units for drug cartels, Raylock would have to do it in secret. Especially now that the El Draco cartel was designated as an FTO. That would put the entire company and its founders in legal jeopardy.

Even if she ran with this crazy theory, finding a secret facility in Mexico would be impossible. The drug war proved that. But maybe her team could look for where the mask had been found?

That Raylock would be part of this scheme still seemed outlandish. On the flip-side, if it was true, it meant her adversary was more cunning and more powerful than an entire country of drug cartels. Raylock Industries was one of the Pentagon's biggest arms dealers. She'd be risking everything going up against someone that well connected and protected. But she had no choice here. She'd already vowed to avenge Will, and she intended to do it.

PART X

MISSION

53

High altitude jumps were not Natalie Nicks's preferred method of infiltration, but Jack Byrne had insisted. "Safest way to get you in undetected. If Raylock is hiding the Pantherix Project in that facility like you believe, his installation will be guarded by the best security tech in the world. After all, he builds the stuff."

Nicks had agreed enough with that assessment to risk the jump. The signal light flashed red, and she stood up.

Military free fall was something many special operations officers were trained in. Nicks had trained as a Ranger and again during her clandestine services training. For this particular HALO—High Altitude Low Open—jump, she would exit the plane at thirty thousand feet and open her parachute at about three thousand feet. Accounting for the extra weight of the gear she carried, she calculated she would be on the ground in about three minutes once she jumped.

Three minutes, and she would know if her theory about Raylock was accurate or a serious miscalculation.

When she'd presented her conclusions to Byrne, he'd put the

team into overdrive. They'd scoured the public and military records about Raylock's construction projects but come up short. They tried another angle and analyzed the history of jade artifacts like the jaguar mask. Similar discoveries had all come from the Yucatan peninsula coastline. Archeologists had uncovered elaborate cities, tombs, ceremonial altars, and even pyramids in places like La Venta in the state of Tabasco.

Using this information, along with what they knew about Gardner's movements in and out of the facility, the team requested more help from General Drummond, who tasked the DIA with compiling an exhaustive list of chartered jets operating in that area. It was Mouse, a fan of Raylock, who had given the effort its breakthrough. He knew Raylock had a childhood obsession with an anime show titled *Eureka Seven* about a boy who fought an evil wizard from within a giant animal mecha he'd built himself.

Eureka Seven Airlines was one of the busiest small jet companies in the region. Its primary destination was a private airfield located outside the small coastal town of Sisal. When they checked the area's satellite imagery, they couldn't find the airfield—or any structure for that matter. It was the absence of these structures that confirmed they had the right location. The circumstances were uncannily similar to those found at El Draco's compound.

The bay hatch of the airplane opened, and the air rushed in like a hurricane. Nicks stepped closer to the lift. She checked her oxygen, then set her FF-2 automatic ripcord release to the minimum. If she blacked out for some reason, or her eye protection cracked and her eyes froze together, the device would open her chute at a preset height of three thousand feet. She didn't want to set it any higher in case she was spotted. She'd rather damage a bionic leg than get shot by whoever was guarding the facility.

Fatima opened a channel to give her an update.

"Diaz is gone. He left Camp Northstar without authorization," she said.

"What!? Why?"

"I don't think he's handling things well. His boy is in the ICU unit here at the base. He's getting the best care possible, but he isn't doing well. A bullet strafed his head. It didn't penetrate the skull, but it was bad enough to leave a small fracture. He made it through surgery, but he's not responsive. Too early to call it a coma, but Byrne thinks it's headed that way," Fatima said. "I'm sorry, Natalie. I know you really like the kid."

A wave of despair washed over her as she stepped closer to the edge for her jump. "Where do you think Diaz went?"

"We don't know. We can only guess. But I can find him. Do you want to go after him?"

"No," Nicks said. "I'm sure it's a reaction to what's happened. He'll come back around. Give him some space."

It made perfect sense the man was wild with grief. She knew facing the death of a loved one changed a person, but this wasn't the right time to muse about such things. As hard as it was, she refused the tears that wanted to come, and forced herself to put the child and his father out of her mind. No more time for human emotions. The machine needed to take over.

It was time for Viper and Viper alone.

The jump master warned her to get ready.

"Flux, engage the protocols!"

"*TALON protocols engaged.*"

She waited for the signal. When it came, she leapt off the airplane and dove headfirst into the dark void.

NICKS FELL with her arms and legs stretched out for stability. It was always a strange sensation to feel them buffeted by the air. She pointed her head at the coast, now only the size of a ribbon, then collapsed her arms, and headed down through the smattering of clouds toward the black sea.

Her HALO altimeter in her heads-up display spun like a slot

machine. Twenty thousand feet, fifteen, ten, nine, eight. The countdown continued as she fell through the radar detection zone.

Because oxygen improved night vision, she kept her mask on. Plummeting closer to her target, she forced her arms and legs out to adjust her trajectory. She needed to come in from the south and land in cover along the beach so any surveillance equipment or security guarding the facility wouldn't see her approach.

When the altimeter hit three thousand feet, the chute deployed and at about two thousand feet, the full canopy spread out and jerked her up under its wing. Now, she was floating, light as she could be under the conditions.

She reached up and engaged her night vision long enough to grab the toggle handles and take control of her remaining descent. Then she switched it off. She wanted her eyes to adjust to the existing light.

She pulled on the upwind toggle to turn the canopy, and her entire body swung about forty-five degrees in line with her landing target. Her airspeed was about thirty miles per hour. She crabbed a bit to the right. She was running with the wind, just as planned. Then, in her peripheral vision, she caught sight of something unexpected.

Giant translucent drone panels.

She was about to crash right into one.

How could she have missed them? They were pieced together in the same megadrone configuration she'd seen on El Draco's estate. They crisscrossed over her target's location. Most likely, synced to the spy satellites spinning high above them all. Now she knew how El Draco had come by them. The same technology that had saved her there was about to kill her here.

Sure she could land on the panel. She'd done it before. But she had too much speed and was coming way too fast. She'd never be able to make a smooth landing. If she survived at all, she'd also be trapped high above the ground. No, she had to get around them somehow, and she only had seconds to do it.

She gauged the wind line, violently trimmed the canopy, and

swung wildly away from the drones. Sweeping past the panels, she scraped one edge. It spun her back around the wrong way. She spiraled into the wind and couldn't correct herself.

The ground was coming too fast now. She pulled the toggles to her waist, forcing the chute into the full braking position. She peddled her feet as if running in the air, getting ready to land. But her landing wasn't pretty. She was moving too fast and the sand was too soft. Her feet scraped the ground and she tumbled hard. When she finally stopped rolling, she was cocooned in her chute.

She lay motionless for a minute, listening. Checking for any sign she'd been seen. Hoping that anyone scanning the beach would see nothing more than a big black lump. A shadow among shadows.

When it seemed the coast was clear, she used her knife to cut herself out of the chute. Then she got on her feet and sprinted toward cover, pulling the tattered fabric behind her. Once in the bushes, she buried the chute and prepped her gear.

Now for the difficult part, she thought. As if jumping out of an airplane wasn't hard enough.

The building she intended to scale was only a few hundred yards away.

54

N atalie Nicks had ended up on a beach about two hundred yards north of the property in question. A five story building loomed directly in front of her. A single road snaked off to the east and there was an airfield with a short landing strip to the west of the property, on her right. The Atlantic Ocean was behind her. She scurried through the sparse cover on the beach, hid behind a decent-sized boulder, and pulled out Quinn's special monocle. Scanning the details of the building told her she was in the correct place.

The facility's existence was the most important thing she observed. All the intel said this stretch of land was an undeveloped coastline. But here was a new compound, with the same design used by other Raylock Industries manufacturing sites.

Also, the outside walls matched images she'd seen of Raylock's Smart Wall demos. That detail made sense now that the threads of the mystery were tied together. Why not test the wall's anti-intrusion capabilities out here, in secret, and kill another bird with the same stone—protect your own covert facility?

These details, coupled with the fact she'd almost been killed by the drone panels camouflaging the area, confirmed to her that the team had found the right location. But she needed to see what was on the inside to be one hundred percent.

She grabbed her pack and ran at bionic speed up the hill. She cleared the beach and stopped behind some cover about seventy yards from the northeast corner of the property. She swept the monocle back and forth, carefully studying the situation.

There was a ten-foot wire fence surrounding the building and guards everywhere. Several on the roof and in pairs patrolling the perimeter. A main entrance with a massive gate was visible to the south. Three black SUVs were parked in a circular drive in front of the building. Along with one brand new, special edition Raylock Quantum. This was all just inside the gate.

From here, she could see the road to the east actually curved back around toward the airfield. It was the only paved road in sight.

She decided she'd seen enough, cinched her pack of gear tight, and made her way carefully to the fence line. The bottom of the fencing was anchored in concrete. She found one loose corner of the fencing and ripped it back like she was folding open a tent flap. She squeezed inside and bent the fencing back down.

From there she headed to the front of the building on the south side by staying in the shadows as much as possible. When she reached the main driveway, she did a forward roll over the pavement, back into cover, and crawled on her stomach up to a position closer to the entrance.

She waited for two guards to pass and did another forward roll right up to the first SUV. Here, she set her magnetic charge under the wheel-well closest to the gas tank. She repeated this for all three SUVS around the entrance and moved back into hiding. They would give her the most bang for her buck and she just couldn't bring herself to destroy another pretty Quantum. It just seemed like bad karma.

When it was safe, she sprinted around the corner and down the west wall to the rear of the building, avoiding the patrols as she went.

There, she found an equipment hub on the northwest corner of the base. All the electrical and air conditioning were housed here.

She set two charges next to the transformers. And two more under the fuel cell station. Giving Flux the appropriate command would blow the holy hell out of the base's small power plant.

With that done, she slinked into the shadows one last time and put on her special gear. When she found an opening, she sprinted to the north wall and leapt, reaching for it with the palms of her hands.

This better work, she thought.

Raylock's engineers designed the walls to discourage scaling, but thanks to Mouse, that wouldn't stop her. As he had explained, the suit's special fibers promised to get her up any surface.

Her hands hit the wall with a dull smack and anchored her in place. The rest of her body swung into the wall and the coverings on her knees and feet anchored themselves as well. She dangled off the wall about fifteen feet above the ground. Another sixty or so would allow her to climb onto the sentry catwalk that circled the roof.

She pulled her right hand away from the wall with a jerk, stretched another few inches, and grabbed the wall again. It stuck to the wall like a hot-glue gun had pasted it there.

She then raised her leg and jammed her toes into the wall like a mountain climber who'd found a good foothold. There was nothing there. The wall was absolutely sheer. But her foot stuck to the surface as if by magic.

The spider-suit worked. She pushed higher, rocking back and forth, repeating the same motions as she ascended. Only a slight scraping and the dull thud of her legs and hands hitting the surface came as she climbed higher.

Everything was working like a dream, when the acrid smell of burning tobacco wafted through the air. She caught the glow of cigarette ash in her peripheral vision. One guard patrolling the roof was coming her way. She froze and pushed herself flat against the wall. She hung there in the shadows like a black starfish when the guard stopped directly over her.

Nicks was at a serious disadvantage. If the guard saw her here, he could blow her head off with his automatic rifle, unless she took the risk of leaping backward off the wall. But now she was high enough to break even her bones. Dying at this point would mean the whole mission was for naught.

She slowed her breathing. Thankful that the ambient noise of the beach and ocean was loud enough to drown out her subtle movements while the guard lingered above her. Did he see her? She prayed that wasn't the case. She dared not even adjust her head to look up.

The guard cleared his throat and spit. The wet spray fell down over her. He coughed, and then she heard his inhale of breath as he took a drag of the cigarette. She was so acutely aware, she could hear the way the man's puff burned away the paper and tobacco.

Move on already!

She heard him take another drag. After a moment of silence, the butt landed in the crook between her neck and right shoulder and lay there on Mouse's spider-suit, burning into the fabric and then into her skin. She pumped her shoulder, and it rolled closer to her neck, making the whole matter worse. That part of her body was original issue. There were no artificial pain receptors to dial down. She closed her eyes and endured the pain, hoping the cigarette would extinguish itself as fast as possible.

Finally, the guard's footsteps receded as he continued his circuit. When she was sure he was gone, she reached down and swept the cigarette away. Then continued her ascent.

To avoid the next guard, she climbed faster up the wall, rocking back and forth until she was on the catwalk.

Seconds after that, and before the next guard circled around, she slinked down a ladder and entered the building through a roof-access door. Finally, she was inside.

55

Nicks had entered on the fifth level, and it seemed to be mostly unused meeting rooms and conference space. The hallways were reminiscent of corridors you'd find in a hospital or a military installation. It reminded her of DR-Ultra's secret lab, Blackwood Lodge.

She continued down the hall, reflecting on the mission defined by the team: gather intel on what was inside. Collect evidence, if possible. Then exfiltrate to the beach where she'd find transportation off the coast. To do all of this, she needed information about the building's layout. That required access to their computer system.

She tried one door and found it unlocked. She peered in; it was empty except for an unused desk and chair. No computer or phone was visible, but along the wall near the electrical sockets she saw ports for the computer network. She reached out and touched one and Flux networked into the system.

After several seconds of processing, Flux's humanoid voice spoke in her ear, "*Five main floors. Two basement levels. Four central elevators. Two stairwells on the eastern and western sides of the building. The security is heaviest in the basement.*"

"Can you bypass the security?"

"*Yes, except for the system protecting the new expansion.*"

Nicks raised her eyebrows. "Expansion? Where is that?"

"*Sub-basement. The structure and the number of levels is unavailable.*"

"Is any part of the facility assigned to Dr. Milton Gardner?"

"*Affirmative. Basement Level Two, Lab Alpha.*"

Having stored the information, Flux disconnected from the port. Nicks stood up and moved to the door. "Give me directions to Lab Alpha."

"*Planning quickest route.*"

"And can you do something about those cameras?"

"*I will disrupt the video feed as you move through each sector.*"

Following Flux's lead, Nicks made her way to the eastern stairwell and down to basement level two and found the activity on this floor was busier. Flux tapped into the frequency used by security personnel. There was no chatter indicating they knew about her, so she continued on.

Gardner's lab was the first door down from the stairwell. She waited for one security patrol to pass and slipped out into the hallway. Then down to Lab Alpha. The door was locked and required a remote access key, which she didn't have.

Kneeling in front of the door, she held her hand over the scanning mechanism. Flux networked in and began decrypting the lock. Seconds later, she heard footsteps approaching from around the corner.

"Flux, we have company on the way."

Nicks held out her free hand. Flux sent out a sonic pulse to mark the distance and gauge the speed of the approaching guards.

"*Echolocation suggests twenty seconds before the guards are in visual range. Estimation for encryption is twenty-three seconds.*"

"Speed that up!" Nicks whispered. There wasn't time to hide. And if she forced the door, the alarms would go off.

Fifteen seconds now. Nicks stood up, ready to take action.

Ten seconds. She was sure she was blown.

Five seconds. She turned ready to fight.

Clickkkk!

The lock released and the door swung open. Nicks rushed into the lab and closed the door behind her. She slid down against the jamb, listening to see if the guards would investigate. To her relief, they continued on past the lab.

Keeping the lights off, she checked her surroundings. It fit what she had imagined Gardner's lab might be. Strange components of various shapes and sizes filled the lab tables and workbenches. Pristine stainless-steel gears and small electronic parts lay about, clustered in like groupings. Several microscopes and computers were at each of the stations. An air conditioning system whined above her as its fans filled the room with cool air. A hint of machine oil filled her nose.

She examined the devices on the tables. Some of these parts she recognized. They were like those on Will's workbench in the Diaz barn. Blueprints encased in plexiglass wall mounts decorated the walls. Several versions of the Pantherix were visible on the plans. Pantherix One, Pantherix Two, and Pantherix Three. This was undoubtedly where the dangerous robots had been created and built.

One blueprint stood out because of the size of the Pantherix. This version seemed to have a special purpose but was unmarked. Nicks wasn't sure what to make of the coding system on the various plans, but according to some memos lying around, the units called Pantherix Fatalis seemed to be the most current focus of the lab. She assumed the Fatalis was the oversized Pantherix. It was larger and looked more dangerous than the Pantherix models she'd already encountered—a true monster—as if Gardner's team designed it for a science fiction movie. Surely, they were not building this thing for a real-world application.

Along the last wall, there were several recently constructed units. These models were the standard size, and like most of the upgrades she'd seen so far, were even more animal like, so much so that Nicks felt hesitant to even approach them. These units were missing their battery core, which nested in the center of their ribcage like a heart and was then surrounded by other components and the robot's metal shell.

As she looked for the missing batteries, a familiar earcon sent a shiver down her spine. Flux was warning her that an old nemesis had walked into range.

The adjacent lab's lights turned on, then the lights for the room beyond that lit up. More labs were beyond Lab Alpha than she'd realized. They cascaded into infinity. All of them filled with Pantherix units and their components. The lab in front of her had one terrible exception.

Mr. Brightside.

He stood in front of her behind the large window separating the two labs. They made eye contact and he smiled mischievously.

"Are you enjoying the tour? I hope so. I've been waiting so patiently for you to arrive."

His voice came through muffled, as if he were speaking from under water.

"I knew you'd eventually crawl out from under your rock, Brightside."

He stepped closer, like he was challenging death itself.

"Here I am. Come and get me!"

56

Nicks and Brightside stared at each other through the lab's adjoining window. They paced like animals stalking their respective prey.

Brightside flipped open his weapon and raked it across the glass.

Nicks could see he'd upgraded it yet again. Electricity sparkled over its sharp edges. The black blades scratched the glass like fingernails and crackled with a surge of dazzling energy.

"You know it's not fair, showing off that ridiculous thing," Nicks said with a sneer. "All I brought were my two little fists."

She hit the window with a right cross. It buckled and splintered. A thousand tiny spiderwebs spread across the surface, but it resisted her attempts at breaking through.

"Reinforced glass," Brightside snarled. "To make sure the animals don't get out of their cages."

Nicks hit the shatter-proof glass again. Her strange colored blood marked the point of impact with a smear. Brightside laughed at her frustration and headed for the door. To speed things up, she picked up a nearby metal stool and hammered the window with the full brutal force of her cybernetic arms and the pane exploded outward in one full piece. She climbed through the opening into the other room and ran after Brightside.

In the hallway, she found he had fled deeper into the building. He hit a red panic button mounted on the wall as he turned a corner. Emergency lights flashed and an ear-piercing alarm blared, making it impossible to track his sound profile.

It got worse when the lab doors flew open and panicked workers spilled into the corridors. Those in charge shouted instructions, reminding everyone how to evacuate. She shoved several workers aside.

"Move it," she yelled. "Get out of my way!"

A pair of guards coming toward her realized, a fraction of a second too late, she was an intruder. Nicks leapt forward, throwing her whole body into them. One man fell back, smacking his head on the hard floor. It was lights out for him. The other attempted to fight her, but a well-placed uppercut to his jaw put him down beside his partner. She got up and continued on.

When she rounded the corner, Brightside had disappeared. She headed down that corridor and turned again and found herself in a hallway labeled restricted. It was dark except for a single red emergency light at the far end, shining like a demonic eye. The glow illuminated the only possible path, a large portal at the end of the corridor.

Wary of being ambushed, she approached with caution. The over-sized door had a rubber gasket around its edge. It reminded her of a submarine bulkhead. A radiation hazard poster hung on the adjacent wall.

As she paused, considering the risk of entering the room, the blare of the alarms faded, replaced by the haunting whisper of a small child.

"Shadow! Shadow! Come on, boy!"

Nicks didn't want to accept what she heard. It was some kind of sick joke. "Natalie, will you keep us safe?" The voice of Will Diaz filled the hallway.

Rage boiled deep within her. The taunt was personal, and it meant Brightside had prepared for her. She wondered about a trap.

She pulled the handle of the door and found it unlocked. As it swung back, the air inside escaped with a hiss. Against her better judgment, she stepped inside.

The room was completely white and covered in pristine ceramic tiles. The only door was the one she'd entered through. Brightside stood waiting for her in the back of the room near a table full of equipment. As she stepped forward, the door closed, sealing them both into the room.

"That door won't stop me. I think you know that."

"I'm not going to kill you with the door," he said.

Nicks found that amusing. At least the big tattooed meathead had a sense of humor. She stepped closer, glancing at the components around the room. She could take him now, but held back. She wanted information.

"What is this place, Brightside?"

"This is where we find out how stupid you really are."

Brightside aimed his macuahuitl and fired at her. She shielded her face and two of his blades hit her in the forearm. They stuck like two little black fangs. She ripped them out, and tiny droplets of blood and biocoolant painted the white tile floor.

She sprung across the room, grabbed his weapon, twisted it out of his hand, and whacked him with the flat part across the head. It was like using a cricket bat and it made her point. He yelled out and stumbled back, trying to absorb the blow.

"Who are you working for?" She yelled.

She saw pain and concern in his eyes. He hadn't counted on her being that fast or that strong.

"You shouldn't have come here," he said. "You're going to die, *painfully*. Just like that little boy."

She swung again, more viciously this time, and he fell hard, ending up sprawled on the floor seemingly unconscious.

While she cursed herself for hitting him too hard and blowing a chance at interrogating him, she noticed the table he'd been protecting was filled with familiar devices. In addition, stacks of US Army crates lined the wall next to it. She compared the parts to the labels on the boxes and realized she'd finally found the missing ground sensors.

She wasn't expecting that. She'd almost forgotten about them.

The sensors had been dismantled, and their battery cores were missing. On the wall, she found the ominous clues why—detailed procedures for handling RTGs or radioisotope thermoelectric generators. The briefing with Drummond replayed in her mind.

My God, she thought, *they were after the atomic batteries!*

Byrne's worst-case scenario was true. She had to warn Reaper Force as quickly as possible. This took precedence over all her other concerns.

As she headed for the door, a new alarm buzzed through the room's speakers. "Emergency lockdown procedure initiated," a computerized voice blared.

A pungent chemical smell polluted the air flowing through the filtered vents. Green smoke followed, filling the room. She didn't understand what the gas was, but its thick cloud of fumes gave it a dangerous appearance. She tore apart a nearby lab coat and fashioned a mask to cover her mouth and nose.

She tried the door and discovered it was locked. Flux networked in and found it protected by the same difficult encryption, but went to work anyway. The smoke stung her eyes as she searched for another way to open it. Across the room, Brightside groaned as he regained consciousness.

In desperation, she tried brute force against the door. Her improvised mask was ineffective. Her sinuses burned, making it hard to breathe.

When Brightside stood up, he was wearing a clear-plastic filtration mask. Clear enough for Nicks to see the smile underneath. Oxygen hissed from some source within it.

She needed that mask. She stumbled toward him, choking as she went. She collapsed mid-stride, and when she attempted to get up, vertigo set in.

The thick smoke rolled up in a great plume around her, and she imagined it as a mushroom cloud spinning its toxic ash out over an incinerated landscape.

Darkness closed in, welcoming her into its comfortable arms. As she gave into its promise of oblivion, she wondered, Camp Northstar, who would warn them?

PART XI

FAREWELL TO KINGS

57

CAMP NORTHSTAR

As far as Colonel Jack Byrne knew, Nicks's mission was still on course. He'd left Quinn in the ops tent monitoring the team's communications rig, fully expecting she'd send him another good report within the hour.

Byrne wasn't worried about Nicks at the moment. He was worried about *logistics*—something he normally never thought about, or wanted to think about. Such things were better left for DoD bureaucrats.

But right now, he was the most senior officer on the base. The El Draco operation was his baby. And the fallout was his problem.

As he walked over to the tarmac, one of the Delta Force operators jogged up to greet him. The young man, who'd been trained to keep his cool in combat, seemed completely frazzled.

"Colonel, I'm glad you're here," he said, shaking his head. "We have a serious problem."

"What's that, Sergeant Major?"

The man pointed to the center of the tarmac where his team milled around two shipping containers. "Those things. That's our problem."

"Where the hell did those come from?"

"Sir, that's the haul from the Draco compound. You ordered us to bring it all here." The young soldier tugged at his Taliban beard and gave Byrne a bewildered look. "And ... uh... excuse my French, sir, but those things are fucking full."

Byrne made his way over to the first container, had one man open it for him, and peered inside. The Delta team had outfitted the container with plywood shelving and packed it to the ceiling with Pantherix units. The robocats were all turned off and laying in a prone position. They appeared to be sleeping with their strange heads on their metal paws. Rows and rows of them. Shoulder-to-shoulder. There wasn't an inch of space to spare.

The Delta teams had been right to bring them here. But Byrne knew Camp Northstar couldn't accommodate the sheer size of the haul. Plus, Mouse was the only one assigned to analyze and catalog all the machines.

"Shit... it's going to be a long-ass night," Byrne said, then checked the second crate and found it was just as full. "Scratch that. Maybe a long-ass week, or two."

"Yes, sir." The Sergeant Major handed Byrne a clipboard with the shipping manifest and a pen. "You want us to move them closer to Dr. Park's lab?"

"Let me break the bad news, and I'll ask him what he thinks."

Byrne turned around and reached for a radio, laying on a nearby equipment crate. He keyed it and called for Mouse just as the first burst of gunfire erupted behind him.

A man let out a blood-curdling scream and there was more automatic gunfire and more shouting. Panic broke out on the tarmac and Delta force soldiers began scrambling for weapons and cover. One man was down in a pool of his own blood. It took Byrne a few seconds to realize it was a surprise attack.

He turned around and ran at bionic speed to the nearest fallen soldier. But the man was already dead. In fact, something had ripped him into three pieces.

Byrne spun around and stared into the closest shipping container. It seemed a million glowing red eyes were staring back at him.

The Pantherix were awake and every one of them looked ready to kill.

58

Natalie Nicks's head pounded with a nausea-inducing thump that finally hammered her awake. She was no longer in the radiation lab where she'd collapsed. She was lying on her back, on a stone platform about ten feet round.

She wasn't restrained, but she might as well have been because moving her body felt nearly impossible. She rolled to one side and immediately vomited. The room continued to spin as she struggled to sit up.

When she was able, she looked around and saw she was at one end of what could only be described as an arena. It was about the size of a high-school football stadium with a dusty, walnut-colored dirt field.

Encircling the arena were stone steps and slabs of rock, resembling benches or ancient bleachers. A rack of human skulls lined one section of the arena's wall, a ghastly display that helped her understand what she was lying on.

It was like a large stone wheel turned on its side. It was covered in images of human sacrifice. Artistically carved, its shape was that of a feathered serpent chasing its tail. The serpent's feathers were inlaid with jade. No doubt it was an Aztec altar from ages past.

She guessed she was below the building she'd infiltrated because shiny steel columns rose through the old stone and joined new construction above her. She could see one floor full of new equipment, more labs, and an observation deck. The entire area was a strange blend of modern hardware and ancient archeology. Perhaps the builders had stumbled upon the ruins, found it was built on bedrock, and constructed right on top of it. This had to be the place the ceremonial jaguar mask was found.

The arena and stone altar were a contrast to the modern observation deck built above it. Several giant screens hung over the platform like teleprompters in front of a podium. A narrow bridge or catwalk connected it to an elevator that ran along one wall past carvings of toads and eagles holding snakes in their beaks. The elevator stretched upward out of sight. She felt safe assuming this was the secret sub-basement Flux couldn't find plans for.

Around her, different teams of people, each group with its own colored uniform, worked throughout the space. The crew on the observation deck, wearing white coveralls and white hardhats, used a crane to lower a large piece of machinery down into the arena. They seemed to be operating one of those giant magnets that junk yards used to stack old cars.

Another crew across the arena sported orange coveralls that matched the little flags marking their excavation area. They seemed to be part of some archeological team investigating a cave-like tunnel that snaked out of her line of sight.

Suddenly, bright floodlights mounted on the observation platform switched on. A man, followed by a group of whispering security guards in blue uniforms, exited the elevator and made his way to the end of the platform. Everyone seemed intent on talking to him at once.

Nicks took that as a cue to do something about her own situation. Despite having difficulty speaking, she managed a whisper.

"Flux, can you blow the explosives?"

"*Negative, not from this location.*"

"Is the signal being blocked again?"

"*Yes, but the interference isn't electronic. It's structural. You're too far underground and ...*"

Flux's voice garbled and faded away, only to be replaced by the voice of the man on the observation platform.

"Welcome back, Ms. Nicks."

Her host's greeting was so infected with his smug, imperious tone it grated every nerve she possessed. He looked down on her like he seemed to look down on everyone.

It was Travis Raylock.

59

CAMP NORTHSTAR

Quinn was worried. Nicks had missed their agreed upon signal exchange. No message from Flux either. She needed to let Byrne know immediately.

She stood up to leave the tent when the gunfire and screaming started.

"What the bloody hell is that?" she shouted.

She reached for a handheld radio to find out, just as a Pantherix tore through the side of the tent. This one was a sleeker version of the machine she'd seen on the ranch. As it rotated its black head to scan the tent, she dropped the radio and ducked under the table, hoping it missed her.

That hope was quickly dashed when the machine trotted straight for her.

Outside, erratic gunfire continued and shouting from the soldiers confirmed the base was under attack. Her radio squelched and came to life.

It was Byrne but he was cutting in and out. "Quinn, we need that... the Pantherix units..."

The robot pounced on the radio and crushed it. Crunching the metal and plastic it in its lethal black fangs.

Quinn sprung from her hiding place and lunged for the gun leaning in the tent's corner. The Pantherix turned, targeted her, snapped its scary jaws, and leapt for her throat. Quinn spun around with the EMP rifle. It flared with light, and she blasted the Pantherix in mid-air. The robot stiffened, its red eyes went dead, and it crashed at her feet.

She kicked the bloody thing for good measure, grabbed another radio, and left the tent. Outside, she saw Byrne and a team of Delta soldiers hiding behind a stack of equipment crates. They were fighting for their lives. Hopelessly surrounded by a horde of Pantherix units.

As soon as they took one robot down, another would take its place, and more were spilling out of the two shipping containers in the center of the tarmac. Thankfully, a new group of soldiers were pouring out of the barracks and running straight for the fight.

Quinn knew they would need the EMP rifle, so she ran toward Byrne's position. But that's when she saw something that turned her blood cold.

A pack of about twenty Pantherix had broken off from the main battle and were galloping toward the center of the camp. There wasn't anything strategic to worry about there except the MASH unit and the migrant detention center. But both were packed with innocent men, women, and children. Unprotected civilians. If the Pantherix made in there, it would be nothing less than a bloodbath.

She gave Byrne a long hard look, turned around, and ran the other way.

60

Travis Raylock stood on the end of the platform, waving his hands like a conductor and giving commands to a foreman who was directing the white-uniformed workers. Nicks tried to speak but began coughing uncontrollably. Her lungs were on fire, and she was so desperate for air it felt like she'd just escaped drowning. She wiped her mouth and nose and found her hand covered in a viscous green liquid.

Raylock glanced her way. "Easy, Ms. Nicks, take your time. I'll be right with you."

He conferred with the foreman again, who then signaled the crane operator to pick up a large steel crate covered in blackout fabric. He pointed to a spot next to the altar, and the crane lowered the crate into the arena.

"You must forgive me. We're in a rush to move the most important research down here. This natural amphitheater is a perfect storage facility. Such a lucky find, not because of the history it represents—no, I don't care about that—but because it makes such a stable bunker. It'll protect the equipment until we can move it offshore."

At the moment, Nicks didn't care what Raylock was doing, she was more concerned with her health. Something was seriously wrong. She tried to stand but fell back to her knees.

Noticing her struggle, Raylock said, "We dosed you with a weaponized aerosol. It contains nanomachines programmed to disable your cybernetics."

Nicks looked up at Raylock, cursing him under her breath. Then she doubled over and vomited again.

"Uh, yeah ..." Raylock smiled down. "They told me the biological effects of ingesting little metal machines are quite dreadful." He shook his head as he watched her. "But I'm so pleased with the results."

He stepped closer to the podium and typed on his keypad.

"Barnes hounded me, saying we should test things like this nanogas on ourselves. I said he was ridiculous. There's no reason to experience the pain my devices inflict on others. He insisted it would preserve our empathy. I don't see the logic in that. Weapons are by their very nature devoid of emotion."

His voice boomed through the loudspeakers hidden around the arena.

"Do you agree or disagree, Ms. Nicks? Did you preserve your empathy when DR-Ultra used their TALON technology to turn you into a weapon?"

At the mention of DR-Ultra, Nicks cast her eyes back on the podium. Raylock's expression said he was enjoying the renewed attention.

"Oh, come on, don't act so surprised. I know all about you. I've known before our first meeting in Mexico City. You don't think I fell for that crazy cover story. You're a spy for the Defense Intelligence Agency. I also know about your team, Reaper Force."

Raylock's company had multiple military contracts, and he was privy to certain information about DoD programs, but the existence of the TALON program and Reaper Force was top secret. They both knew he shouldn't have access to that level of classified information.

"Honestly, it's very frustrating to find someone so beautiful and capable, so misguided. I can't think of anything more un-American than the suppression of innovation. Our country needs men like me, doing the things I'm doing, I'm convinced of it."

He was angry now. His collection of dharma beads jangled against his silver Rolex as he shook his finger at her.

"I should be celebrated. Instead, my government sends spies to sabotage my work as if I'm some terrorist. Do you think destroying what I've built will make this country any safer, or better, or freer? No, the opposite! You're killing the American dream by moving against me. Who needs a secure border when your own government is traitorous to the very ideals it espouses?"

Several video feeds materialized on the monitors. Seeing this seemed to brighten his mood.

"Speaking of borders," he said, watching the video with great interest, "I've had to push my schedule forward because of your interference. But you know what? Good for you, getting in there and showing me the flaws in my plan. You're a true disruptor. I like that."

Raylock went back to typing, so Nicks scanned the video feeds. Each one gave a variation of the same perspective—a low point of view. The angle told her all of these feeds were being filmed secretly. Raylock was spying on various teams of people: soldiers, technicians, and scientists in white lab coats.

She watched until a man yelled, and the crane lowering the big crate stopped right above the arena floor. Workers scurried over to it and, using guide-ropes, swung the crate into its proper position.

"Right there is good," Raylock said. "Not too close to the altar. Give Ms. Nicks some space to take it in. More dramatic that way."

He smiled as he watched the men make their final adjustments. He gave them a thumbs-up, and the crane's massive electromagnet let go, and the crate dropped into place.

The workers then grabbed the corners of the black fabric and pulled. The drapery peeled back like curtains on a stage, unveiling Raylock's surprise—a monster-sized Pantherix worthy of a horror movie.

The blood drained from her face.

"You look positively shocked." The pleasure was obvious in his voice. "Perfect!"

She'd seen the plans for this version in the lab and assumed it was a joke. How wrong she'd been.

Raylock held a tablet now. When he tapped a few commands, the monster moved. It had all the features of the standard Pantherix, but it was ten times the size. The unpainted stainless-steel armature that formed its massive legs and wide ribcage gleamed like polished chrome. The red camera eyes were recessed into a metal skull more catlike and intimidating than the previous units. Its most unique feature was perhaps its deadliest—a pair of long teeth protruding from its jaw like double-edged daggers—making this Raylock's twisted version of a saber-toothed cat.

The monster scanned its surroundings, and when it found Nicks, it roared. The sound reverberated through the arena and echoed up through the sub-basement. Everyone in earshot turned. The excavation team packed their gear.

Nicks would have thought it absurd were it not for her previous experiences with Raylock's machines and—the two giant fangs—made of sharpened obsidian. They'd decapitate her with one swipe.

"One ton of bite pressure," he said, flashing his own teeth in a wide grin. "You'd do well to stay away from those fangs."

Nicks rode out another wave of nausea and pulled herself up on her knees, still too weak to stand.

"I just don't understand men like you, Raylock." She found it hard to make herself heard. "You're successful, rich, and have the world in the palm of your hand. But dig a little deeper, and what do I find—a little boy playing with toys in his giant man cave—you're a complete disappointment."

He threw up his hands in mock resignation. "I should've known it would take a lot to win you over. And you're right. My childhood love of anime inspired the design. Always wanted to build a real mecha, and this is as close as it comes. But you shouldn't be so dismissive.

This *toy* can rip your sexy bionic legs off in a hot second. Don't believe me? Well, we'll see in a few minutes, won't we?"

"Killing me won't save you. My team has you in its crosshairs. You've been sloppy, left enough breadcrumbs: the stolen sensors, El Draco's tech, and this secret facility. If I go missing, that'll be one more clue leading back to you. They won't stop coming after you. It doesn't matter how many of these things you build ... this ... what did the plans call it? The Pantherix Fatalis?"

Raylock threw his head back and laughed.

"Here I thought you'd figured it out. But you have no idea, do you?" He was gleeful at that realization. "This sabertooth is the *Pantherix Destroyer*. A one-off. *Pantherix Fatalis* is something completely different."

Raylock tapped on his pad and pointed at the monitors.

"Look more carefully, Ms. Nicks."

The video feeds changed. On one monitor she saw Byrne along-side his Delta team on Camp Northstar's tarmac. They were fighting a group of Pantherix. On another monitor, she saw Quinn. She had her back against a chain-link fence and she was firing her EMP rifle as fast as she could. And there was Mouse. Hovering over his computer as if nothing was wrong. He did not know he was in danger.

Her heart sank.

"Despite your meddling, the plan is right on course. In fact, I'd say your team's interference helped me make sure of it."

She assumed Raylock was trying to intimidate her by showing her this. But for what reason? What did he mean they were helping him?

"That video feed is transmitting in real time from some of my Pantherix Fatalis units. Reaper Force quarantined them all at Camp Northstar, just as I'd hoped."

One feed showed a new closeup of Mouse. He was dissecting the components of one unit.

"Your team is smart, but they haven't figured out the special tactical purpose of those units. The armature is cast from plastic explosives that surround specialized shape charges. Each one has a core packed with the Strontium-90 we extracted from the ground sensors. Individually, they pose little threat, but it's another story if you gather the entire production line in one place and detonate them simultaneously."

"You can't be serious," Nicks gasped.

"Oh, I'm very serious. Fatalis will be the first nuclear weapon detonated on American soil, and thanks to Reaper Force, the weapon is right where I want it."

She couldn't believe Raylock was that insane. There were hundreds of innocent people at Northstar. Military personnel. Migrant detainees. Immigration authorities. And the people she was most worried about at the moment, Reaper Force, Brett Diaz, and his son Will.

"You'll never get away with that. Every military and intelligence officer America has will be on the case. They'll hunt you without mercy."

"You're right. The key to success is complete deniability. No one can know I'm connected to this operation. So Reaper Force is a concern. But they won't be in a few minutes. Once Fatalis detonates, it will vaporize your team and all the evidence they've gathered about me."

Nicks hated Raylock, but now she had a taste of how evil he was.

"It will be easy enough to trace the detonation to the Pantherix units, but that trail won't lead to me."

"So you weren't helping El Draco, you were setting him up," Nicks said. "The Pantherix units were confiscated from his compound. The sensors were stolen by his people. He'll be blamed for the dirty bomb."

"Exactly, Ms. Nicks."

"But what could you possibly gain from this?"

"Senator Snell's Smart Wall contract. That's the endgame."

"Money!? You're willing to detonate a nuclear bomb to win a

contract? That's complete madness. Especially when you have all the money you'll ever need."

"It's about money, yes. This will cement Raylock Industries' position as the premiere defense contractor in the world. But it's more than that. It's about the power to protect America's future."

"You've been playing both sides this whole time. A hero ready to save America with your smart wall and a villain supporting El Draco's takeover of the black market."

"I didn't fry that pretty little brain of yours, after all." He winked. "The data I've gathered supplying security for that narco-peasant will go directly into my Smart Wall. Nothing will cross that border without my say so. The black market will only survive if I can profit from it. Otherwise, it'll get shut down."

"Barnes. You said your partner, Barnes, argued about tactics. He'd never agree to this."

"Barnes was always in the way, but I do miss having an audience. I enjoy having at least one peer around to appreciate what I've accomplished. I can't post this to social media, so I guess you're it for now."

"You murdered him, didn't you?"

"No, I didn't." He pointed over her shoulder. "He did."

Nicks turned. Mr. Brightside was standing on the ledge of the arena right behind her.

"So you're on Raylock's leash," Nicks said to Brightside, who stared at her like he was admiring his next meal.

It seemed he'd been there for some time, but she'd never detected him.

"Flux, system check."

"*All TALON protocols disengaged. Operational system down to five percent.*" Flux's voice was barely intelligible, as if the AI was drunk.

"What does that mean?" she asked.

"It means the nanogas has done its job," Raylock said. "Now Brightside has a fighting chance against you."

Nicks wondered how he was hearing Flux. Somehow he was eavesdropping on her internal systems. She reached up and felt the back of her neck. The protective patch covering the sigillum was gone. Damn it!

Nicks realized Raylock had played her team well. They'd never considered an American company would be behind the sensor theft or the Pantherix units. Now she knew that was a big mistake. And everyone who knew the truth was about to die. She had to do something, and quickly.

"You're a smart man, Raylock. But are you ready to be a mass murderer? A nuclear weapon on American soil? That kind of evil puts you in Hitler territory. Don't do it. You have time to back out. Kill me. Pack up your toys, go into hiding. You fooled us once, you can do it again. In a month or two, Reaper Force will find bigger fish to fry. You can move on."

Raylock's fingers danced across his tablet. The video feeds minimized into one corner of the screen to make way for a digital clock set to ten minutes.

"Good speech. The two things that stand out are: First, I'm a *smart man*. Check. I agree. Glad you're finally noticing. Second, *kill you*. Check. That's part of the plan. As for the rest, you underestimate my level of commitment to saving America from the likes of you, Ms. Nicks.

"The incident at Camp Northstar will show the world's worst terrorists the United States is vulnerable to attack. We both know the Pentagon won't let that stand. By the end of this day, your bosses will be on my phone begging me to make sure it never happens again. I'm the only man for the job.

"Sometimes to do great things, you have to break all the rules. So let's get on with it, shall we?"

He hit the tablet and the countdown began.

61

CAMP NORTHSTAR

Mouse had checked his theory several times and found it hard to accept. The new units Byrne's soldiers had found had different rib cages, and the design choice didn't make any engineering sense.

The previous design had been better in every way. This new one served a completely different function, and he didn't understand what it could be. But he got the first clue when the electron microscope spit out the chemical analysis of the material.

Military-grade explosives.

A new formula that Raylock Industries held a patent for.

The second clue he found in the computer code. The project that had created these units was named Fatalis.

His only working theory about their purpose was one he didn't want to accept. The Pantherix Fatalis were suicide bombers.

But there was more. The Pantherix's rib cage made of explosives protected a heart of Strontium 90.

"Shit! This damn thing is a dirty bomb," he shouted.

As if responding to that revelation, the four Fatalis units he had lined up along his work bench woke up. It was as if they'd been playing dead and waiting to see if he'd uncovered their plot. The minute he did, they came alive and began scanning the room. Easily targeting him, since he was only a few feet away.

Mouse reached for his backpack and fished out a radio and called the Colonel.

"Byrne, I need you in the containment tent. ASAP!"

Byrne responded with a shout. Then there was gunfire. Screaming. More shouting. Followed by static and dead air.

What the hell was going on out there?

He was slowly backing out of the room now. The Pantherix watched his every move. When they stood up, he dropped the radio and pulled out a pair of black gloves.

The first unit jumped off the table. The second one did the same.

There was a wall behind him, maybe he could get there and climb it with his spider gloves. He slipped them on. It was the only way he could think to get away.

The third and fourth Pantherix joined their companions but circled around to his blind spots, flanking him.

Mouse turned and ran for the wall. The first unit leapt after him. Mouse screamed and ran right into the chest of Jack Byrne. Byrne grabbed him with a bionic arm, and threw him across the room, out of harm's way. The Pantherix attacked Byrne.

Byrne caught the first unit by the throat and tore its head off completely. Using the head like a boxing glove and the metal body like a shield, he savagely smashed the other units apart. Mouse had never seen his friend this angry or this deadly.

The Pantherix did their best to fight back, but they were no match for the bionic man. In the space of a minute, he'd torn them limb-from-limb, and scattered their parts throughout the room.

When the robots were down, Byrne rushed to Mouse's side.

"Are you hurt?" he asked.

Mouse shook his finger at the scattered parts. "No. But Byrne, these things are weapons."

"No shit," Byrne growled. "They've killed most of the soldiers on duty."

"You don't understand. It's more than that. Raylock, it has to be him. He built them as dirty bombs." Mouse pleaded. "He's made a nuclear weapon!"

Byrne stared at Mouse in disbelief for a few seconds as his mind wrapped around the possibility.

"He has them moving to specific coordinates," Mouse said. "I found it in the code." He pointed at the numbers on the whiteboard.

Byrne said, "You're right, they're not killing us. They're getting us out of the way." He looked at the coordinates, making quick calculations in his mind. "That's the center of the base. Jesus, come on. That's where Quinn is, we have to go help her."

62

As the digital timer ticked away, Nicks considered her dwindling options. She scanned the arena for anything that might give her an edge. The closest possible escape might be through the excavation tunnel, but a retreat was out of the question. And even if she could run, Raylock seemed to have other plans for her.

"You have it all figured out," she said, her voice finally coming back. "So why am I still alive?"

"So we can have some fun, of course." He played with his tablet again. "A little entertainment while we wait."

The Pantherix Destroyer jumped off its platform and circled the altar. Still some distance away, but way too close for comfort, it growled and clacked its long fangs. Nicks wondered how long she could last against it in her weakened state.

"Don't worry about him," Raylock said. "He's there just to keep you two in the ring."

Mr. Brightside stalked her from the arena wall. He wore black tactical pants and boots but had stripped off his shirt, exposing a tapestry of Aztec-inspired designs and leopard spot tattoos. They covered his muscular chest, arms, and neck. He had his damn macuahuitl again but seemed to bide his time, waiting for some signal from Raylock.

Watching him move along the wall reminded her of their previous fights. Brightside was a sniper when it came to hand-to-hand combat. He used distance as his primary defense, relied on the reach of his weapon, and rarely had his guard up. She'd caught him once in the face by surprise at the museum. Taken him down again in the lab. A partial plan formed in her mind, a Hail Mary for sure, but something that might give her a chance.

"You should've killed me, big guy," Nicks taunted. "I held back before, I won't this time."

"Oh, he doesn't want you to," Raylock said. "In the Aztec culture, prisoners are ritually sacrificed, cut into pieces, and gifted to the warrior responsible for the capture. But sometimes the most fierce prisoners got one last ceremonial battle to prove they deserved death. Mr. Brightside insisted we follow the tradition, and for the hell of it, I've agreed to play along."

If getting to Raylock and the Fatalis controls meant facing off with Mr. Brightside, she'd have to play along too. Even though she wasn't in any shape to match his power or deal with that damn weapon again.

"The good news is I won't let your body parts go to waste," Raylock chuckled. "The bad news is Brightside wants them for himself as payment. A little cybernetic recycling if you will."

"And if I win, which one of you do I get to dissect?" Nicks sniped.

"Brave words," Brightside said, jumping down onto the other side of the altar. He waved his macuahuitl, and it crackled with electrical energy. "It'll be an honor to kill you finally."

Still sitting on her knees, Nicks edged backward, anchoring her feet on the lip of the altar, hoping to coax Brightside toward her. The sabertooth, sensing she might step off, crept up behind her and stopped, watching and waiting for her next move.

She beckoned Brightside with a wave, but true to form, he kept his distance.

She leaned forward as if to stand up and Brightside advanced, swinging his weapon. Barely dodging it, Nicks readied herself for another swipe, which came faster than expected. The macuahuitl scythed through the air. She ducked, evading it once again. But instead of fading back, she moved closer for the next swing. As it came down, she gritted her teeth and raised her arm like a shield.

The macuahuitl hit her, making a sickening *thunk* as its obsidian teeth sunk into her flesh and hit her metal skeleton. Had it been a normal bone, she would've lost the arm for sure.

Frustrated, Brightside savagely ripped the weapon away, tearing her flesh and leaving several jagged puncture wounds that immediately hemorrhaged. Nicks screamed as biocoolant splashed onto the altar, mixing with the ancient blood of its former victims.

A satisfied smile curled on Brightside's face as he stepped closer and leaned in for another slash. It was the moment she was waiting for. She yelled and whirled her body around, catching him off guard with a reverse roundhouse.

The kick was so ferocious it appeared to unhinge Brightside's jaw, and he went down hard. His head slammed into the altar with a brutal smack, and he collapsed.

His macuahuitl clattered down on the stone within Nicks's reach. She picked it up and advanced to finish him.

Raylock's incessant banter broke out over the loudspeaker.

"I'm beginning to think you are bad for business," he groaned. There was stress in his voice this time. "I've invested too much in this operation. I can't have you messing it up."

Nicks ignored him. She couldn't let Brightside get up. When she swung the macuahuitl back for a killing blow, she sensed she was in danger. She looked up in time to see the crane lowering the electromagnet over her. It dropped fast. The macuahuitl flew from her hands, and she followed, levitating by the force of the machine's magnetic field. She was sucked up and magnetized to the steel casing.

"Susceptibility to magnets—one disadvantage of the nanogas."

The crane reeled in the magnet, lifting her higher.

"Flux," she moaned, straining against the magnet. "Do something!"

Fibrous threads grew from her fingernails and crawled like living vines around the magnet and into its power supply. There was a sudden surge of energy as the force of the magnet increased, painfully smashing Nicks more violently against the base.

"Overloading power supply," Flux reported.

The hum of the electrical current roared as Flux pushed the magnet past its limits. Nicks felt crushed by the increasing pull, but there was one surprisingly helpful side-effect. The green mucous-like substance she'd coughed up was seeping through the wounds in her arm. As the power of the magnet increased, so did the flow—the magnet was leeching the nanomachines from her body.

"Machine failure imminent."

As the last of the nanogas oozed through her wounds, the magnet overheated and exploded. Nicks dropped free and fell right on top of Brightside. He groaned from the impact and rolled over, rubbing his jaw, slowly regaining consciousness.

Before she could get up, he pounced, and their fight continued. They struggled with each other until they rolled over the edge of the altar into the arena.

The Destroyer charged straight at them.

63

CAMP NORTHSTAR

Quinn had positioned herself in the chute, a gated alleyway created by a ten-foot fence on either side. The chute led to the most protected area of the base called the square—a spacious courtyard flanked by the base headquarters, medical tents, and the migrant detainee center. The center was one of the few permanent buildings on the base and it held the most women and children. That included Will Diaz, who'd been moved to the ICU housed in the newest wing of the building.

Behind her a team of soldiers stood shoulder to shoulder, M16s at the ready, trying to hold a defensive line to protect the square. So far, no Pantherix units had made it in. But Quinn was worried that was about to change.

The battery on her EMP rifle was at fifteen percent. Hardly enough power to shut down the army of robots that were amassing just outside the chute. If they didn't find a way to stop the bloody things soon, they were all dead.

Thanks to Dr. Milton Gardner, the Pantherix acted autonomously. Which meant that every second they remained online, they were processing their environment, and learning.

Quinn had already disabled a pile of units and ordered the soldiers to stack them against the gate to add another barrier. But the result was pretty pathetic. Even now, the Pantherix were purposely sending in one or two units at a time to test the chute's defenses.

The rest organized themselves in perfectly proportioned clusters. They looked like human troops presenting themselves for inspection. Some units were gathering their fallen. Dragging and depositing them in a pile near the chute. She stared at the closest group of robots and imagined they were biding their time. They seemed confident they'd eventually overcome the humans.

A pair of Pantherix galloped into the chute, one behind the other. Quinn aimed carefully and took them both down with a single charge. The rifle barely had time to reset, when three more units tried a similar strategy.

She side-stepped to get a better angle, fired, and took them down. That's when she saw Byrne appear in her peripheral vision. He was running toward the chute. Mouse was clinging to the old man like a human backpack.

Several yards from the fence line, Byrne leapt skyward and hurdled himself and Mouse up and over the fence into the chute. They landed hard, tumbled in the dirt, and ended sprawled flat in front of Quinn and her line of soldiers.

One of the younger men raised his rifle, ready to fire. Quinn stepped in front of the bewildered soldier.

"Stand the bloody hell down," she shouted. "That crazy geezer is the goddamn Colonel."

Mouse rolled over, holding his ribs. Byrne got up and helped Mouse. Then he stepped up next to Quinn as she was getting a bead on the next wave of units coming down the chute.

"What took you so damn long?" she asked.

Purple goo covered Byrne. A result of blood and biocoolant congealing all over his body. The Pantherix had shredded almost all of his artificial skin from his arms and legs, exposing his TALON components, and making it obvious to everyone around him. He was something other than a normal human. It was no wonder the young soldier had reacted the way he did.

"Good to see you too," he said, and leapt forward a few yards, kicked the approaching Pantherix in the head like he was punting a football. The machine sailed across the yard, hit a metal fencepost, and broke into two pieces. The mouth was still snapping its nasty teeth when Quinn took down its brother.

Byrne picked up the zapped robot. Pulled it over near Mouse. And the two went to work networking Mouse's battered laptop into the Pantherix's computer ports. When Mouse was sure it was connected, he looked up at Quinn.

"How much charge you got left in that rifle?" he asked.

"Five percent. Only a couple more shots and it's toast."

"That should be enough," he said.

"Enough for what?" she asked.

"To turn the damn thing back on," he said. "It's the only way I know to stop them."

64

Nicks's strength returned as she grappled with Brightside. He'd given up on fighting her with finesse; she'd hurt him too badly. Now he was relying on sheer strength and his penchant for brutality, doing his best to subdue her before her bionics kicked back in.

He was also ignoring the fact they'd fallen into the arena and were within the sabertooth's reach. The Destroyer galloped toward them and swiped at them with its frightening teeth. Nicks pulled Brightside on top of her in time, and the fangs raked across his back, ripping into the big man's muscular shoulders. He cried out, let go of Nicks, and tumbled away.

As the sabertooth circled back around, Nicks reached for the altar, and using her renewed power, heaved it up on its side. Positioning herself behind it, she rolled it forward.

The Destroyer locked onto Nicks and galloped toward her. She pushed the stone forward until they collided. Nicks hadn't generated enough momentum to knock it down completely, but the Destroyer was no match for the weight of the stone, which crushed its front legs. The sabertooth stumbled, trying to correct its balance, then fell over.

Nicks let go of the stone and it fell across the robot's torso, pinning the creature in place. It roared in protest but couldn't free itself.

Brightside charged Nicks, but she was one step ahead. She cocked her fist and leapt toward him, landing a devastating punch to his already wounded face. The hulking assassin stumbled backward, weak-kneed and disoriented.

Nicks continued attacking him. An upper cut to the stomach. Another hook to the nose. Then she kicked him in the chest with such power he fell backward into the jaws of the pinned Destroyer.

The monster bit down and Brightside's head tumbled across the arena like a loose soccer ball. It rolled into the gruesome display of skulls and the wall of bones collapsed in a heap, burying Brightside's head among the remains of his ancestors.

So much for rituals, Nicks thought.

She checked the clock. Five minutes were left on the countdown.

65

CAMP NORTHSTAR

Byrne and Mouse explained their plan to Quinn, and she agreed it was worth a shot. Quinn's soldiers positioned themselves to hold the line, and the team retreated to the center of the square with the EMP rifle, Mouse's computer, and the dead Pantherix.

Quinn stripped down the EMP rifle to jerry-rig its battery.

"I'll rewrite the code for this one," Mouse said. "Programming it so it becomes the lead unit. A master for the whole damn lot of them. If it works, it will trick all the other units into rebooting, and when they do, they'll come back online as slaves to this one. Then we can move them away from the camp."

"Use these coordinates," Byrne said, he'd written the numbers on a clipboard.

"Where will they go?" Quinn asked.

"Into the open desert south of us, there's nothing out there. We'll get them just far enough away that the blast wave won't touch the camp."

"But what about the radioactive fallout?" Mouse wondered.

"There's nothing we can do about that now. If we can get the damn things on the move, then we'll retreat into the migrant center. It's made of concrete and sturdy. If the wind blows away from us, we should be safe, until the DoD can send the proper help to evacuate us."

Quinn did her best to hot-wire the Pantherix to the EMP rifle, and when all the proper wires were twisted, she was ready to fire it one last time.

"Byrne, you'll have to hold the damn thing down until I get the new code uploaded," Mouse said.

Quinn pulled the trigger on the rifle and instead of firing a pulse, it kick-started the Fatalis unit. The robot came back to life. It struggled to move, but Byrne had it pinned. When it clacked its jaws like an animal in distress, Quinn turned the butt of the rifle on the thing and began knocking its teeth out.

"It don't need those bloody things to be our little Pied Piper, now does it," she said.

Mouse gave the upload command and watched as the code spooled down the screen. When it stopped, he tested his program by entering the new coordinates.

"Okay, let the damn thing up. We need to see whether it worked."

Byrne let go, and the Pantherix rose to its feet. It scanned the square, while Mouse watched the code send a transmission to the rest of the units.

"I think it's working," he said.

There was a brief pause, and the Pantherix walked right past them, headed to the center of the square. It stopped and sat down.

Mouse followed it with his laptop in hand. "That's the old destination, but I think it's recalculating."

Byrne and Quinn jogged over to the fence line to check on the units that had encircled the square. Suddenly, the entire group moved in unison. But not the direction Mouse had hoped. Instead, no matter where they were, each unit advanced about ten feet, and stopped. Then their red eyes turned bright orange.

That concerned Byrne. "What's happening. That's a new color. Orange. What does that mean, Mouse? Talk to me."

"It's hard to know, but I think it's some kind of countdown." Mouse said.

"How many minutes do we have?" Quinn asked.

"It's not minutes, it's the level of concentration," Mouse said.

"What does that mean?" she asked.

Byrne understood. "Whoever's controlling these things will only detonate the units when they are close enough for maximum impact."

"That's right," Mouse said, his eyes still scanning the code. "When it reaches the correct density. Their eyes will turn green."

Quinn seemed to understand. "So, the closer they are to each other, the stronger the bomb."

"Exactly," Mouse said.

"God help us," Quinn sighed.

"We can't let that happen," Byrne said. "We have to detonate these things now. Otherwise every person around us will be vaporized and the nuclear fallout will last a generation. We can't let them get any closer."

"You're crazy man, I'm not blowing these things," Mouse said, frantically. "Let me try another patch, we have some time before those eyes go green."

The team argued back and forth for a few seconds before someone else broke in.

"Reaper Force, come in, over!"

They stared at each other, dumbfounded. They were being hailed through a speaker inside the Pantherix unit. It was like they'd heard the voice of the Almighty.

"Quinn, Byrne, Mouse, anyone? Do you read?"

It wasn't God, but maybe their savior—the one person who could stop Fatalis and cancel their impending trip to the pearly gates.

Mouse hit the right key and responded.

"The is Reaper Force. We read you loud and clear!"

66

Nicks ran into the center of the arena, directly toward the observation tower. Above her, Raylock was furiously attempting to get his sabertooth out from under the stone altar to no avail. He switched over to the crane's controls and swung the dead magnet in a wide arc toward Nicks.

She leapt onto the service ladder, avoiding the magnet, and started climbing to the top. Raylock took another swing with the crane, and the magnet bashed into the side of the platform, barely missing Nicks and battering the main support so severely the structure buckled.

Raylock's remaining workers tried to lead him away from the controls and to safety, but he rejected their help.

"Stop where you are, Ms. Nicks, or I'll blow this whole damn chamber and bring it down around us."

Nicks ignored him and continued up the ladder.

As she climbed, the observation deck lilted. The strain of the metal columns caused a massive groan, announcing the impending disaster. The whole thing was on the verge of collapse.

When she finally reached the top, she grabbed the edge of the platform and vaulted over to confront Raylock. But the coward had already fled down the walkway back to the elevator.

Nicks analyzed the panel and the information on the monitors. Her first thought was to radio her team. But she was still too far underground to get a clear signal, so Flux networked into Raylock's communication system and radioed Quinn through the Fatalis units. Mouse responded immediately.

The team was okay, but just as beat up as she was. They compared notes about the Pantherix Fatalis situation, and Mouse walked her through what to do next.

As the last minute ticked away, she found the proper control, turned the key, and a long, shrill alarm sounded, signaling the end of Fatalis countdown.

When they confirmed all the Fatalis units had been deactivated, and were permanently offline, there was a collective sigh of relief.

"We can handle these things on our end. You get the hell out of there and get your ass home," Quinn said.

"I will, but first there's someone I need to find," Nicks said.

Hoping to stop Raylock from getting away by using his vehicles, she switched to a broadcast frequency, and Flux detonated the charges she'd set on them. Even at her current depth, she could hear the muffled sounds of the explosions wreaking havoc topside.

After double checking the Fatalis program was completely offline, she punched through the controls, destroying them for good. Then she headed for the elevator to find Raylock.

She hadn't taken two steps when the platform under her feet failed.

67

T he observation platform, a cantilevered deck-like structure, lurched to one side and Nicks half fell, half slid down to the edge. She clawed her way back to her knees and got back on her feet.

Despite the obvious dangers, two blue-uniformed security men came running down the plank, guns drawn.

The platform swayed to one side, all of its support beams creaking as it did, reminding Nicks the crane had done serious damage to the structure's main column. She grabbed a rail to steady herself.

"Shoot her, you idiot." One man shouted as they moved in.

The guard in front had drawn his gun and was leveling it at Nicks. "Sorry, hot stuff. The boss said it's a million each if we bag you."

The platform lurched again and tilted dramatically, causing everyone to lose their footing. The lead guard dropped his gun, and it slid toward Nicks, who bent over and grabbed it before either guard could react.

She aimed and fired, emptying the clip into the two men. Their lifeless bodies slid over the edge into the arena.

The platform corkscrewed again and wouldn't stop. Then its most essential support snapped. Nicks, who wanted to chase Raylock upstairs, had no choice but to retreat to the service ladder she'd climbed before. She leapt just as the entire structure tilted one final time and tipped toward the arena.

She clung to the ladder, trying her best to ride it down as the structure crashed into the Aztec's granite auditorium. As it fell, the platform ripped other parts of the structure away. Several of the giant monitors tore from their mounts and, as they dropped, took a bank of lights with them. Sparks flew as power lines ripped away and an electrical transformer blew.

At the last minute, Nicks leapt off the ladder, saving herself from being buried underneath the collapse. She hit the arena's dirt floor and tumbled into one of its granite walls.

Above her, fires erupted on the sub-basement level, and smoke filled the cavern. Nicks looked up to see Raylock's elevator had made it to the highest visible level. He'd finally escaped.

As the fires and smoke spread, the compound's emergency alarms blared. A few stragglers left in the arena ran into the excavation tunnel and disappeared. Nicks decided following them was the safest route out. At least that's what she thought until she saw another security guard with his gun drawn blocking the entrance. She'd have to go through him if she wanted to escape. She raised her hands in surrender as he approached.

"Ms. Nicks, how fortunate to find you here," The guard said. "I'm afraid you have a terrible habit of destroying my places of employment."

It was Alejandro from El Draco's compound. The man gave her a wry smile and holstered his weapon.

"I don't know how or why you're here," she said, staring at the man in disbelief, "but we need to go—*now!*"

Overhead, the fires had grown into a roaring blaze. Parts of the

building's structure were giving way, and pieces were falling down
into the arena.

"Agreed," he said, and gestured at the tunnel. "Follow me, I know
the way out."

THE TUNNEL WASN'T easy to navigate, but it eventually led them
into a cave that opened up to one of Sisal's white sand beaches. From
the beach, they could see Raylock's compound on the hillside overlooking the coast.

"Flux, blow the power station!"

Flux sent the signal, and seconds later a fireball lit up the dark.
Flames and smoke engulfed what remained of the building. Satisfied
the compound wouldn't last the night, they made their way down the
beach, following Nicks's exfil coordinates.

When they were a safe distance away, Nicks turned to Alejandro
and said, "You want to explain yourself? How the hell are you mixed
up in all of this?"

"You're right, a proper introduction is in order," he said, holding
out his hand. "Victor Aguilar. CNI."

"You're an intelligence officer?" Nicks asked, surprised.

"Mexican CIA, bet you didn't know there was such a thing."

Nicks smiled. "Well, I sure as hell do now. You've saved my ass
twice."

He laughed. "Thanks to you, Ms. Nicks, I'll finally get to drop
this cover, and go home. You just single-handedly took down the
Draco cartel."

"I think the correct term is *disrupted* the cartel. Draco's still alive
and so is Raylock. It's not over until we get them both."

He nodded his agreement. "In the meantime, let's get the hell out
of here. You don't look so hot."

Nicks wasn't offended. She didn't feel that great, but she made it
down the beach to her exfil. It was a spot where the coastline jutted

out into the water, creating a small cove. In the corner, they found a cave to hide within.

Nicks radioed Quinn and Byrne again. Quinn reported the coordinates of the *Sea Dagger* anchored offshore.

"I'm with an Agent Aguilar. We can't swim that far. Can you bring it in?"

"No, but the Blackfish can come in undetected and pick you two up," Quinn replied.

"Copy that," Nicks said. "Flux, send the Blackfish to our location."

"Blackfish underway. It will arrive in two minutes."

"Blackfish?" Aguilar asked.

"A remote-controlled jet ski," Nicks said with a faint grin. "Got a problem? We've got a drone for it."

"All of this damn technology. It seems to have made the world worse, not better." Aguilar said as he leaned into the shadows of the cave.

Nicks tried to respond, but felt too ill. There was a flash of pain in her neck, confirming something was wrong.

"Hey, are you okay?" Aguilar reached for her as her knees weakened.

She tried to speak, but before the words reached her lips the night closed in around her, and she collapsed in his arms.

PART XII

CARAVAN

68

While Natalie Nicks was fighting her battles on the Yucatan peninsula, Brett Diaz stood on a hill overlooking the arroyo he'd chosen for a special meeting. The wide ravine, flanked by two natural ridges, stretched out before him like an ancient road, which seemed appropriate. At the moment, three black SUVs were using it for that exact purpose, driving straight toward his position.

Diaz had insisted on the meeting place because he knew the land and knew it well. A face-to-face with the leader of a drug cartel needed to be planned to his advantage.

The vehicles pulled in close to Diaz's truck and stopped. As if they'd choreographed it, every door in the caravan opened, and men with automatic rifles poured out.

A large man at the front of the pack took charge. He yelled up at Diaz, "Tienes la máquina?"

Diaz nodded confirming he had the machine and pulled back the tarp showing that the Pantherix One unit was in the back of his truck.

Satisfied, the man spoke into his handheld radio. Some of the gunmen moved down the ravine and formed a circle around the middle SUV. After a few moments, their leader emerged from his vehicle.

Diaz had never seen him in person. But he knew about his infamous mariachi jacket. The one with the embroidered dragon that had given him his name El Draco.

"Let's make this quick," El Draco said as he marched up to Diaz. "You wanted to speak to me before turning over the Pantherix. So, here I am. Speak."

Diaz, who had one hand on his revolver, regarded the man for a few seconds then said, "Solis, you've committed so many crimes in Mexico, I can't even count them. But when you sent men across the border, to my ranch, you went a step too far."

El Draco looked amused. "Sheriff, you may have a badge. But you're in no position to dictate anything to me."

Diaz scowled, fingered his gun, and leaned forward. "My son is fighting for his life because of you. I should shoot you in the face right now. But I'm going to do the right thing and give you a chance to turn yourself in. Do that, and we can avoid more bloodshed."

El Draco laughed out loud. "You're either crazy or the bravest man I've ever met." He pulled out his gold-plated pistol and pointed it at Diaz's face.

"Give me the keys to your truck. We're taking that and the fucking machine. You can live. But say another disrespectful thing, and I'll shoot you dead right here."

"You promised no killing," Diaz said. "I thought you were a man of your word."

"No, Sheriff. I'm a man of blood."

"Oooh... you are *scary*," Diaz said. He gave his shoulders a fake shiver. "But I'm still going to arrest you."

"If your plan was to arrest me, you shouldn't have come alone."

Diaz smiled, "I'm not alone."

Diaz whistled, and a thin white man with a long gray beard and matching braids stood up. He was standing on the east ridge overlooking the ravine. Every gun Draco's men had turned his way.

El Draco gave him a sideways glance. "Who the hell's that?"

"Don't recognize him?" Diaz asked. "Hey Riley, wave to Señor Solis here, he doesn't remember you."

Frank Riley flipped El Draco the bird with both hands. The only problem was he was missing one bird. El Draco had cut it off many months back.

"Fuck you, man. Fuck you!" Riley yelled. He sounded stoned. "Fucking dickless wetback."

"I also brought Frank's brother, Joe," Diaz said. "And *all* of his friends. They're excited to meet you."

The rest of the Sierra Vista militia revealed themselves. A long row of men had taken strategic positions up and down the eastern ridge. An equal number formed a second row of men on the western ridge. The cartel had driven into an ambush, and his men were outnumbered three to one.

El Draco's tough exterior melted away. He lowered his handgun, and his lip started quivering. Something which Diaz had never expected in a million years.

"Please, you're a man of the law. I didn't want to do this, they made me—"

BANG!

El Draco went down hard. A single bullet through the side of his skull. Diaz stepped back and cursed.

In that almost infinitesimal moment before the barrage of gunfire broke out. Frank Riley held up his four-fingered hand to take ownership of the misfire.

"Sorry 'bout that guys. Trigger finger's jumpy," he shouted. "But the fucking spic deserved it."

Frank slid back down into cover and the Sierra Vista militia opened up, raining down hot lead like they were trying to fill the ravine with bullets. Diaz dove for cover behind his truck.

El Draco's men opened fire in retaliation, but the fight didn't last long. The Sierra Vista militia wiped the entire crew out like they were shooting fish in a barrel. Which they were. Even when the men were dead and unmoving. The gunfire didn't stop. Later, over beers, they'd celebrate the victory as the highlight of their lives. They'd been fantasizing about a battle like this for years, and they made sure to use every last bullet they owned.

Diaz wasn't as happy with the outcome. He'd wanted to shoot El Draco himself. But at least the bastard was dead. Now he could rest easy, knowing Will would be safe. That was the most important thing.

69

Escaping both Reaper Force and Natalie Nicks filled Travis Raylock with the feeling of significance. It was the kind of emotion that permeated everything he believed about himself and life—destiny had called him to greatness—nothing would stop him from realizing his purpose. That sense of specialness was reinforced when he found his Quantum prototype had survived Natalie Nicks's sabotage. Despite the interference of his enemies, he knew he still had time to win the day.

He climbed into the car, used the palm print scanner to turn it on, and drove away just as a giant fireball exploded behind him. It looked like a small star had winked into existence. Its fire and heat engulfed the Pantherix lab, ensuring all the evidence of his covert project would be destroyed.

With the car, it took only a few minutes to race to the private twin-engine jet waiting on the airstrip. As he approached, he flashed his headlights three times to signal his crew he wanted an immediate takeoff.

The Gulfstream G650 ER was the most expensive private jet money could buy. His seventy-million-dollar investment meant

Raylock could travel almost anywhere in the world. The ER stood for extended range because the aircraft could fly over 7500 nautical miles or about fourteen hours without landing. As he climbed aboard, he told the pilot and stewardess to set a course for his private home in Aspen, Colorado.

He buckled in, and the stewardess served him his favorite cocktail. With the drink in hand, he took a moment to relax and think up the best way to salvage his pièce de résistance. He would detonate the Pantherix Fatalis remotely from the air. Even if he had to risk flying within range of Camp Northstar, it would be worth it to see the plan through. Surely, Reaper Force hadn't had time to move all the units to a safe distance from each other. The attack wouldn't be as elegant as he'd conceived, but even with an asymmetrical epicenter, the explosion would serve his main purpose: destroy Reaper Force, frame the Draco cartel, and scare the Pentagon into granting him the Smart Wall contract.

When the plane reached a safe cruising altitude, he retrieved his secure laptop stowed in the nearby credenza, sat down on the plush divan, and logged into the airplane's network. Thanks to the encrypted ka-band uplink, he had a stable and lightning-fast internet connection. The next step was some quick computer coding to mask his IP address and hacking a communications satellite his engineers had left a backdoor in.

He smiled. No one, not the bitch, not the fat drug runner, no one would stop him. Hell, he didn't even need Brightside—poor prideful and dead Brightside. The next hitman he hired would be free of any peculiar attachments to bizarre weapons or warrior culture—just a run-of-the-mill professional killer. Someone that wouldn't confuse wet work with a spiritual calling.

Just as he established the satellite connection, the lights in the cabin flickered. Music played over the loudspeakers.

Then the uplink dropped, and his detonation program froze. He banged his fist on the table. "Damn it, come on!"

"Always quick to temper," a man said as the door to the stateroom slid open.

Raylock knew the voice, but it took a moment to recognize the man using it. In fact, he couldn't accept who he was seeing. Could anyone when confronted by a ghost? Dylan Barnes had risen from the dead.

This undead Barnes was disturbingly different from his old partner. His bald head sported the faint shadow of his former stylish blond mane. There was an angry red gash across the side of his face. A shiny piece of obsidian had replaced his left eye. One side of the man's head was still handsome and embodied his famous boyish-charm, while the other side stared at Raylock with its frightening gaze. He raised a cigar to his mouth with his right hand, exposing his missing thumb. His customary anxiety and hysterics were also gone. He lit the cigar, and the pungent smell of marijuana filled the cabin. Dylan Barnes must have found peace in death because he looked so devilishly serene.

"There's no need to detonate the Fatalis units, now. They've served their purpose."

"Fatalis? How do you know about Fatalis?" Raylock wasn't sure if what he was seeing was real. "How ... are ... you here?"

"You wouldn't deny me access to the company jet since I'm a founder of Raylock Industries, would you?"

"But you're supposed to be dead."

"You mean *murdered*, don't you?" Barnes said with no hint of emotion. "You hired Mr. Brightside to *murder* me."

Raylock was, for the first time in recent memory, stunned into silence.

"I realize it's a shock seeing me like this. You've always felt the arc of your life has bent to meet your desires. How shocking it must be to learn everything you believe is a lie."

"Barnes, I don't know how you got here. But I'm glad you're alive."

"I don't think you'll be glad for long."

"What does that mean?"

"Let me give it to you in bullet points, like you've always preferred. First, I've always known you killed my father. In fact, I let it happen because I wanted it to happen. I hated him with a passion, and before the idea ever crossed your mind, I was pushing you toward that scheme. You think you conned me, but I was the one who planted the seeds. It's always been me. I knew we could do something marvelous with my inheritance, but it was important that I was blameless and above reproach. It was the only way my family would've ever cut the purse strings.

"Second, I realize you've always thought I was the sucker, but it's the opposite. The scared, anxious Barnes that annoyed you night and day was painstakingly rehearsed. I let you believe the success of the company resulted from following your leadership. But you've actually been following mine."

Barnes stopped his speech and waved the cigar in the air like he was erasing a blackboard.

"Strike that, since my alliance with my new partners takes precedence over even my personal goals. I should say you've been following the plans of the Dharmapala. They're using Raylock Industries—and you—to accomplish one of its major goals.

"But you do get credit for a job well done. Despite my incessant bitching, I always believed in you, Travis. And you delivered on this one. By sunrise, you'll be gone and I'll emerge with the horrific story of how I was imprisoned by my former partner. Senator Snell's Smart Wall project will be awarded to Raylock Industries. And I'll take the reins of our company on behalf of the Dharmapala. You've had a good run, but now it's over."

"Over? What the hell are you talking about? Nothing is over!"

"Yes, it is. I'm afraid you've outlived your usefulness."

Raylock laughed. "Are you going to kill me now?"

"Not me. The nanogas. Did you know it's soluble in water? It tastes just like carbonated soda? You've been drinking it for the last thirty minutes. I told you once to test these things on yourself. Had you listened, you might've noticed.

"Turns out you can tweak those little nanomachines so they function like a lung full of VX nerve agent. Once I turn them on, they'll disrupt the signaling between your muscular and nervous systems, causing you to suffocate. Prepare yourself. This is going to hurt like hell."

Barnes pushed a button on a small remote control he held.

Raylock tried to yell for help, but his diaphragm seized, and his throat closed. His final word wheezed through his open mouth. "Why?" he gasped.

"Why? Because our partnership has run its course," he said over Raylock's gurgling death rattle. "I sense you understand."

70

Miguel Solis had survived a long time because of his shrewd criminal mind. But it was mainly because of that stupid fucking jacket he wore. He actually hated the shitty mariachi jacket as much as he hated his shitty loser father who'd worn it proudly when he was a child. He hated it, but he kept it around for a good reason.

It was part of his brand. His story. His legend.

And most people who wanted him dead, namely the gringo faggots in the DIA, couldn't pick him out of a crowd of Mexican men even if their lives depended on it.

Dirty Mexicans all looked the same to the Americans.

It was the same story with his enemies in the other cartels. They didn't know what the fuck Miguel Solis looked like. They just wanted to kill El Draco. And El Draco wore the stupid fucking jacket.

Wearing the thing had been a genius move, but it had come with a price. Literally, it was expensive. The intricate bead work added up when he'd had hundreds of copies in various sizes commissioned.

The worst part was he could never take it off. In fact, the only place he'd been free of it was in his secret Valle de Guadalupe compound. That place had been a fortress and a sanctuary. But the American bitch had ruined that for him. He wouldn't forget that—ever!

The only reason he'd agreed to meet with the sheriff was to get a lead on her. He'd suspected the meeting would be some kind of half-ass trap. But he figured he had to go through with it if he wanted revenge. And he needed that damn robot panther to turn his luck back around.

When they'd arrived at the meeting place, he'd forced Esteban to put on one of the many duplicate jackets, get out of the SUV, and greet Diaz.

Sure enough, it was a fucking ambush.

He'd warned the men about just such a thing. Even had one SUV stay half-a-kilometer back in case. His soldiers promised him they'd get the Pantherix and get him out safely, but now they were being slaughtered by a bunch of rednecks.

He jammed the barrel of his pistol into the temple of his closest bodyguard and, using him as a shield, forced the man out of the truck. It only took a few seconds for him to get peppered with automatic gunfire.

His bullet-ridden guard toppled over and El Draco fell with him, twisting in such a way that the corpse landed on top of him. As the gun battle continued, he inched his way out from under the dead man and then under the SUV. And from there he crawled on his stomach until he made it to the third and final vehicle.

He continued on like the snake he was until he cleared the truck and rolled into a muddy crevice of the ravine. Slowly but surely, he pulled himself out of the line of fire and into the shadows of the arroyo. Now it was just a matter of time and luck. When night fell, he'd be able to make his way to the backup SUV, only about a ten-minute jog through the desert.

He wasn't confident he'd survive. But if he made it, his first order of business would be to kill the fucking cop who'd set him up and his whole fucking family, and then he'd go after that bitch Natalie Nicks.

Hell, when people heard about the ambush and gun battle and then saw that he had survived, his legend would only grow. Thanks to that stupid fucking jacket, the dragon would rise again, stronger than ever before.

PART XIII

TIME STAND STILL

71

Natalie Nicks woke up in luxury. A pleasant ocean breeze flowed through the large glass doors of her villa, past a balcony of lush vines and palm fronds. Beyond the garden was the beach and the turquoise water.

A silver tray rested beside the bed with white linen napkins, polished silverware, a steaming silver pot of coffee, a small carafe of cream, and a bowl of bright raspberries dusted with sugar.

Golden sourdough toast was stacked next to square pads of real butter. A newspaper, so neat and well-folded it must have been pressed on an ironing board, was tucked under a plate of perfectly browned bacon.

Colonel Jack Byrne, still damp from his swim, stood on the balcony in a pair of tight-fitting swimming trunks sipping from a steaming coffee mug. A white towel hung over his shoulders, catching the trails of water dripping from his blonde hair. His tan, muscular body gleamed in the sun.

She rolled over and winced. Muscles she forgot she had made themselves known. She wouldn't slip out of this bed with ease; she was a living bruise.

Someone had wrapped both her arms and legs in Quinn's special regenaderm bandages, which facilitated the growth of her self-healing artificial skin.

"Mmmm ... Nice view." She stretched and yawned and tried to sit up in the bed.

"Is that sarcasm? I sure hope so," Byrne laughed. "That would tell me you're feeling better."

"Not sarcasm, not yet. I feel like I was run over by a—"

"—giant robotic sabertooth?"

"Something like that, yeah," she groaned.

Byrne poured her a glass of orange juice from a crystal carafe bathing in a bowl of ice. Nicks took it and drank half in one continuous gulp.

"Is this paradise?" she asked, marveling at her surroundings.

"It may be." He walked around the bed to be closer. "Five grand a night. But worth every penny."

"I'm not sure my credit card can handle that."

"Don't worry, DR-Ultra is covering it. We picked the location because it was close to the operation, and it's an exclusive resort. We bought out most of the place. Also, since it's a wellness spa, they restrict Wi-Fi and cellphone access. No signals for miles. Only old-fashioned landlines, and even those aren't in the rooms. They communicate in written letters." He pointed at the basket of notes and envelopes near the door.

"Sounds good to me," Nicks said.

"We thought this would be the safest place for you until we get that signal-blocking patch back on you. Quinn is back at the Cage, working on a new one as we speak. She'll be back tomorrow."

"And what about Brett and Will?"

"Diaz is squared away. Fatima was about to go track him down when he finally resurfaced. He wouldn't tell us where he'd been, but maybe he'll tell you when we get stateside," Byrne said. "He's in Denver at Granite Nine. That's where we moved Will to get him better care. I'm happy to say, there's been a bit of improvement."

Nicks let out a big sigh. She was so relieved to hear that. Finally, some good news.

"How are you really?" He touched her on the shoulder and stroked her arm.

She reached out and squeezed his hand. "Not sure yet? Can we stay here forever?"

"You've been here a week already."

"What!? *A week?*"

"Yeah, so have I," he smiled. "First real vacation I've had in ten years."

"How's that possible?"

"Agent Aguilar got you on the Blackfish and onto the Sea Dagger. But you were in bad shape. We found a lot of the nanogas still in your system. I had to sedate you, and Quinn took some of your TALON systems offline while you were in that thing." He pointed to an enormous machine that looked like a space-age tanning bed in the room's corner.

"What the hell is that?"

"It was hard putting you in the damn thing. Looked too much like a coffin. It works like a hyperbaric chamber to remove the nanomachines from your bloodstream. Dylan Barnes sent it over to help our team."

"Dylan Barnes? I thought he was dead."

"Yes, we all did. Turns out, Raylock had him locked up like a prisoner."

"And what about Raylock?"

"He's dead," Byrne said. "Autopsy says he was exposed to the nanogas. He had an adverse reaction and died."

"That doesn't seem right, if he was exposed. I would have seen some evidence of it."

"Honestly, I don't care how the bastard died. He almost detonated a nuclear weapon on US soil. Would've killed our whole team and scores of innocents. He tried to murder you several times. If he were still alive, I wouldn't let that go unpunished, I promise you that."

"What about Snell's Smart Wall contract? He was obsessed with that."

"Raylock Industries got the contract. The brass at the Pentagon recommended it despite what we uncovered. The reasoning is, their technology is the best for the project and the country's security."

Exactly what Raylock had been counting on. Nicks didn't think it was a good move to hand the southern border over to the company. But with Raylock dead, she understood why the powers that be would make the choice.

She swung her legs over the edge of the bed as if she would get up.

"Please stay in bed," Byrne said. "You've earned the rest. You did good, soldier."

"Thank you, sir," Nicks said, adding a wry smile and a quick salute.

"I know you don't need my permission. I'm just ..."

"At ease, Colonel. Let me try this." She stood up but felt too dizzy to walk. Then gave up, sat down, and rolled over into the pillows. "Come feed me some of that toast with that orange marmalade."

Byrne removed his wet trunks and put on one of the white cotton robes. He laid the other one down at the foot of the bed for her. He sat on the bed and opened the small jar of jelly and did as she requested. They continued to talk about the operation, the events after, and how the team was doing. As the conversation continued, they fell into an easy rhythm with each other. She knew Byrne could be with many other women if he wanted, but since they'd worked together, he'd chosen the job over pursuing romance. Maybe because, with all its strange complications, the job was *her*.

"How's the arm?"

"I don't feel a thing."

They laughed. It was a common joke between them.

"Well, Mouse had more upgrades. You know he's become a little obsessed at figuring ways to turn that thing into a modern-day Swiss army knife."

"More power to him. I've used about ever upgrade he's made," she said solemnly. "It's saved my ass several times now."

"If you could ..."

"Would I want my old arms back?"

"Yeah, I've wondered. Because I've been thinking about it myself."

"No."

She waited to see if he would push the conversation into the territory that would derail the nice moment they were now sharing.

He didn't. He just smiled at her and fed her more toast.

He was learning to navigate her turbulent waters, as she was learning his. This was a welcomed development.

Perhaps some emotional wounds were healing as well. Surely, it would take a lot more time, but this was progress worthy of a love-making session. The desire rose in her but stalled out; her body was too exhausted to do anything about it. Right now, she would have to settle for another bite of toast.

THE NEXT DAY, Nicks ventured out of her luxurious bed.

"If I stay in here any longer, as wonderful as it is, I'm going to scream," she complained to Byrne who had been by her side dutifully, playing nurse and helping Nicks finish reports about the operation that were sent to DR-Ultra at Blackwood Lodge.

"Well, Quinn and Mouse are coming down. But they won't be here for another five hours. You should explore the resort. It's pretty damn nice. There's a spa and wellness classes. Check the inbox." He pointed at the basket near the door.

Nicks walked over and rifled through the letters and notes. There was an embossed invitation to a transcendental meditation class attached to a small bouquet of sage, mint leaves, and dragon fruit.

"They've sent one of those for the last five days. I guess everyone that stays here gets a complimentary meditation lesson with the resident guru," Byrne said. "I almost went myself when you were still in that damn compression chamber."

Nicks picked it up and looked at it. It had a room number and her first name written in beautiful script. It looked like it had been hand drawn.

"How much did you say this place cost?" Nicks smiled.

"Most expensive place on the peninsula."

"Only the best for me," she chuckled. She picked up the sage bundle and tossed it at Byrne. It spiraled into his chest and bounced off into his hands. "Burn that sage and clear the room of all my bad juju. I'll go do a little mind yoga and come back a new woman."

She grabbed the invitation and ventured down the hall to find the guru.

It sure as hell couldn't hurt.

72

A beautiful Hispanic woman, wearing white linen pants and a sheer halter top stood near the entrance to the meditation room. Her jet-black hair was tied in a ponytail and laced with small pink and ivory flowers. She was so lovely that Nicks couldn't help but feel drawn in. She greeted her, took the invitation, and glanced at it while opening the door.

"Welcome, Natalie. Are you ready to begin your lesson?"

"I think so." Nicks smiled.

"My name is Valentina," she said as she escorted her inside. "I'll get you started, then the teacher will complete your training."

The room seemed perfect for meditation. A fragrant aroma of vanilla and lavender candles filled the space. The lights were dim, and because the sun was setting, there was no bright glare through the windows. A refreshing ocean breeze tickled the chimes hanging from a metal hook in the bay window.

Valentina sat with Nicks and explained the basic process of meditation. When the lesson was over, she took her to a small altar to perform a brief ceremony. A picture of Valentina's guru, covered in a chiffon handkerchief, mysteriously veiling the teacher's identity, sat next to a collection of candles.

Valentina chanted in Sanskrit while she waved the dragon fruit and mint leaves through the candle's smoke. After a few minutes, the ceremony was over.

"Please take a seat, close your eyes, and try the technique I described." She said. "The teacher will join you while you're meditating and introduce you to your mantra."

Nicks, who had never had much success with sitting still, smiled weakly. "I'm not sure this will work, but I'll give it a shot."

Valentina smiled politely, nodded, and quietly left the room.

Nicks closed her eyes and took some deep breaths. She tried Valentina's instructions but a brief moment of quiet gave way to images of the recent operation, Raylock, El Draco, Mr. Brightside, and the giant Pantherix, flashed through her mind making it difficult to unwind. She folded her hands into her lap and relaxed her shoulders and tried again.

She found a few more moments of calm before thoughts of Will Diaz surfaced. She felt tremendous guilt for what had happened, and that was compounded by the realization she'd been avoiding talking about him, first with Brett, his father, and lately, with Jack Byrne. Why did the boy have to suffer? A wave of despair rose in her. She wanted to cry but refused to let the tears come. She shook her head and tried to find that elusive place of serenity hiding somewhere within her darkness.

As she slowly allowed her muscles to relax, she floated off into a place she'd rarely visited. It was a place of surprising tranquility. Here she found the embrace of nothingness. Why didn't she come here more often? Was she afraid of it? Did peace and death feel too similar, were they in some ways related, somehow mirror images of each other? Below her, a deep well of freedom was making itself known. She sank into its pleasurable depths when she heard the teacher's voice in a whisper.

"Peace ... do you feel its embrace?" The teacher asked.

Nicks nodded.

"Good. I want you to remember it. Because from this day forward, you'll never feel it again."

Nicks opened her eyes.

"Death," Riza Azmara said. "That will be your new mantra!"

73

D read filled Natalie Nicks as she stared at the person in front of her. The young woman was about twenty years old with high cheekbones, tan skin, and dark eyebrows. Her tiny frame was covered by a tight-fitting dark outfit accentuated by a blood-red hoodie. She pulled it back, revealing her cold, black eyes which were an unwelcome and disturbing sight—she'd seen them before.

Nicks didn't feel quite right and wondered if she'd fallen asleep and was having some kind of nightmare. Maybe the nanogas or the pain medication was causing her to hallucinate. But none of those theories could argue with reality—Riza Azmara—Codenamed Starfire by DR-Ultra—sat before her alive!

Riza pulled her hoodie back and let it collect around her neck. Her appearance was a strange blend of beauty and the surreal. Reminding Nicks why she was called the Demon Queen by her followers in the Dharmapala.

Nicks recalled the Japanese temple where she'd seen Riza last. One side of the girl's head had been covered in her lush brunette hair, while rows of fiber optic cables sprouted from the other side, and connected her to an elaborate computer system. Each strand had been capped with a red micro-antenna that blinked. She had looked like Medusa with a head full of living snakes.

Now, those weird dreadlocks were gone along with her scars, which was odd because they'd been so conspicuous. Her dark hair was still there, but the cable ports, if you could call them that, were capped off with translucent discs. They pulsed with colorful light, as if her different thoughts and emotions generated their own unique hue.

"Hello, Natalie." Nicks cringed and braced herself as she felt Riza using the sigillum to invade her mind and memories. "So close to death, once again? Strange how our experiences keep mirroring each other's."

"How are you even here?" Nicks asked, still stunned by what she was seeing.

"We're one and the same, you and I. We share an origin and a strange ability to escape death."

Nicks had the impulse to kill Riza on the spot. She'd tortured Maggie Quinn, and Jack Byrne, and almost murdered her whole team. She wanted to grab the woman by the throat, but something stopped her.

Then Riza asked, "Did Travis Raylock's plot convince you I'm right about the dangers of military technology?"

"Travis Raylock is dead," Nicks said, matter-of-factly.

"Yes, but you didn't stop him," she said. "I did."

Nicks raised an eyebrow. "*You* killed him?"

"I gave the order once he'd outlived his usefulness. Some of his schemes aligned with my plans, but our visions weren't *perfectly* aligned."

Riza brushed her hand along the silver discs embedded in her scalp. They glowed in strange alternating patterns of indigo, green, and purple.

"Are you confessing you were behind all of this?"

"Confessing? There you go again, Natalie. Why do you still

believe you can stand in judgment of me?" A blaze of crimson erupted among Riza's tranquil colors. "You and your government have no authority or power over me anymore!"

"Are you aware of how many died because of Fatalis?"

"I'm aware of everything. Why don't you understand that by now? Even though my consciousness is still re-indexing, I see all and feel all. The entire world is in danger and I'm the only one trying to save it."

Riza's colorful discs flashed red again while her face remained a mask of unnerving calm.

"I understand they've brainwashed you. You're vulnerable because of the guilt you carry, and your shame demands I play the villain so you can act the heroine. That explains why you did what you did in Japan and why you keep working against me. You still don't see the truth. Or your greater purpose. Our fates are inter-twined. What's happened with Raylock proves we have to work together."

"I won't join your cult, Riza."

"Would ordering the death of that little boy change your mind?"

Nicks body went stiff. She'd forgotten how audacious the young psychopath could be. "What did you say?" She asked daring her to repeat it. "*What boy?*"

"You know who I'm talking about, Natalie. I see his sweet face in your mind. I can feel how much he means to you. I'd hoped his injury would trigger your memories of what we suffered. I was sure it would open your eyes. How many children have to die before you accept the truth and join me?"

Nicks lunged at Riza, grabbed her by the throat, and lifted her off the floor. "I'm going to kill you now." Nanofibers crawled up Riza's neck and into her colorful ports. Riza's eyes widened in disbelief. Nicks smiled as Flux decrypted the woman's firewall. "But I'll kill you slowly so Flux has enough time to download all your sick secrets."

She squeezed harder, and Riza gasped for breath.

Flux cracked one layer of the security. The flow of information across the sigillum seemed to stop and reverse course. Riza went slightly limp, as if the life was finally draining from her body.

"Hopefully, you'll suffer like Will Diaz is suffering."

Riza's head snapped up, and her body flexed. Still connected, Nicks squeezed her grip in surprise. Riza's voice, when it came, was laced with rage. "Don't you remember, I already have. And I'll never let it happen again!"

Like a possessed child in an exorcism movie, Riza levitated, pulling them both toward the ceiling. Her features changed; she grew fangs and demonic horns. In seconds, she'd transformed into the living embodiment of the Dharmapala symbol—a true demon queen.

Riza's transformation dumbfounded Nicks. It wasn't possible. Another high-tech illusion, perhaps? She suppressed her astonishment and fought back the only way she knew how—by punching Riza in the face, savagely.

It had little effect, Riza countered, butting Nicks with her horned head, stunning her. Despite being dazed, Nicks refused to let go of Riza's throat and pummeled her severely. But the woman endured each punch as if she were impervious to the pain.

"I gave you another chance. But I see there's no saving you," Riza said.

Leathery, bat-like wings unfolded behind her and buffeted the surrounding air. Nicks tightened her hand around Riza's thickening throat, attempting to choke her unconscious. Riza laughed, grabbed Nicks's hand, clawed all the nanofibers away from the cerebral ports, and disconnected Flux.

Then, before she could land another punch, Riza ripped Nicks's arm from its socket and tossed it across the room. Nicks screamed so loudly it seemed to distort the fabric of reality. Riza glitched like a bad video.

"I want you to know, before I sever our connection, that my final plan is already in motion."

Riza's dark eyes sparkled with electricity that traveled down her arms and into her hands, electrocuting Nicks. All the muscles in her body contracted. Her back went into a severe spasm.

"Prepare yourself. Piece-by-piece, I'm going to destroy your life. Your family, your friends, and your precious country—all of them will die, and it will be your fault."

The energy surged again around her neck, and everything went dark, Suddenly, a curtain of inky blackness surrounded Nicks. She couldn't see a thing.

"Next time we meet, there'll be no mercy."

"I'll find you," Nicks yelled into the darkness. "This isn't over!"

"No, it's not," Riza said, her voice fading like a whisper. "There's so much suffering yet to come."

The sigillum shorted out, and Nicks screamed from the intense heat and pain. Her eyes popped open. She was still in the meditation room, sitting on the floor. Everything was as it had been before she'd closed her eyes. The candles flickered on the ledge. The chimes tinkled in the wind. But no one else was in the room. Then the realization hit her.

No one had ever been in the room!

The gentle ocean breeze wafted by, filling her nose with the unpleasant smell of fried electronics and singed skin. Nicks felt her neck. It was warm to the touch, and her skin was raw. It seemed everything she'd experienced had been an illusion created by the sigillum, except for one thing—her terrible enemy was somehow alive.

Seconds later, Maggie Quinn and Lee Park rushed through the door in a panic.

"Nat, are you okay?" Quinn yelled.

"We heard you scream all the way down the hall!" Mouse said.

Nicks filled in her alarmed teammates, and Quinn did a quick check of the sigillum. "I don't know what the hell just happened, but this thing is completely trashed. It looks like it just shorted itself out."

She reached into her backpack, found a pair of tweezers, grabbed the sides of the sigillum, and yanked.

"Thank God in heaven," Quinn said as it slid free. "The bloody thing's finally out."

Mouse and Quinn had spent countless hours trying to figure out how to remove it, and now it was done. They gave each other a high five to celebrate. But when they reached out to do the same with Nicks, she left them hanging. She was staring at the ocean through the window.

"Nat, are you okay?" Quinn asked.

"Yeah," she lied.

Mouse and Quinn stared at each other with concern.

Nicks knew she should be relieved that damn thing was finally out of her body. But all she could think about was what Riza Azmara had said. If that bitch could make good on a fraction of her threats, everything she cared about was in danger. The time for her recovery was over. Despite her serene surroundings, Nicks sensed the real war had just begun.

PART XIV

VITAL SIGNS

GRANITE NINE, DENVER INTERNATIONAL AIRPORT

Nine secret levels above Natalie Nicks, a herd of pronghorn sheep gathered close as the sun dipped below the beautiful Rocky Mountains. Nearby, hundreds of jetliners crisscrossed runways and took to the air, shuttling their passengers to destinations across the globe. No one except the most hardened conspiracy theorists would believe Granite Nine, the DR-Ultra station, existed below Denver International Airport. But it was there, fully operational and staffed to capacity, thanks to the recent breach at the other Ultra-site Blackwood Lodge.

Fatima, Quinn, and Nicks, along with General Drummond, peered into the specialized decontamination room. Mouse was behind a thick window of safety glass, managing a cadre of robotic tools. It looked like an assembly line running in reverse. Instead of cars, he was disassembling Pantherix Fatalis units.

Drummond leaned forward, watching over the top of his glasses. "Mr. Park has handled the analysis of these machines very well. And he's also full of advice on what to do with the other technology we recovered from Miguel Solis's estate. He's been a real asset. I've suggested to Penbrook that he should become a permanent member of the team."

"He loves the work but doesn't like to commit," Nicks said.

"Give him a sizable R&D budget and a wide berth, and you'd have him hooked for as long as the money lasted," Quinn offered.

Drummond cracked an eyebrow. "I'll look into that."

Quinn keyed the intercom to speak. "Hey, hotshot, how's it going?"

"Almost have all the cores extracted." Mouse rubbed a hand over his stubbled chin. "Another hour or so."

Fatima crossed her arms. "This couldn't be more boring."

"Yeah, but it has to be done," Quinn said. "I give Mouse a hard time, but I don't think we'd know what to do about these things without him. He's a genius at this stuff."

"Can't believe that's coming out of your mouth," Nicks said, throwing some side-eye.

"I can't either, and if you ever tell him, I'll disassemble you just like those bloody bots."

Nicks didn't doubt her.

An amused smile fractured the marble facade of General Drummond's face. "Well, Reaper Force, you've achieved the original mission. All sensors accounted for—and much more to boot. That should satisfy the Pentagon."

"What about the militia in Sierra Vista?" Fatima asked. "Any of them facing jail time?"

"There was talk of that. And they threatened legal action from their side. However, Diaz intervened and found a solution," Nicks said.

"Yes, that was a *creative* compromise your sheriff friend came up with." Drummond eye-checked Nicks. "I applauded his ingenuity when I spoke to him about the troubling news."

"Troubling news?" Nick wondered.

"I'm afraid Miguel Solis aka El Draco slipped the net. DNA analysis shows he was not among those killed in the action. He somehow escaped. Sheriff Diaz wasn't too happy about that."

Nicks was disheartened to hear that too and knew she'd need to talk it over with Diaz. As long as El Draco was in the wind, his family's security would be a concern.

"What about the Milton Gardner mess?" Quinn asked. "A DARPA scientist building tech for a narco? These machines were operating autonomously. How'd that happen?"

"Talk about letting the genie out of the bottle," Fatima added.

"The DIA issued a broad agency announcement for new background checks and security clearances on all current and former DARPA scientists. We need to keep a better eye on our people, after what you discovered with Gardner," he said.

Nicks nodded. "That's a good idea, if you remember Dr. Victor Vargas did the same thing. Selling black market body parts, seems we should stop that going forward."

"Let's start with this Dylan Barnes," Fatima said. "What do we really know about him?"

"Dylan Barnes has agreed to cooperate," Drummond said. "He shouldn't be a problem."

"Do you trust him, General?" Nicks asked.

"Trust is not in my job description, and it shouldn't be in yours. We need to keep an eye on that company after what happened. But we have to do it by the book. American law gives corporations the same rights as people. We won't roll over those."

Nicks stared at Fatima and Quinn. It seemed to her they'd earned the right to roll over Dylan Barnes and anyone else in charge of Raylock Industries if they thought it was necessary.

Drummond added, "You've made a friend in the senator, too. Jason Snell wants to meet you, Captain Nicks."

"That's unnecessary," Nicks said. "I'm not sure we'd see eye-to-eye on much."

"I understand, but he's ready to put your name on that damn wall of his, if you want it."

A brief smile flickered and then vanished on her face, and Nicks said, "A wall won't protect us from what's coming, General."

"On that, we both agree." He turned to her and shook her hand. "We owe you a debt, soldier. You stopped a serious disaster."

Nicks thanked him politely and added, "It's a team effort with us. It always is."

"Your damn straight it is. Glad you have a good one." He gave her a wink, as if her answer had passed a secret test, then thanked Fatima and Quinn before turning to leave.

As Drummond headed for the exit, Quinn told Nicks, "We traced the signal source of Riza's attack. Penbrook wants to discuss it with you."

That reminded Drummond of something, and he turned around and offered. "I almost forgot. We have some intel on your suspect. The woman calling herself Valentina. The targeting package is on Penbrook's desk."

"Good, I'd love to pay her a visit," Nicks said. Then to Fatima: "Ready to go?"

Fatima rolled her eyes. "Fucking mothers, yes."

They waved to Mouse, said their goodbyes to the General and Quinn, then headed to Penbrook's office on the executive wing.

75

A few minutes later, Fatima and Nicks were in the waiting room outside Director Penbrook's Granite Nine office. Marisol Flores brought them coffee, and after a brief wait, Penbrook opened his office door and stepped out.

"Nicks, Nasrallah, good to see you both. Follow me, please."

He led them into a small waiting room with a set of four plastic chairs, a table with magazines, and one fake potted plant. Opposite the entrance was a heavy steel door. It had an iris scanner rather than a handle. Nicks had seen this set up before. The door led into a Sensitive Compartmented Information Facility. A very elaborate one, she guessed—this was DR-Ultra after all.

Director David Penbrook used the scanner, and the door clanged open. He held it ajar, allowing Fatima and Nicks to enter. When they passed into the vestibule controlling access to the larger conference room beyond, Marisol tried to follow. But Penbrook blocked her from entering.

"Marisol, would you give us a moment? I need to speak to Captain Nicks and Agent Nasrallah, privately."

Marisol's bright green eyes flashed about, as if searching for a different response. For a split second, Nicks saw her flushed face betray a hint of anger. But these subtle cues had no effect on Penbrook's resolve. He held her gaze, smiling serenely, looking at her as if she was the most understanding assistant he'd ever worked with.

"Oh, uh ... of course." She turned around. "I'll just return some emails. Call me if you need me."

"Thank you," Penbrook replied.

Marisol returned to her desk and busied herself with her computer.

As Penbrook swung the heavy metal door shut, Nicks scanned his poker face, wondering what was up. Something was on his mind, something off his normal track, and when he joined them, he seemed unsure how to start. He opted for a quick tour of the small room since, he explained, it was the first time they'd used it together.

The SCIF, pronounced *skiff*, was like the Cage back at Angelos Grove. Per Pentagon orders, doors had alarms, the latest surveillance equipment, and motion detectors. They had no exterior hardware, and the hinges hung inside the room. Every equipment panel had tamper-proof casing. Not even the Dharmapala could penetrate these rooms without being detected. It shocked Nicks to learn that was why Marisol had been kept out.

Penbrook walked over to the CCTV monitor that covered the office where Marisol worked on her computer. The three of them watched her as Penbrook explained his plan.

"I want you to run a counterintelligence investigation on Ms. Flores."

Fatima crooked an eyebrow. Nicks's eyes widened as she leaned in.

"I have an intuition she's leaking information," he said. He looked at Marisol and sighed. Then a mask of resolve covered his face as he took a deep breath. "There's no solid evidence. But something tells me she has secrets that may be important for us to uncover."

"She's in a very sensitive position. Why not shut her down right now, if you have any concern?" Nicks asked.

"Yes, I'll happily get the truth out of her," Fatima said.

"I'm sure you could," Penbrook said, like it tempted him to let her try on the spot. "But if the Dharmapala has penetrated DR-Ultra again, we could use that to our advantage. They've been a step ahead of us. It's time we reversed that. Riza Azmara is too dangerous. We have to think outside the box, think like she would."

Nicks agreed. "She'll do anything to destroy us. She said as much."

"Yes, we have to take some risks, I'm afraid. Radical tactics. If we're to bring her down. If she is truly back."

"If? Do you doubt what I experienced?" Nicks searched his face, then looked away as she recalled the strange encounter. "Because I know I've doubted it. It seemed like some kind of hallucination, like I was going crazy."

"No one here knows exactly what happened. Or, if Riza is truly alive. But we underestimated her once, we can't do it again. I *won't* do it again. That's the reason I'm making this request. Can your team handle Flores and the search for this Valentina?" he asked and pointed at a picture of the woman who'd lured Nicks into the meditation room at the resort.

"Yes, sir." Nicks looked at Fatima who gave her a confirming nod. "We sure can."

"Good, I knew I could count on you." Penbrook shook Nicks's hand. "Now, Agent Nasrallah, if you would stay and help me devise some plans for this operation. We'll let the Captain head down to the medical wing."

Nicks wrinkled her brow.

"Colonel Byrne called a few minutes ago. He has some news for you about your special patient."

76

Nicks rushed down the hallway of the medical wing until she found Colonel Jack Byrne. He stood outside one of the intensive care rooms holding a paper cup of steaming coffee.

"He's awake," Byrne said as she jogged up. "But just barely. Make it a short visit. The kid needs all the sleep he can get."

She peeked around the door frame into the patient's room. Will Diaz was groggily rubbing his eyes and sipping from a box of apple juice. Erin Diaz, who Nicks had only seen in pictures, sat next to him.

Nicks hugged Byrne and thanked him a million times in the space of a minute. "You did good, Colonel. Very good. I owe you."

She turned to enter the room. Byrne grabbed her arm gently to stop her and said, "Listen, one more thing. I kept you in the dark about his condition for a reason."

"Quinn explained it to me," Nicks said. "She picked up the Dharmapala's attempts at hacking the sigillum. You guys were worried she might eavesdrop through me."

He nodded. "I know it was terrible to keep you in suspense, but we didn't want to risk the boy's safety. Of course, we never suspected Riza Azmara was alive, and we thought the resort gave us the perfect safety net. But you know how that worked out."

"It was smart to be cautious. I get that," Nicks said.

He went on, explaining how Fatima had brought Will's mother to the base. "Erin Diaz died in drug rehab from withdrawals. At least, that's what the records will say from here on out. We're giving the Diaz family new identities, new cover stories, but first we'll make sure they're all okay.

"Brett's okay with that? He'll leave his job and home?"

"Well ... he said he needed time to think about it. I hope he agrees, he'll be back soon."

"Be back?" Nicks asked. "I thought he was here?"

"He's been by the kid's side night and day, didn't take a break until his ex-wife was here. Then he said he had to tie up loose ends, his job, and some issues related to the attack on his farm."

"You mind if I take the ARES down and check on him?"

"Nat, I'm so glad you're okay, I don't care what you do, just stay safe. Let me know when you get back, and we can have a rematch. Lot of open space to run, around DIA."

"You're on," she said. "But no cheating."

Byrne chuckled. "No promises." He stepped closer. "You need to know, I won't ever lie to you again."

"I believe you, really I do." She smiled and touched his forehead, smoothing down his crinkled brow. A playful holdover from their days of when the sex and the romance was new. "This kid needs to stay alive and safe. You made sure of that. I couldn't ask for anything more."

He squeezed her arm affectionately and let her go. She turned and entered the room feeling like she was walking on sunshine.

Will caught sight of her and yelled gleefully, "Natalie!"

"Hey, little man. How ya feeling?" she asked.

"Kinda tired and kinda good." He shrugged. "Mom, this is Dad's friend I told you about. She's a cybernetic super-soldier created by a covert DARPA program. But it's a *secret,* so don't tell anyone, okay?"

Erin Diaz looked at her son like he was speaking a foreign language. She smiled politely at Nicks as Will gave her a brief lesson in bionics, explaining some details that Nicks wasn't sure she understood herself.

When he stopped to open another box of apple juice, Nicks shook Erin's hand and they chatted about Will's last surgery and how the doctors reported he would make a full recovery.

Nicks turned to Will and said she had a present for him. She made him close his eyes, then dropped a plastic sleeve of Oreos, fresh from the vending machine, into his little hands.

"Double-stuffed? Cool!"

Will opened the cookies and passed them around, then watched as Nicks dissected hers. Laughing, he grabbed another one and copied her, pulling the cookie apart.

"Hmmm. Pretty good." He raised his eyebrows and grinned. "Hey, do you know what they gave me?"

Will turned to the side, exposing a fresh scar along the back of his head. They covered it in a clear adhesive bandage.

"Regenaderm, just like you had. Remember? Cool, huh!?"

"Super cool, for sure!" She gave him a high-five.

They continued talking and eating cookies until a nurse entered to replace his IV. Nicks used that as an excuse to end the visit. She squeezed the little boy's hand, said goodbye to his mother, and headed for the door.

As she turned into the hallway, she looked over her shoulder, capturing the image of Will and Erin like a snapshot. The scene of a mother and a son together, loving each other, lingered in her mind. It was like a premonition of what could be, but also a shadow of a life she may never have. Was it a promise or a fool's dream? Either way, she knew the image would haunt her for some time to come.

77

EPILOGUE

N atalie Nicks watched Brett Diaz, hoping he would abandon the entire crazy, stupid plan. A row of knee-high cypress trees bent toward the Tijuana River as if they were making the same petition, praying the man standing in their midst would see his folly. While the sun set, Diaz watched the murky water as if judging the depth and where to cross. The shadows, unhindered by the petitions of the cypress, cast their dark magic on the land to the south, giving more weight to its obvious dangers.

Nicks wondered how such a barren and desolate place could hold so much meaning. Evil was not restrained by lines on a map. Nor was danger confined by such things. Even now, Brett Diaz was determined to prove no border provided sanctuary.

"This was my paradise, a poor man's paradise, maybe," Diaz said. "All the same, El Draco invaded it, hurt people I love, and started a war. Now I'll end it."

He wouldn't look at Nicks, but he seemed to have picked the place he would cross the river. He'd told her, the entire time he'd lived here, there had never been one moment where he'd even considered crossing into Mexico. All his thoughts about the border were focused on stopping bad people and bad things from coming his way. It was strange to think about the reversal. Now he would be the illegal alien, invading another country, hell-bent on staining its ground with blood.

"The Sheriff's department has given me a leave of absence. But I've conveniently forgotten to tell them about this detour. I'll either be back in a week, or I won't."

Nicks crossed her arms over her chest. "I won't lecture you about that beautiful boy needing a father!"

"That boy needs to live in a world where he'll never have to look over his shoulder. And I want him to be able to do it without changing his name or running off to some other state to hide. If I don't settle scores, he'll always be in danger. Plus, there's the guilt. I failed to protect him. So I'm going to do something about that."

He left the edge of the river and joined her near the DARPA Sandbug.

"Anyway, Erin is out of practice. She needs some time with him. And Will needs time with her."

He zipped up one duffel and placed it in the cargo box. Nicks bent over to help with the other bag. She paused as she noticed it was full of guns and ammo, zipped it up, and handed it to Diaz. She couldn't hide her disapproval.

"This is a personal matter for Will, of course, but let's not forget Sheriff Turner, Vegas Santos, and the family I found—Rafael, Araceli, and Alejandro Garza. They all deserve real justice."

With the gear and bags packed, he shut the tailgate.

"You can't fight a one-man war against a cartel," Nicks protested. "Let me help you. *I want to help you.*"

"You already have." He kicked the tires of the ATV. "I've got wheels and gear, and you took care of the big problems. Just like a badass ranger should. You cleared the way. I can handle it from here."

"What happens when you find El Draco? He's got enough money to raise a new army, and you're one man."

"Oh, I'm not going alone," he said, and whistled.

A familiar sonic profile sounded in her auditory processor.

A pantherix bounded across the ranch and skidded to a stop next to Nicks. The robocat turned and examined her with its camera eyes.

"I've got all the help I need," he said, a sly smirk on his face. "Ain't that right, Shadow?"

Shadow purred with its strange electronic growl. Nicks rolled her eyes.

"Look," he said, holding out his arm. He was wearing a leather fingerless glove that covered his forearm. The controller Will had built was fastened to the leather. "Quinn made a few adjustments for me."

"I think mine's better looking." Nicks shook her new arm at him.

For a moment, he looked at her like she was the last woman on earth. "Everything about you is better looking," he said. "Can I kiss you goodbye?"

"Saves me from doing it," she said.

He reached around her waist and pulled her close. One last kiss. That would be it. Somehow, she knew it. But one wasn't enough. When was it ever?

She forced herself to let go and tried to shake the impulse to use her power to restrain him, tie him up, break a few small bones, or anything to stop him.

He kneeled in front of her. "Come here, Shadow."

The pantherix responded obediently, and Diaz used a pair of pliers to do some impromptu neutering.

"Truck Nuts—nice touch! But they cut down on his stealth capabilities." He handed them back to Nicks, who grinned as the weight of them filled her hand.

"But, Will insisted Shadow was a boy," she protested.

"Neutered cats live twice as long. Plus, Will needs to learn how much females kick ass."

He tapped out a command on the controller, and Shadow—the first Pantherix, which they had encountered only yards from this same spot—stood up and waited for its next order.

"Come on, Shadow. We have a man we need to find. I hope you're ready for some fun."

A strange growl emitted from the cat's angular head. It clacked its obsidian fangs and jumped into the Sandbug.

Diaz tightened his body armor, bent down to cinch up his boots, climbed in, and secured his rifle in the seat next to him. When he was satisfied everything was in order, he fired the engine and rolled up to the edge of the river.

He stopped there for what seemed like an eternity—turned, giving Nicks one last look—then passed through the murky water and disappeared into the dark land on the other side.

PLEASE LEAVE A REVIEW
REVIEWS HELP ME KEEP WRITING!

That concludes VIPER FATALIS. I hope you enjoyed it!

If you liked the book, you'd make this writer very happy if you'd please leave an honest review on Amazon.com (or the online store where you bought it). Reviews are critical. They feed the algorithms and allow more eyes to see my books. Despite being a bit of a hassle, they are essential to my success.

So, please take a moment to leave a review. If you do, I promise not to send a blood-thirsty Pantherix to the location of this reading device.

Thank you very much!

— Mark

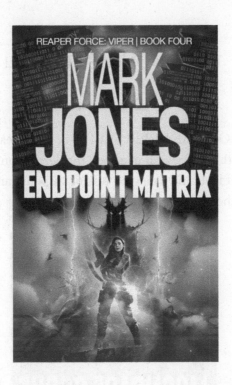

**Natalie Nicks Will Continue Her Adventure In...
"ENDPOINT MATRIX"**

If you join TEAM VIPER you'll be the first to know when the next book is out. I'll send you information about my Advanced Reader Group and the chance to read all my new books free of charge!

Click Here To Join Team Viper:
http://jonesmarkc.com/teamviper

BUY MOONBASE ROGUE!

PRAISE FOR THE VIPER SERIES ... "This really did have everything I look for in a good thriller: action, danger, characters I love, and a tangled web of suspense artfully woven by the author! Five Stars!"

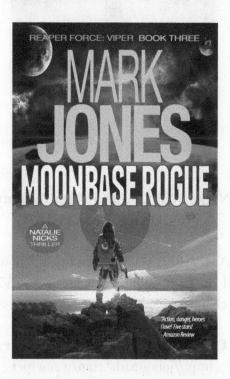

Click Here To Get MOONBASE ROGUE Now!

LIST OF CHARACTERS

Reaper Force
Captain Natalie Nicks [Viper]
Sergeant Margaret Quinn [Gremlin]
Colonel Jack Byrne [Spartan]
Intelligence Officer Fatima Nasrallah [Cartwheel]
Dr. Lee Park [Mouse]
Director David Penbrook
Marisol Flores
Flux

Supporting Characters
General Drummond [DIA]
Sheriff Brett Diaz
Will Diaz
Miguel Solis [El Draco]
Travis Raylock
Dylan Barnes
Mr. Brightside

The Dharmapala

Riza Azmara [Starfire]
Lida Laram [Scorpio]
The Rook
General Marcel Bishop

Other Characters

Uncle Wilco [Natalie Nicks's Uncle]
Victor Aguilar [CNI]

Programs

DIA: Defense Intelligence Agency
DARPA: Defense Advanced Research Projects Agency
DR-Ultra: DARPA's Covert Branch
TALON: DR-Ultra's Bionics Program
Reaper Force: Joint DIA-DARPA Task Force
Pantherix One: Pantherix Mk I [Shadow]
Pantherix Destroyer: Limited Edition Pantherix unit.
Pantherix Fatalis: Covert Tactical Pantherix unit

ACKNOWLEDGMENTS

Thanks to the team of people that helped me finish this book and supported me along the way: Hannah Sullivan, Linda Nguyen, Joel Gladden, Diane and Larry Jones, Laura Kate and Jonathan Brandstein, Hannah Jones, Juliette Jones, and Maverick Jones.

ABOUT THE AUTHOR

Mark Caldwell Jones is a novelist and screenwriter living in Los Angeles. *Viper Fatalis* is the second book in his Reaper Force: Viper thriller series. Learn more about Mark and get free content like news about, *Moonbase Rogue*, the next book in this series, by visiting him online.

For more information:
www.jonesmarkc.com/teamviper
mark@jonesmarkc.com

9 780991 037650